Angie Amalfi Mysteries by
Joanne Pence

COOKING UP TROUBLE

AN ANGIE AMALFI MYSTERY

JOANNE PENCE

AVON BOOKS

An Imprint of HarperCollinsPublishers

This is a work of fiction. Names, characters, places, and incidents are products of the author's imagination or are used fictitiously and are not to be construed as real. Any resemblance to actual events, locales, organizations, or persons, living or dead, is entirely coincidental.

AVON BOOKS
An Imprint of HarperCollins*Publishers*
10 East 53rd Street
New York, New York 10022-5299

Copyright © 1995 by Joanne Pence
ISBN-13: 978-0-06-108200-9
ISBN-10: 0-06-108200-7
www.avonbooks.com

First Avon Books paperback printing: September 2006
First HarperPaperbacks printing: May 1995

Avon Trademark Reg. U.S. Pat. Off. and in Other Countries, Marca Registrada, Hecho en U.S.A.
HarperCollins® is a registered trademark of HarperCollins Publishers Inc.

Printed in the U.S.A.

20   19   18   17   16   15   14   13   12   11   10   9   8   7

To Aaron and Zachary, with love.

Special thanks go to Roberta Grant Flynn and Doris Berdahl for their help and support, to all the SCRIBEs, and to everyone at Book Passage for so warmly and generously putting up with us.

1

"*I wouldn't feed this swill* to my cat!" Martin Bayman announced.

Angelina Amalfi watched the older, gray-haired man stand, throw his napkin on his plate, and storm from Hill Haven Inn's dining room.

The lentil-soybean cutlets were not a hit.

Angie had to agree with Bayman. The cats she knew would have tried to bury them.

"Some people are so insecure, they have to make a big deal out of everything." Disgust dripped from Finley Tay's voice. Tay was the owner of the inn and would be its head cook when it opened to the public in another three weeks. In his midforties, he was a gaunt man with thinning brown hair pulled back in a ponytail, a long, angular face, small eyes, and sharp, jutting cheekbones. He was also Angie's new boss. "Eat up, Miss Amalfi," he commanded cheerfully.

"Oh, I will." She cut a bite-size piece from one of the patties. "This is so interesting. I've never heard of making cutlets with beans. I mean, they're usually made out of meat."

Finley Tay's fork froze in midair. The four-letter word she'd just uttered brought a look of shock to his face and a gasp to his lips.

"Delicious," Angie lied, stuffing the forkful of cutlet into her mouth. It was better than the foot she currently had in it.

Maybe her new job wasn't going to be such a piece of cake after all. From the time she first spoke to Finley Tay over the telephone, she should have known the job he described was too good to be true.

He had told her he was opening an inn in an elegant Victorian mansion built in the 1870s by a man who'd amassed a fortune in the goldfields. It stood atop the windswept cliffs of a secluded promontory overlooking the rugged northern California coastline. Everything in it would be of the finest quality. To go with this setting, he was looking for a student of fine foods to assist him in developing a series of menus for gourmet dining.

Angie wanted this job. The setting had decided her, as visions leapfrogged from Manderley to Wuthering Heights. She could easily imagine herself in such a place, even if Finley Tay, charming though he was on the phone, was unlikely to be a Max de Winter or a Heathcliff.

The only minor proviso, Finley said, was that the food must be vegetarian.

This gave her pause. But only for a moment. She was a student of *cordon bleu* cooking, so how much of a problem could a vegetarian menu be? Nothing a spicy imagination couldn't solve.

"Your job offer sounds like a wonderful opportunity," Angie had replied. A wonderful opportunity to add to a résumé sorely in need of a current entry. She was out of work. Again.

There was a second even more minor proviso, Finley added. Rather than a salary, she must be willing to receive room and board at the inn for a week, since he was strapped by opening-day expenses. She asked for room and board for two.

He agreed so readily, she was almost sorry she hadn't asked for more. He sounded ecstatic to have her, as if her cooking skills were the answer to his most heartfelt dreams.

Gleefully, she took the job.

After two weeks of reading every book about vegetarian cooking she could get her hands on, and talking to every chef she knew who had ever worked in a vegetarian restaurant, she had arrived at the small, windswept airport near the town of Hayesville.

As she stood off to the side of the runway, her bags at her feet where the copilot left them, she saw a man awkwardly heading her way. Long, skinny legs stepped over rain puddles, and pointy elbows flapped, giving him the appearance of an overgrown flamingo.

"Hello, Mr. Tay," she said, holding out her hand. "I'm Angelina Amalfi."

"Right, right." Without shaking her hand, he scooped up all three of her bags. "Got to hurry, Miss Amalfi. Storm's coming."

She had to run to keep up with him. "Is the inn far?"

He stopped in front of a battered VW van that sported gingham curtains, a crumbling GET OUT OF VIETNAM bumper sticker, and a faded peace symbol. "Hop right in."

She stared at the vehicle, a definite relic of the sixties. "They just don't make vans like they used to," she said.

Finley ignored her comment as he tossed the bags behind the front seats, climbed in, and then faced her for the first time. "I should explain to you, Miss Amalfi, that I create the perfect balance of foods at each meal."

"That's important." She smoothed the front-seat upholstery over a bare spring, then got in beside him. "I always try to do the same thing. To begin each dinner with a small but elegantly arranged appetizer as the first course, let's say warm *bouchées* or cold *amuse-gueule*—"

"Food needs to be soft, easy to digest, and yet centered in simplicity, without nonessentials." He scarcely waited until she was settled before he tore out of the parking area. The van rocked precariously at each turn.

"Pardon me?" She must not have heard right over the roar of the engine.

"What we eat," Finley said, "must not impede our spiritual journey. It must not arouse the baser passions that deny us enlightenment."

Baser passions? Enlightenment? She forced her mouth to remain shut. Being slack-jawed made one look so foolish. She searched for something to say. "Enlightenment is important when eating," she murmured. "I hate heavy meals myself. As I was saying to my good friend, Chef Raymond DuTuoille of Greengrocer— a true master of vegetarian cooking, as I'm sure you know—"

"No. I pay no attention to those who choose to make names for themselves in this world."

She retreated into silence, trying to remember the alleged pluses of this new job. Finley Tay did not appear to be one of them.

"Nurture the spirit as well as the flesh, Miss Amalfi," Finley cried. He turned and smiled at her, taking his eyes off the narrow coast highway just as a sharp curve loomed ahead.

She clutched the dash. "But there's much to be said for the here and now, Mr. Tay."

"Here and hereafter! Don't you agree?" He looked

back at the road just in time to avoid a sudden plunge down the embankment.

"Oh, God," she murmured, her heart in her throat.

"Ah, Miss Amalfi, I knew you'd appreciate my food philosophy, but it's not *that* grand. Yet."

She stared at him as if he'd lost what little sense he might have had.

Blissfully, he continued. "It's important for the well-being of this inn that we see eye-to-eye this way. I have some business partners, I'm afraid, who aren't the best judges of proper food and nutrition. But together we'll convince them that we know best. Together we'll develop food that sings."

She took a deep breath as the road momentarily widened. "A sort of Zen and the art of eating," she said.

"A woman after my own heart." With that, he began talking about soybeans. He knew seventy-three ways to prepare them.

He was on number twenty-six when they reached the inn. It was a massive wood-framed house built on an outcropping overlooking the Pacific. Gingerbread and fancy millwork etched scalloped patterns along the roofline and around the windows and doors. The imposing middle section stood three stories high, the topmost floor having two dormer windows looking much like two beady, peering eyes. Jutting out from it were a mismatched pair of two-story wings. The west wing, nearest the ocean, ended in an octagonal turret.

Angie got out of the van and stood looking at the house, trying to remember what it reminded her of. Then she knew. Tyrannosaurus Rex.

The house was badly in need of paint, and didn't at all resemble the elegant mansion Finley had described to her on the phone. But she could imagine how lovely it could be if done in the multicolors that were so popular among San Francisco's Queen Anne and Victorian painted ladies. "It's distinctive," Angie said finally, without much conviction.

"It is," Finley replied. "And much, much more. It's a quiet, mystical place. A place to make your dreams come true."

"Really? Well, in that case I'm especially glad I'm here," she said—and glad she'd convinced Paavo to tear himself away from Homicide to come and spend the week with her. Perhaps here her dreams about herself and the big, tough detective might come true as well.

While Finley gave her a quick tour of the property, he introduced her to his sister, Moira, who would be helping him run the inn; Miss Greer, who served as general housekeeper and assistant cook; plus six "investors"— people who owned a share of the inn and now were here to see that it got off to a good start: Martin and Bethel Bayman, Greg and Patsy Jeffers, Chelsea Worthington and Reginald Vane.

As Angie spoke with the investors, it became clear that it had been they, and not Finley Tay, who felt her services were needed.

Now, as Angie looked over the meal of lentil-soybean cutlets, seasoned tofu, and steamed vegetables, she realized the investors had been absolutely right. If the menu didn't change, the inn would close within a week.

Few of the investors had chosen to eat here this evening. Even Finley's sister, Moira, claimed to have an upset stomach. The message to Finley couldn't have been much clearer.

When Martin Bayman left, the only others beside Finley

and Angie were Chelsea Worthington, a pleasant, round-figured young woman, and Reginald Vane, a formal middle-aged gentleman from Vancouver, British Columbia.

"I think," Reginald Vane said, smoothing his bow tie and casting a sidelong glance from Angie to Chelsea Worthington, "the soy-lentil cutlets are superb."

Angie couldn't believe her ears.

"Why, thank you," Finley said smugly. He glanced at Angie's plate and his brows lifted. "You're not eating, Miss Amalfi." His hurt tone failed to mask his irritation. "You must be hungry after your long trip up from San Francisco this morning and your tour of the inn. Surely a student of gourmet cooking has more of an appetite than this."

She wished he hadn't reminded her. Without thinking, she reached for the basket of coarse black bread.

"Soy bread," Finley said.

Angie's heart sank. "Is there any butter?"

Finley handed it to her.

"Soy butter?" she asked.

"Naturally." He smiled. "Get it?"

She hoped her wince passed for a grin. "Yes."

"This evening, in about a half hour, I'll go on my after-dinner nature walk. It's good to stir the blood and speed the digestive juices so that the nutrients are pumped into the body, not merely broken down and expelled. Please feel free to join me."

"Thank you, but I may retire soon," Angie said. "As you mentioned, I've had a busy day."

Angie paced, unable to relax enough to lie down, let alone sleep. Her mind raced with the sights, sounds, and impressions of the day, all swimming in a meatless stew. None of the investors seemed to object to Finley's basic vegetarianism; it was just the blandness of his particular soybean-based food philosophy that gave them pause— or brought them to a screeching halt.

She stopped pacing and added Algerian vegetable stew to the growing list of menu possibilities she was putting together. She knew a delicious recipe that mixed butternut squash, new potatoes, chickpeas, and North African spices, and was served with couscous.

She had to stop this and get some rest. Tomorrow her work would begin in earnest. She walked over to the windows.

The room Finley had given her was large and octagonally shaped. Windows on five of the eight walls provided a breathtaking view of the ocean, the rugged cliffs, and the thick redwood forest that spread over most of the promontory. Dark clouds covered the moon in a portent of rain.

Tomorrow Paavo would arrive. She felt excitement coupled with raw anxiety over having asked him here, taking him from his job. Too often he acted as if being a homicide inspector for the San Francisco Police Department was a way of life or something. Sort of like being a priest.

She thought of shoulders broader than a tollbooth on the Golden Gate Bridge; of strong arms, legs, and hands; of his kisses. . . . No, he was no priest.

He'd just come off a difficult case involving the highly publicized murders of two San Francisco restaurant owners. Throughout much of that time, she'd seen more of him on local news broadcasts than in person. The man needed some rest.

That was why she "just happened" to mention that going away alone to such a remote area made her uneasy. Of course, she hadn't reminded him that she'd traveled halfway around the world alone, or that a remote area in Northern California was a hundred times safer than most of the big cities she'd ever lived in.

But he rose to the bait and told her he'd go with her. She didn't allow herself too much guilt.

She began to pace again. He'd hate the inn's vegetarian food, but he was driving up here in her Ferrari Testarossa—a gift from her father a couple of years ago. What better use was there for a fancy car than to drive around in search of a good restaurant?

All of a sudden, she stopped pacing. Chefs were always the first ones up in the morning. They'd have to make the coffee, mix biscuit batter, do all those get-ready-for-breakfast things before the guests arose. She'd been so busy worrying about everything else, she hadn't bothered to think about the most obvious. She wanted not only to watch, but also to assist Finley in preparing breakfast, as a kind of damage control.

Since she wasn't a person who functioned well at the crack of dawn, she decided that this evening, in a leisurely manner, she'd go down to the kitchen to familiarize herself with the supplies and how they were arranged. Better tonight than to wait until morning, when she'd be harried and sleepy.

Under the bed she found the pink satin mules she'd kicked aside earlier, put on a matching quilted satin bedjacket, and left her room. Just before the stairs down to the first floor, the hall ended and a galley opened onto the large, silent drawing room below. The room was dark and empty except for a single night-light.

In the foyer, another dim night light burned. Two hallways radiated out from it, one into the east wing and one into the west, like tunnels with no lights at the ends. The kitchen was in the east wing.

In the still darkness, the smell of decay hit her. She'd vaguely noticed it earlier while being whisked from room to room, meeting the investors and hired help, and taking in all the antique Victorian touches that she was sure were original. Now, though, she could almost feel the rot in the house, coupled with a scent of wet earth—the scent one finds at a newly dug grave.

She tried to shake off the feeling. Big old houses like this could be terribly creepy at night. Perhaps the next day she could convince Moira Tay to open up some windows and let sunlight and fresh air come in.

The kitchen was just a little way past the dining room. Before she reached it, the hall became pitch-black. She stiffened, then tried to laugh away her uneasiness. Wasn't it always this way? she asked herself. When it was dark, that was when you began to sense all kinds of hidden creepy things. That was when something always went bump in the night.

Like that.

She froze, listening, afraid to take another step.

The sound of someone crying quietly seemed to float on the air. Angie's goose bumps stood so high she was surprised she didn't levitate. "Hello?" she called.

No answer. The crying continued a moment longer, then abruptly stopped.

It was the wind. That, or the creaks and groans of a house this old. Continuing forward in the darkness, she reached out until her fingers found the door frame, the kitchen door, and then the doorknob's clammy metallic chill.

She twisted it and gave the door a push. Its hinges squealed as it swung open. When she was young, she and her fourth sister, Francesca, used to shake in their shoes watching ghoulish movies about Freddy Krueger or

Friday the 13th. She remembered thinking how stupid the people in those movies were to go into dark, mysterious rooms.

There was no way in hell she was going to step into that kitchen without first turning on the lights.

Running her hand along the walls past the doorjamb, she found the light switch and flicked it on.

The kitchen blazed almost too brightly. The countertops and sink were all stainless steel. Yellow-painted cabinets lined the walls. She waited, listening, a part of her still convinced something was wrong here.

What nonsense! She was being childish.

She marched straight to the middle of the floor. The kitchen was spotless. But glancing at the range top, she saw a large, unwashed platter.

Slowly, she walked toward it, her mind refusing to accept what her eyes saw. Then she stopped and stared.

On the platter was a ring of cold lentil cutlets, and in the center, draped around an open package of rat poison, was a fat, gray, very dead rat.

2

"*I don't want you* in my kitchen." Miss Greer, the cook, stood in front of the kitchen door with her arms folded. She was a severe-looking woman, dressed in black, her gray hair pulled back and twisted in a figure eight held in place with a big black barrette.

"What do you mean, your kitchen?" Angie asked. "It's Finley and Moira Tay's kitchen, and Finley hired me to work with him on the menu. Is he in there?"

"I haven't seen him this morning."

"That's odd. I couldn't find him last night, either. Moira said he probably went into town and would be back in the morning." Moira had appeared curiously indifferent to Angie's tale of the rat in the kitchen. She said she'd tell Finley, and Angie should go back up to bed.

When Angie told her she'd be downstairs early to help with breakfast, Moira had said cold granola and oat bran muffins were all she planned to serve. There'd be nothing to help with.

Angie didn't need a picture to know when she wasn't

wanted, so she decided to sleep in. She usually skipped breakfast, anyway, to spare a few calories for the irresistible temptations of the day.

But now it was ten in the morning. Finley or no, she was ready to get started.

"I'm afraid he still hasn't returned," Miss Greer said.

"So he still hasn't seen the rat?" Angie asked.

"Rat!" Miss Greer sneered, as if Angie were personally responsible for rodents. "Whatever are you talking about?"

Angie stood her ground. "I'm talking about the rat that obviously ate poison that someone—you, perhaps?—left in the kitchen! Do you know what would happen to this place if anyone from the state came by and saw rat poison so close to food storage? I can't believe you or Finley are so out of touch with the world."

"You're having hallucinations. The only rats in my kitchen are the strange people who keep coming in here! I think it's the Sempler ghosts playing tricks on you. Maybe they'll get you to understand that you're not needed here—and not wanted."

Did she say ghosts? Angie wondered. Not only was Miss Greer hateful, she was a nut case besides. "You don't know—"

Miss Greer stepped closer. "I know plenty. If Mr. Finley wanted to work with you, he'd be here. But he isn't, is he? I think you'd better go right back where you came from and leave us alone."

"I'm here because I have a job to do. In that kitchen!"

"Over my dead body."

"You can join the rat, for all I care." Angie stormed away.

◇   ◇   ◇

Homicide Inspector Paavo Smith turned the Ferrari into a truck stop along Highway 101. He had driven through Hayesville twice already, as well as ten miles up and down the highway on either side of it, trying to find the turnoff Angie had told him to take. He gave up.

She'd laugh, he knew. Hotshot city detective and he couldn't even find a rural road to a public inn. At least someone would find his day humorous. He didn't.

It had started about six A.M. with him going to the office to spend a few minutes finishing up some last-minute details before leaving for a peaceful week in the country. Sometime, years ago, he'd taken an honest-to-God vacation. But he couldn't remember when it was.

He'd been at his desk a couple of hours when his partner, Yoshiwara, came in with the news that one of the cases he'd thought had been wrapped up suddenly had begun to unravel. A guy he'd charged with stabbing his wife to death had always claimed someone wearing a black mask had broken in and done it. No evidence at all of a break-in existed, and plenty pointed toward the husband. Now, a black ski mask had been found in a dumpster three blocks away. Even though Paavo knew Yosh could handle the investigation and that the lab report on the mask wouldn't be completed before his vacation ended, he hated going off and leaving something like that hanging.

His mood had turned sour having to walk out on an unfinished case, but now it was downright ugly over his inability to find the inn. A vacation had turned into a lot more trouble than he'd ever expected. No wonder he never took the damn things.

A couple of truckers outside the diner eyed the Ferrari, then him, then the Ferrari again. He did his best to ignore them, even though driving Angie's car usually made him feel like he ought to be a car thief, drug dealer, or at least a high-priced trial attorney.

Inside, the waitress pointed to a rotary pay phone on the wall. He dialed the number Angie had given him, but instead of Hill Haven Inn, he heard a message saying the number wasn't in service. A repeat try netted the same result. "What the hell?" he muttered, then called Information. The number was correct. Finally, he called an operator for assistance.

"I'm sorry, sir," the operator said, "but we're unable to make a connection with that telephone line. I'll have to send a service repairman out to see what's wrong. Do you know if this number has a service contract with us?"

"No, I don't."

"We'll have to check on that first," she said.

"Thanks loads." He hung up, scowling at the phone. "Terrific."

"I can feel the presence of Jack Sempler here," Chelsea Worthington said. "Can't you?" She took a big bite of the avocado, tomato, and alfalfa sprout sandwich Moira and Miss Greer had served, along with barley soup, as a late lunch. Finley Tay still hadn't returned.

Angie sat at a table on the patio with Chelsea and Patsy Jeffers, a plain, nervous young woman. No one else had shown up for lunch. Light morning rains had washed the land clean and sparkling. Despite the slight chill, the air was too fresh and clean to eat in the stuffy dining room.

"I don't know Jack Sempler," Angie said.

"You don't?" Chelsea nearly choked.

Patsy sipped her Evian. "He looks a lot like my husband."

Angie remembered Greg Jeffers—tall and tan, with a big jaw.

"My Greg's the handsomest man I've ever seen in my whole life," Patsy added as she carefully picked the avocado out of her sandwich.

"Except for Jack," Chelsea said.

"But at least Greg's alive," Patsy replied.

Just then, a few large drops of rain began to fall.

Angie ignored them, her looking from one woman to the other. "Jack isn't?"

"No." Chelsea picked up her soup and sandwich and hurried toward the doors to the drawing room. "He's one of the ghosts who live here. And I love him with all my heart and soul."

"Hill Haven Inn? Never heard of it." The young man, his hair shaved to the skin along the back and sides, while long and bluntcut on top, propped his back against the Coke machine, raised a can to his mouth, and drank.

Paavo tamped down his temper. "What about Finley Tay?"

"Nope."

The waitress in the diner, a Shell station attendant, and now this fellow had all given Paavo the same answer. The same lie. He heard it in their voices, saw it in their eyes, and he didn't like it one damn bit.

It was already nearly six in the evening. "There's supposed to be a turnoff marked Hill Haven Road somewhere south of here," Paavo said. "I couldn't find the sign, but I've been told that it's a road that leads out to the ocean."

The man shrugged. "Lots of roads around here. I can't think of one like that, though. I sure can't." He draped his arm over the Coke machine, then grinned.

"Give it a try." Paavo's voice was deadly quiet, but the

irritation and frustration he'd felt made it seethe with anger.

The grin vanished as quickly as it had appeared. "You might want to talk to the sheriff, mister." The young man took a step back. "Maybe he can help. His office is behind the red building on the other side of the highway." With that, he hurried to an old pickup and drove off.

Paavo watched the man go. His muscles ached with tension and he realized how close he'd come to punching the punk. Christ, he'd just spoken to a perfect stranger as if he were a hardened criminal rather than a wannabe tough who'd stopped off for a soft drink. Maybe everyone was right. Maybe he did need a vacation.

He gazed up and down the main street. Hayesville was no more than a gathering of small, dingy buildings along Highway 101. This was campground, lumber company, spotted owl, and Bigfoot country. *Trees of Mystery* bumper stickers were nearly as common as pinecones.

The tall pines and redwoods surrounding the town's buildings were dark in the wintry light of early evening. It had rained earlier, and now wet roads and a cloudy sky had cast the whole area in shades of gray.

Paavo got back into Angie's Ferrari, hung a U-turn, and soon skidded to a halt in front of the sheriff's office.

3

"*That was Susannah Sempler.*" Moira Tay spoke to Angie in a slow, wispy voice as she glided across the high-ceilinged drawing room toward a large portrait that hung over the mantel. "Her father built this house."

Moira was a tall, striking woman with long blond hair worn in a single braid draped over her shoulder. Her floor-length black skirt and black turtleneck sweater, along with makeup-free, deep-set brown eyes, gave her a timeless look of mystery, while her precise, delicate movements carried an air of otherworldly serenity.

"All I've heard about since I got here are the Sempler ghosts," Angie said, gazing up at the portrait. "Is Susannah supposed to be one of them?" Angie sat on a red velvet chair surrounded by dark Victorian tables and chests and knickknacks. Small rugs overlay larger ones scattered over the dark hardwood floors. Each table and chest had a velvet cover with a smaller lace cover over it. The place was stuffed and cluttered and smelled of dust, not because Moira and Miss Greer hadn't dusted, but because the surfeit of doilies and antimacassars and rugs seemed impervious to cleaning, as if they'd carried the dust from years and years of lying about in this room and weren't about to relinquish it.

Moira shook her head. "Everything you might hear about the ghosts is no more than make-believe. Susannah lived here alone until she died at age ninety-two. If you're going to search for signs of the Sempler ghosts, I'm afraid you'll be very disappointed."

Angie didn't want to admit how relieved she was to hear that. "That doesn't bother me at all. I prefer the dead to stay quietly buried." The portrait showed a lovely young woman with blond hair puffed out at the sides, then pulled up in a small chignon, 1890s style. She wore a pale blue dress with a lace neckline. "It's hard to imagine someone so pretty living alone all those years, isn't it?"

Moira sat on a green-and-gold sofa with a high, stiff camelback and high rolled arms. "Yes. But then, this is a very remote area."

"That's true," Angie said quickly, realizing that except for her brother, Moira also seemed to live a solitary life.

Angie glanced at her watch. Six o'clock. Paavo should have been here hours ago. What if something had happened to him? She'd tried calling earlier, but the phone was still out of order, just as it had been yesterday.

She'd wanted to call Paavo and her mother, to let them both know she'd arrived safely. Angie might be twenty-four years old, but she was still Serefina's baby, the youngest of five girls, not to mention the only one still unmarried, which her mother never failed to mention. To keep peace in the family, Angie made sure Serefina knew of her comings and goings. But not Paavo's. She didn't dare tell her mother he'd be here with her. Much as Serefina fancied herself modern, there were some things Angie didn't talk to her about—like sex.

But where was Paavo? Angie hated waiting and worrying, and Moira wasn't the most fascinating person to while away the hours with. "So tell me," Angie said, "who are the other Sempler ghosts? Not that I believe in such things, of course."

"Of course." Moira smiled knowingly, her speech slow and precise. "Let me go back to about 1870, when Ezra Sempler built this house. He was a recluse, and after his wife left him, he lived here alone with his two children, Jack and Susannah. The brother and sister were very close and depended on each other completely."

"Like you and Finley," Angie interjected.

Moira's already pale face turned a shade whiter, but Angie wasn't sure why. "Perhaps," Moira said. "In any event, everything changed when an orphaned cousin, the fiery, beautiful Elise Sempler, came to live here. She and Jack fell madly, passionately in love. Ezra objected to the match, though, and had Jack forcibly sent away to sea. Elise thought he'd abandoned her and jumped from the cliffs right out there." She pointed toward the barren land and jagged rocks just past the gardens of Hill Haven.

"My God," Angie said. The ocean seemed such a cold, forbidding tomb for someone young and in love. These days, Angie knew all about being in love. She glanced once more at her watch. She could all but see Paavo walking into the room. He'd probably be wearing tan Dockers and a black pullover. He'd stand in the doorway, looking casual and uninterested to anyone who didn't know him; but those who did could tell that he was checking out the place very carefully, making sure everything was as it should be and that he wasn't walking into any surprises. A cop's way, eerily similar to a criminal's.

"When Jack returned and found out what had happened to Elise," Moira said, "he also died soon thereafter. Many say it was from a broken heart."

"How awful." So that was the ghost Chelsea insisted she loved. One who'd died because of his love for someone else. Did that make sense?

"The local people say that at times they can hear or see one of the ghosts. Or just feel their presence. But I assure you, Angie, I've lived here for four months and I've never felt them near."

"That's good." Angie drew in her breath. "I hope I never do either."

"Excuse me," a soft, masculine voice said.

Angie started and turned quickly to see Quint, the gardener, standing in the doorway, his cap in his hands.

"Miss Moira," he said, "should I contact the sheriff about Mr. Finley's absence?"

"Still no word?" Moira asked, brows puckered.

"None. I walked over all his usual places," Quint replied. "But no luck."

"Wait a minute." Angie turned to Moira. "Didn't you say he drove off somewhere last night?"

"No," Moira answered. "I thought he had. But his van is still here."

Angie couldn't quite believe what Moira was saying to her. She stood. "Let me get this straight. Finley hasn't left Hill Haven, but you don't know where he is?"

"No one has seen him."

"You're kidding! And you're not out there looking for him? All of us should be."

"I don't want to alarm the investors," Moira said, then turned her gaze outward, toward the ocean. "We'll contact the sheriff. I'm quite sure I'd feel it if anything had happened to him."

Angie didn't go for this touchy-feely spiritual stuff. "How?" she demanded.

Moira shut her eyes for a moment, then with her hands folded gave Angie a serene look. Instead of answering, she said, "You'll understand in time."

"Why are you looking for this place?" Sheriff Butz asked, leaning back in his chair. Paavo had talked his way past the desk clerk and now stood in front of the head honcho.

"I have a friend who's taken a job there for a week," he explained. "A young woman named Angelina Amalfi. She flew up yesterday, and Finley Tay was supposed to meet her at the airport. When I tried to reach her today, the phone was dead."

Butz stood up and walked around to the front of his desk, then half sat on it, facing Paavo. He was built like a boxcar, square and solid. "Calm down. I'm sure everything's okay with your lady. Maybe she just wanted to be alone for a while. Gave you a line about where she'd be. It happens all the time. They get over it soon enough."

"She wouldn't do that."

Butz chuckled, his gold tooth flashing. "Now, son, no man can ever say what a woman will do."

Paavo had reached the end of his patience. He pulled out his identification badge and handed it to the sheriff. "I'm with the San Francisco police. Homicide. I know what this woman will do. She came up here, and I intend to find her. With or without your help."

"San Francisco, hmm? Inspector Pay–vo Smith. Pay–vo. That's a new one." He handed back the badge.

"*Pah*–vo. It's Finnish."

"Hmm." Butz' beady eyes passed over Paavo dismissively. "I guess you S.F.P.D. homicide boys see dead bodies all the time. Go to work in the morning and take your pick of corpses, right?"

Paavo steeled himself. "Not exactly, Sheriff."

"Well, we don't get many homicides up here. Don't get a lot of wacko big-city crimes either. You know why, Pay-vo?"

Paavo's teeth ground. "Why?"

"'Cause we're very particular about who our neighbors are."

"Meaning?"

"Meaning that maybe this community wants no part of people like Finley Tay." He pulled a pack of Tiparillos from his breast pocket and offered one to Paavo. Paavo shook his head.

Butz lit up and went to the window, staring at the street as he talked. "It's easy to take down road signs. Easy to cut a telephone wire. Now, I'm not saying that goes on. It's against the law."

"So I've heard."

"People up here might not be as sophisticated as some, but we know which way the sun comes up. We also know we don't want any part of these psychics and spiritualists. It stinks of cult, like you guys have in Frisco. Any cult who tries to set up here is asking for a whole hell of a lot of trouble."

Paavo hadn't heard that Tay was involved in a cult. He wondered if Angie had heard anything about it.

"My friend is only here as a cook," he said.

Butz folded his thick arms, his jowls puffed up and his slitted eyes grew even narrower. "I say, let 'em starve."

"Sheriff Butz!" The desk clerk knocked on the door at the same time as he pushed it open and stepped into the office. "Excuse me. Telephone. Sounds important."

"Hell." Butz glanced at the blinking button on the phone. "Give Inspector Smith here a map to the old Sempler place." He grinned maliciously at Paavo. "Watch out for ghosts. Word is, the place is haunted."

4

The rocky, potholed road narrowed as it rose steeply up from the highway toward a promontory that edged the Pacific. The road twisted through a damp, forbidding forest, roller-coastering up knolls one minute, plunging into chasms the next. The sky had darkened and towering redwoods pressed in on Paavo in the small sports car. Still the inn was nowhere in sight.

He reached for the car's heater control and turned it on. A line from a poem he'd read years ago came back to him. "This is the forest primeval." He could scarcely see the tops of the redwoods overhead, and below, the ground was dank with ferns and moss.

If he knew Angie was all right, he would most likely enjoy this ruggedly beautiful setting. But the town's animosity against the inn and its proprietors was ugly and potentially dangerous. Butz didn't seem to be the sort to throw warnings about casually, and he'd given Paavo a clear warning.

Angie shouldn't be here.

Damn it, that rankled. He had wanted this job and this place to be everything Angie had hoped for and needed. During the last two months, friends she'd had in the restaurant business had been murdered. She'd had to handle the aftermath mostly alone, since low staffing and high crime meant he'd had to put in too many hours at his job to help.

That she wanted him to spend time with her had been clear, even before her playing her afraid-to-go-alone-to-a-remote-country-inn game.

For some reason, though, the idea of going away with her had bothered him at first. Hell, there was nothing about Angie that didn't get to him. He'd never been involved in such an offbeat relationship before.

He was a cop. What life could he offer her? He glanced around the interior of her Ferrari. Not much, if he stayed honest. This week, at least, they could give each other time without her family or his job getting in the way. Time for serious thought about this relationship and where it was going.

If anywhere.

The road suddenly veered out of the forest and cut a narrow ledge along the side of a high cliff. The terrain rose steeply on one side of the road while dropping straight to the ocean on the other.

As he reached a section where rocks and mud had slid from the cliff onto the roadway, he slowed to a crawl. There wasn't any room to go around them, and he was forced to drive over the loose, slippery rocks. Tires spun and the car fishtailed slightly, despite the care he took and the death grip he had on the wheel. He glanced up at the cliff looming high overhead. The rains must have caused the slide. If more heavy rains fell, the road would be closed for sure, and the people at the inn cut off from the rest of the world.

Yet another reason to get Angie away from there as soon as possible.

As the road doubled back inland, rising steadily, a sharp curve brought him to the crest of the promontory. He stopped the car. Before him stretched an expanse of barren land. At the topmost point, silhouetted against the moonlit sky, a monstrous wood-framed house perched, gargoylelike, upon the landscape.

The house was shrouded in light mist. Dense fingers of fog crept over the cliffs from the ocean and inched toward the house as he watched.

Hill Haven Inn.

Paavo could understand why the locals said it was haunted.

A couple of cars were parked in the driveway. He pulled alongside them and went inside.

"Hello?" he called from the small oak-paneled foyer. His voice seemed to echo through the house.

Touches of faded gentility—from the intricately laid oak parquet floor to the stained-glass peacock window over a hand-carved staircase—told him this had once been a beautiful home.

He heard footsteps and turned in their direction. From the darkness of a side hall, he could see the shadowy figure of a tall woman with long blond hair worn in a single braid hurrying toward him. She stopped. "You aren't the sheriff," she said. Her words were softly spoken, her breath hushed.

He stared. The sight of her pitched him back to years earlier, before he'd become a cop. He almost spoke the name he hadn't allowed himself to even think for nearly a decade, but then she stepped closer, into the light, and he saw he was wrong. "Excuse me for just walking in," he said.

Her steps were featherlight, as if she were floating. Gray, clear eyes met his. "Who are you?"

"I'm—"

"Paavo!" Angie came in through the French doors at the far end of the drawing room. It'd been only three days since she'd met him at his tiny house to say good-bye. The memory of that good-bye made his skin warm under his black sweater.

She wore a little green stretch top that dipped in front lower than he quite approved of and hugged her ribs tight, and white slacks that flowed wide and easy down to funny lime-green shoes with thick wooden soles. Her short, wavy brown hair, streaked with gold highlights, was brushed back from her face in a loose, casual style. Seeing him, she paused just long enough at the door that her wide smile and sparkling brown eyes brightened the room. Although she tried to run toward him, her shoes made it hard for her to do much more than walk fast.

Suddenly, all the hassle, all the trouble he'd gone through to get here to her, was worth it. He grinned and left the foyer and the blond woman to hurry across the room to Angie.

She was in his arms, kissing him and talking all at once. It was all he could do to kiss her back. "Where have you been?" she asked. "I was so worried about you, and with everything else here—God, I was so glad when I finally heard the Ferrari and knew you'd made it safely."

He heard a tremor in her voice and his arms tightened. "It's all right now," he said quietly into her dark hair. "What's wrong? What's upset you?"

She pulled her head back and stared at him. "We've been searching and searching all evening. Everyone said not to worry. But I should have known. From the time I saw that rat. I could just feel something was dreadfully wrong."

"Slow down, Angie. What's happened?"

"My boss, Finley Tay. He's disappeared."

✿   ✿   ✿

"The sheriff's here." Moira Tay stood at the front door, holding it open.

Angie heard a car door slam and a moment later footsteps on the front porch. "Sheriff Clark G. Butz," the big man announced. Keeping his teeth clamped on a Tiparillo, he tugged on the wide brim of his beige hat, which was covered with an ill-fitting plastic rain protector.

"I'm Moira Tay." The tall blond woman shook his hand. "Thank you for coming."

Butz sauntered into the drawing room. Only the movement of his puffy eyelids told Angie he was carefully observing everything around him. He waved his thumb over his shoulder and without looking back said, "That's my deputy."

A lanky fellow bounded through the door. He snatched off his hat and pressed it hard against his stomach. "Deputy Sparks here."

Butz passed a slow glance over Angie, Paavo, and Moira. "That's what'll fly if he gets riled."

Sparks gave an embarrassed smile at what was clearly a worn joke between them. Angie didn't think the sheriff was in any position, though, to joke about anyone else's name.

"Well, Inspector," Butz said, facing Paavo, "I see you made it. If I'd known the phone call coming in was about this place, I'd have led the way here for you."

"Call?" Paavo glanced at Moira. "I thought your phones were out?"

"They are. Quint, my . . . my gardener, went to a neighbor's house out on the highway to phone the sheriff."

Angie loudly cleared her throat.

Paavo glanced her way, then put his arm around her waist and guided her forward. "This is Angelina Amalfi, the woman I told you about." He introduced her to the sheriff and deputy.

"I'm here to work with Mr. Tay on his menu," Angie explained to the sheriff.

He didn't look impressed.

"Shall we sit?" Moira interjected. They did, the three men fidgeting uncomfortably on the stiff Victorian furniture. Angie sat next to Paavo, but forward on the seat, her hip against his thigh and her hand on his knee. That didn't add to his comfort level.

"I haven't seen my brother since last evening," Moira began. "He often goes out after dinner for a nature walk, so—"

"A what?" Butz interrupted.

"A walk in the woods."

The sheriff nodded.

"Anyway, around ten or so last night, Angie—Miss Amalfi here—thought she saw a rat in the kitchen and tried to find him."

"Him, meaning Finley?" Butz asked. "Or the rat?"

"My brother."

"I didn't *think* I saw a rat," Angie said. "I know I did."

"I'm sure, Sheriff," Moira said, "all she saw was a little field mouse. Angie lives in an apartment building in San Francisco. She's not used to such things."

Angie folded her arms. "I know the difference between a small mouse and a large rat. Besides, it was dead."

"The mouse was probably so scared it froze in its tracks," Moira said.

"Then why was it draped around a box of rat poison?" Angie asked.

"Hold it, ladies!" Butz said. "Are we here to discuss a man or a mouse?"

"I called you here to find my brother," Moira said.

"All right, then."

Angie clamped her mouth shut, annoyed that they wouldn't listen.

Paavo didn't get it. Why would Moira Tay try to deny any connection between a poisoned rat and her brother's disappearance? Was it too obvious a warning, or too silly to be one? Or was she simply too close to see it?

On the other hand, Paavo couldn't help but wonder if he was being too suspicious. Too much the big-city cop, as Butz might say.

"I wasn't worried," Moira continued, "when Finley didn't come home last night. He enjoys meditation—sometimes does it for hours. He'll occasionally fast as well, to achieve an even higher level of spirituality."

"So your brother has stayed out all night before this?"

"A few times."

One of Butz's eyes twitched a couple of times before he turned again to Angie. "Where is your dead rat, miss?"

"It disappeared."

"Just like Finley Tay," he said.

Angie noticed Paavo's blue eyes sparkle and his lips begin to break into a grin—until he caught her disapproving glare.

"Not only did the rat disappear," she said, facing Butz again, "but so did the whole platter he was on, the one with the lentil-soy cutlets. Even the box of poison was gone."

"Lentil what?" Butz asked; then before she could answer, he dismissed it with a wave of his hand. "Never mind. Who took it?"

"I'm not sure."

"Any guesses?"

"Well, if I had to guess, I'd say it was Miss Greer."

"Hilda Greer?" the sheriff asked. "From town?"

"She's a terrible person," Angie said, not caring that

the sheriff knew her. "She wouldn't let me go into the kitchen in the morning, or let me help with lunch or dinner. What does she think I'm here for?"

"Good question," Butz murmured.

Deputy Sparks snickered. Paavo noticed that he'd been spending the whole time sitting across the room staring at Angie. Paavo put his hand possessively on her waist and glared back at the man. Sparks scrunched down in his seat.

Angie folded her arms and leaned back against the sofa.

Butz turned to Moira. "Is anyone else here besides you two, the cook, and the gardener?"

"Yes. The inn's investors have all gathered to be sure that when we open in three weeks, all goes according to plan."

"Investors? Hmm. So Finley Tay isn't the sole owner after all."

"That's correct."

"Okay, who are those investors?"

"We have Mr. and Mrs. Greg Jeffers. He was a house-painter until he married." She hesitated before adding, "Mrs. Jeffers is wealthy."

"I see."

"Then there's Chelsea Worthington; she's a student, but her parents are well-to-do and saw this as a worthy investment for her. Reginald Vane, an electrical engineer from Vancouver, and Martin and Bethel Bayman. She's a popular channeler, with quite a following."

"A what?" Butz asked.

"She communicates with the spirit world," Moira explained. "A spirit speaks through her body."

Butz's face wrinkled in disgust. "Cult stuff."

"Not at all," Moira said.

"Where are these fine people?"

"Some are up in their rooms, some outside looking for Finley. And I believe the Jefferses are having an OBE."

Butz started to ask a question, then clamped his mouth shut and instead rubbed his chin, "Is your brother's car gone, Miss Tay?"

"No."

"Any reason to suspect foul play?"

"None at all."

"Was anyone here who could have given him a ride into town?"

"No." Moira looked dejected.

"What about those men finishing up the hot tub?" Angie asked.

"That's right." Moira's voice sounded hopeful for the first time that afternoon. "They didn't want to have to come all the way out here again on Monday, so they stayed late to finish up."

"All right." Butz stood up. "Get me the names, addresses, and phone numbers of those hot tub boys and we'll check them out. Right now, I'd like to talk to the investors."

Moira also stood. "I'll get them for you."

"Good. And don't worry about Tay. He probably went off to town with someone and simply hasn't come back yet. He's a grown man, after all."

"But, Sheriff," Angie said, "what if he didn't leave? What if he's out there hurt?"

Butz slowly turned her way. "I've seen those swamis on TV walking on nails. Going through fire. They say they do it all through meditating. His sister here just said Tay knows how to meditate. And nothing out there's as bad as nails or fire. Don't you ladies worry none. He'll turn up, fit as a fiddle."

5

Paavo, his canvas carryall slung over his shoulder, followed Angie up the stairs and across the second-floor gallery toward the west wing. A large oil painting of Hill Haven and the cliffs near the house hung prominently beside a brilliant stained-glass window. It proclaimed to one and all the beauty this house had once possessed.

Paavo stopped at the entrance to the room he and Angie would share. It was simply furnished and was eight-sided, with so many windows it felt as if they were in a tree house. Angie stood in front of the west window, the last glimmer of light from the setting sun behind her. The softly rounded contours of her cheeks took on a reddish glow from the sun, while her big dark eyes, cast in umber shadows, looked even deeper and larger. Her full mouth had a gloss of lipstick, and the golden highlights of her hair created a glow that framed her head. His breath caught, as it so often did when he looked at Angie in repose or in some unexpected setting where he could reflect on how beautiful and special she was to him.

He knew then, beyond doubt, that he'd been right to come here to spend this week with her.

"I hope you like the room," she said, her outspread arms taking in the two plump rose-colored chairs facing a small fireplace, the king-size bed piled high with pillows. The walls were white, the floor uncovered hardwood.

He shut the door and walked toward her.

"There's a fully mirrored dressing room through the door on the left, and a private bath just beyond it," she said.

He dropped his bag on the floor.

"I guess that means you don't want to see the dressing room?" She knew she was babbling.

"Come here," he said, scarcely recognizing that choked whisper as his own.

Angie didn't remember moving, or that he did, but in a moment she was in his arms. His hands rubbed against her waist, sliding under the edges of her green stretch top. She touched his face, scratchy with five o'clock shadow, and buried her fingers in his hair, pulling him closer, wanting more of his kiss.

They sank onto the duvet-covered feather mattress, the piles of pillows against the headboard. But in a moment, Paavo propped himself up on one elbow and looked down at her, his gaze burning as his hand slowly, lingeringly slid from the side of her breast to her waist, her hip, her thigh, then back up again.

Angie couldn't move, too languorous from the heat of his kisses, and too much in need of more. Slowly, she touched his broad shoulders and hard chest. He lifted her hand away and kissed the back of her fingers.

Why did he stop her? she wondered.

"I've got to talk to the sheriff," he said. "Before he leaves. You look beautiful right there. Don't go away."

He kissed her again, then got up from the bed and carried his bags into the dressing room.

She felt like a balloon that'd been deflated. He had to talk to the sheriff in the middle of their big vacation welcome. Why didn't that surprise her? She rolled onto her side. "Do you think the sheriff will have found out anything about Finley's disappearance this quickly?"

"I don't know," he answered from the dressing room. "He made it clear earlier that this town doesn't want the Tays or the inn here. The phone lines aren't simply out of order, they were cut."

"I can't believe it."

He stepped back to the bedroom, leaning against the door frame. His sweater sleeves had been pushed up to just below the elbows, his hair was mussed, and his mouth and eyes were soft. "The road signs to the inn have all been taken down. No one in town would even admit knowing about this place."

"Maybe they were telling the truth. It doesn't open for another three weeks."

"Look at the size of this town, Angie."

"Doesn't mean a thing." She knew she was being obstinate.

He gave the kind of cold stare he was a master at. The kind that made you ready to confess to any crime, because you were convinced he'd nail you one way or the other. "If your boss doesn't show up tonight, I think we should leave."

Her heart sank. This was what she was afraid of. All she had wanted out of this trip was to be alone with Paavo, to have him all to herself for once. Damn Finley Tay and his disappearing act, anyway! "You're letting your imagination run away with you," she said finally. Never mind that Paavo was the most coldly logical person she'd ever met. "Finley will be here soon. It's not a problem."

"I hope you're right," Paavo said. "For now, I'll take a quick shower and go back downstairs and see what the sheriff has to say before he leaves."

"Okay. I'll take one next. It should be dinnertime soon."

He disappeared into the dressing room. She got off the bed and stood where she could watch him. Maybe Finley would show up soon and she could get on with her plans for Paavo.

She watched him take a clean shirt from his bag, then lift out a pair of Levi's and some underwear. She watched him set his shaving things out on a shelf in the bathroom. She would have watched him take his shower, but she didn't want to seem pushy.

As she sat on the bed listening to the water running in the bathroom, she ran her fingers over the satiny duvet, the lace on the pillow coverings, the indentation where Paavo's head had lain. Here she was, miles from home, her boss was missing, the house was supposed to be haunted, and all she could think about was that the bed in this room seemed to be about the size of the Queen Mary. And she was ready to pull up anchor.

She was ninety-nine point nine percent certain that she was head over heels in love with this man and wanted to spend the rest of her life with him. This time together would make or break their relationship, of that she was certain.

As such, this might be the most important week of her entire life, deciding her whole future.

She could handle it.

Then why were her palms perspiring?

◦   ◦   ◦

Outside lights illuminated the driveway well enough that Paavo could see Butz standing beside his car talking with a stiff-looking middle-aged man. As soon as Deputy Sparks started the car's engine, the man gave a bow and turned back to the inn. Butz reached for the car door handle.

"Sheriff," Paavo called. Hurrying toward the sheriff, Paavo registered the stranger's slicked-back brown hair, black suit, black bow tie, and white shirt as they passed. "I'd like to talk to you."

"Sure." Butz rested his elbow on the top of the car. "What's up?"

"I was wondering if you found out anything about Tay's whereabouts."

The sheriff shrugged, his eyes slowly going over Paavo. "Well, I'll tell you," he said. "The more I look at it, the more convinced I am that the fellow just took off."

"Why?"

"Well, one of these people here said they saw him talking with the hot tub boys by their car."

Paavo was surprised. "Who was that?"

"It was that big blond guy. The one with the muscles. Jeffers, his name was."

"Jeffers." Paavo wondered why this Jeffers hadn't mentioned that fact to Moira or Angie earlier.

The sheriff leaned his backside against the door of the car. Sparks shut off the engine. "In fact," Butz said, "Deputy Sparks thought he saw Finley Tay riding through town this very morning. Ain't that right, Sparks?"

"Sure, Sheriff."

This was a new one, Paavo thought. "He's sure of that?"

"Let's say he saw a skinny guy with long brown hair worn in a ponytail."

Paavo nodded, then spoke quietly, stating the obvious to Butz, but not letting his own suspicions show. "This area is a mecca for aging, displaced hippies. How many of them fit that description?"

"Plenty." Butz pulled out a Tiparillo and lit it. "That's why marijuana's the second biggest crop in the area. Right after lumber. Hell, these days with what's happened to the timber industry, maybe it's the first biggest crop. But that's exactly why the folks in this town wouldn't care what happened to someone like Tay. We don't want his type here. These dope-smokers killed our livelihood, and with the spikes they put in trees, they've even killed some of our neighbors when their saws hit the spikes. They say earth first. We say home and family first."

"That's why you're not doing anything to find Tay," Paavo said.

"Well, goddamn, Inspector, I resent that. I do. Does this look like I ain't doing anything?" Butz spread his arms wide, taking in the whole of Hill Haven Inn and the promontory it stood on. "I spent damn near an hour here. Only to learn that even these so-called investors—like that gray-haired boozer—don't think Tay's hurt at all. All he talked about was Tay's money troubles."

"Which one was that?"

"Hell, I don't know. Bayman, I think. Martin Bayman. In fact, he said he lent Tay a lot of money for the inn, and he'll lose it if the inn doesn't open. He wondered if Tay might have taken them all for a ride."

"A con?" Paavo asked.

"Could be. Anyway," the sheriff continued, "when I get back to the office, I'll contact his bank and credit card companies. If anyone tries to get at any of his accounts, we'll learn about it right away, then track him down."

"What about doing a search out here in the meantime?" Paavo asked.

Butz's eyes narrowed. "After forty-eight hours someone can file a missing person report if they want. Even then, I'd have to get some of the townspeople to help search an area this size. Right now, I'll tell you frankly, I don't think I'd be able to get three men to join me. If Finley Tay's disappeared, the last thing anyone in this town would want to do is to find him. Second to last is to help anyone connected with this wacko group. If you're smart, you and your lady will get into that fancy car of yours and go right back home. Like I'm doing. Big Pacific storm's headed this way, and I want to get off this damn hill before the rains hit. That's when this whole hilltop turns into one big water slide. Why else would a nobody like Finley Tay be able to afford this place?"

"He wasn't very helpful, was he?" Moira Tay was waiting in the foyer when Paavo entered the inn. The way her hands were clasped in front of her, her voice so serene and slow, and with her all-black, floor-length clothing, she reminded him of a nun. But then, when he lifted his gaze to hers, the image was shattered by the bold, knowing look she gave him. A look much like that of the woman he'd known many years ago.

The wind had kicked up to almost gale force, and the storm the sheriff had talked about was sure to strike soon.

"He thinks Finley took off," Paavo said.

"I don't know what to think." Moira's only sign of agitation was the twisting together of her long fingers with their short, unpolished nails. "Dinner's ready. Won't you join us? Everyone's in the dining room."

Good, Paavo thought. He'd finally get to meet the mysterious investors. Just then a lightning bolt shot across the sky, followed almost immediately by a loud peal of thunder.

"Let me see if Angie's ready. We'll be right there."

It must have been the sound of their footsteps on the hardwood floors that caused all eyes to turn toward the doorway, Paavo thought, as he and Angie stepped into the dining room.

"Hello, Angie," a plump young woman called. "I saved a place for you and your friend right next to me."

"Thank you, Chelsea," Angie said. Paavo's hand stayed at her back as they crossed the room to the table.

Woodpaneling covered the lower half of the walls, topped by redflocked wallpaper and a series of small seascapes. An enormous crystal chandelier hung over the massive mahogany dining table, and smaller tables along the walls bore colorful vases of dried wildflowers. But by far the dominant feature was a portrait of an old man with muttonchop sideburns, hung so it was seen as soon as one entered the room. One of the original owners of the house, Paavo suspected.

"Good evening, everyone," Angie said. Paavo held her chair out for her as she sat. "This is Paavo Smith. He's also from San Francisco."

The investors murmured their hellos. Paavo sat next to Angie and beside him, seated at the head of the table, was Moira.

She nodded at him in greeting.

"You look pretty tonight, Angie," said Chelsea, seated next to her.

Pretty was an understatement, Paavo thought. Angie had blown him away in her red silk jumpsuit and matching high, spiky heels. Dangling diamond earrings flashed big bucks with each saucy turn of her head. That she'd gone to such trouble just for him made her even more beautiful in his book.

"It's nice to have someone to dress for," Angie replied to Chelsea's compliment, with a smile in Paavo's direction. He rested his wrists on the table, and she reached over to place her small, smooth hand atop his large, rough one. The heat from her touch seared all the way to his toes.

"Yes," Chelsea murmured, "I know exactly what you mean."

Paavo tried not to let his skepticism show as he took in Angie's new friend. She reminded him of an upside-down turnip. Her purple sweatpants amply filled the seat of her chair, while her purple sweatshirt rose to narrow, pinched shoulders. Heavy, unkempt red hair sprawled over her shoulders, springing from a head way too small for the rest of her.

She leaned forward to better see around Angie and smiled at him. "I'm Chelsea Worthington," she said. "From Malibu."

"Nice to meet you," he replied.

Chelsea's dumpiness was in counterpoint to the flamboyance of the older woman seated across the table from her. The woman's turquoise caftan, dotted with silver starbursts, was topped by a turquoise turban with a large crystal in the center of it. A short fringe of wiry gray hair crinkled out from under the turban, framing a face that had clearly been tanned once too often. Her cheeks had the look of dried, minutely cracked leather.

She stared intensely at Paavo, her gaze almost as charged as her hair. Then, to his surprise, she stood and raised her arms, a little like the pope giving a benediction.

"I am Bethel Bayman. And this," she indicated the man at her side, "is my husband, Martin."

She sat down, and they exchanged hellos. Paavo remembered Moira telling the sheriff a famous channeler was in the group. So that was she.

"Cheers." The fifty-something man beside Bethel lifted his water glass in his left hand as if he were toasting them, while at the same time standing and reaching across the table with his right hand to shake Paavo's. Paavo, too, stood.

Seated again, Bayman took a sip from his glass and put it down with a look of disgust. Water was for fish, not for Martin Bayman. It was clear he'd drunk lots more than water already. With his heather-colored houndstooth jacket, white shirt unbuttoned at the neck, and dark blue cravat, he gave off a sophisticated, slightly degenerate air.

Thunder boomed, and the lights flickered. The people at the table shifted uncomfortably while exchanging quick glances.

Paavo glanced down the opposite side of the table. Beside Martin, another place sat empty. Then, directly across from him, was a younger man.

"My name," the man declared in a deep, sonorous voice, "was once Greg Jeffers, but since my enlightenment I call myself Running Spirit. My home is Earth." Obviously pleased with this announcement, Jeffers smiled as he and Paavo half stood to shake hands. The fingers of Jeffers's right hand were heavily encrusted with slightly tarnished silver rings. "Oh, I almost forgot," he said with an indifferent toss of his shoulder-length blond hair. "My wife, Patsy, is sick tonight."

That explained the one empty place setting. Another, at the foot of the table across from Moira, must have been Finley's seat. That left one more, on the far side of Chelsea. It must belong to the stiff-looking fellow with the bow tie whom Paavo had seen talking to the sheriff earlier. Paavo raced through the names of the investors— the Jefferses, the Baymans, Chelsea Worthington, and Reginald Vane. Okay, so Vane was missing.

"Angie's friend," Moira said to the others, "is an inspector of some sort. He knows our local sheriff. Tell us, Mr. Smith, what it is you do?"

She faced him fully, and with her large eyes set in that pale, ethereal face, a sense of déjà-vu rocked him. He stared at her, perhaps a little too long. "I work for the San Francisco Police Department."

"How interesting," Bethel said from the far end of the table. "What do you inspect?"

Paavo glanced at Angie, then back at Bethel. "Homicides."

Bethel opened her mouth, but no sound came out for a moment. Then she said, "Oh," and leaned back in her chair.

"Since Finley can't be with us tonight," Running Spirit said, "I will take it upon myself to lead our little group in thanks for this meal."

"You?" Martin asked. He glanced at the others. "Who gave Running Mouth the right to lead anything?"

"Let us all join hands," Running Spirit intoned, ignoring Martin. "We need to form a circle and use our energy to bring Finley back to us safely."

Moira took Jeffers's hand. Eyes shut and heads bowed, they sat with their free hands outstretched, dangling in the air, waiting for the others to grasp them. The others glanced about uneasily. Martin folded his arms.

Angie could have gladly knocked all their heads together. Here she was, trying to convince Paavo this was a fine place to stay for the week, and this group, previously a little strange, had now totally weirded out on her.

"We must join hands," Running Spirit repeated solemnly, "so we will be cleansed and purified. Mind, spirit, body. We will use the pure and nutritious food we are about to receive to renew and energize ourselves. To cleanse our minds, our stomachs, and our bowels."

I'm not hearing this, Angie thought. Was Running Mouth—she liked that—saying grace or lecturing them on laxatives?

"I don't want my mind clean," Martin said lecherously. "I like it just the way it is."

Chelsea rolled her eyes. Bethel adjusted her turban, which had a tendency to list toward her left ear. Moira kept her eyes shut, and Angie snickered, then clasped her hand against her mouth, pretending to clear her throat.

"Let us pray," Running Spirit said.

Had she heard right? Running Spirit didn't look like he prayed to anything but the god of Nautilus equipment. On this cold February evening he had come to dinner practically bare-chested, wearing only a white leather vest. The man had the kind of sculptured, muscular build achieved only by months of workouts in front of a mirror.

Still, despite this brazen display of narcissism, Angie couldn't keep her eyes off him. Even egomaniacs could be good-looking, and that scantily covered bronzed chest didn't hurt. What was funny about him, though, was that he seemed oddly familiar, with his small eyes, huge jaw, long blond hair, and rugged good looks. She must have seen a picture of someone who resembled him. Some pirate movie, maybe? She just couldn't remember.

"Where's Reginald?" Angie asked. "Shouldn't he be with us?"

"He's got another migraine," Chelsea said. "He's very sensitive to stress."

Martin snorted. "His bow tie's probably too tight."

"Will you shut up, Martin, and take our hands?" Bethel said shortly. "I'd like to eat tonight." She grabbed his hand. With an exaggerated shudder, he reached across the missing Mrs. Jeffers's place and took Running Spirit's hand.

Bethel reached across Finley's unused place setting, offering her hand to Chelsea who in turn took Angie's.

Everyone's hands were linked except Paavo's. Angie turned to him.

Paavo could see the consternation on her face. She knew he hated things like this. He took her hand and saw a flash of relief light her eyes. Next, he reached over to Moira. Her eyes opened at his touch. Her mouth upturned ever so slightly in a smile, and she moved her hand so that their fingers entwined. She closed her eyes again.

He didn't shut his eyes and didn't bow his head, nor did he look at Angie. He was certain she had taken in Moira's smile with some interest. Angie didn't miss much where he was concerned. Across the table, he was surprised to catch Running Spirit's glare of obvious anger.

"Breathe deeply," Running Spirit bellowed, averting his gaze from Paavo's. "Think pure thoughts of being cleansed and refreshed."

"I smell something strange," Bethel cried, her eyes still squeezed shut. "I hope it's not perfume. I'm allergic to such smells. I thought everyone knew that."

Angie couldn't imagine anyone being allergic to her dab of *Quelques Fleurs*.

Running Spirit, barely hiding his irritation at the interruption, tried again. "Let us thank the Supreme Oneness that is all, with whom we communicate with our every

action, for bringing us together today to share this meal.
We ask for his or her help in keeping Finley safe."

They observed a moment of silence, then began to
release hands and relax. "Excellent," Running Spirit
loudly proclaimed.

Paavo kept Angie's hand in his.

"Yes, yes." Bethel's voice was fervent, tinged with a
hint of hysteria as she raised her eyes to the chandelier
and lifted her arms. "I felt your energy, Allakaket,
directed at me to keep Finley safe and well."

"What are you talking about, Bethel?" Running Spirit
snapped.

"You want him safe, don't you? To return to us?"
Bethel shut her eyes and clasped her hands. "Allakaket
said—as I channeled him earlier today—that he and I
will lead the way for Finley to come home."

Running Spirit snorted. "A four-hundred-year-old
Eskimo knows where Finley Tay is?"

"The proper name is Inuit, not Eskimo," Bethel retorted.

"Inuit or idiot, you need to start smoking better quality
stuff. Your Eskimo boy's wires are crossed."

"They are not." She smacked her turban back in place.
"I channel him perfectly."

"Lady, you're off the dial. If there ever was an
Allakaket and he had any sense, he wouldn't talk to the
likes of you."

Paavo tugged on Angie's hand. She nearly burst out
laughing. Whatever those two were talking about hardly
sounded like English.

"Oh?" Bethel leaned forward. "How did you come to
know so much? No spirit guide has ever contacted you."

"I know what I've been granted," Running Spirit said,
smugly superior. "At least I don't peddle make-believe
drivel from an imaginary igloo."

Paavo hadn't seen a display like this since watching films about dysfunctional social groups at a psych class at the police academy. With each fired salvo, heads swung one way and then the other, as at a tennis match.

"You are so ignorant, Greg Jeffers," Bethel hissed. "I don't know why Finley ever had anything to do with you. You poor man's Hulk Hogan!"

"You should talk. Everyone knows your name should be Brothel, not Bethel, you old—"

"Dear friends," Moira interjected in her most serene, otherworldly voice. "It's so nice to have you all here with me in this time of stress."

Shamefaced, the combatants fell silent.

Running Spirit placed his hand over Moira's. "Forgive me. Here I was thinking of myself, of my calling as a guru who one day will fully flower, already trying hard to burst forth, to lead others . . . but I was forgetting your pain, your loss."

"It's all right, Greg. I mean, Running Spirit." Moira pulled her hand away. "Ah, here's our meal."

Miss Greer rolled a cart to the table. She gave a haughty glance at Angie, sniffed, then walked away.

The meal began with appetizers of sliced mushrooms, eggplant, and broccoli. Raw. Angie took a sliver of each. If she'd been in the kitchen she'd have sautéed them, or at least steamed them, perhaps served them chilled with a nice vinaigrette. This way, they were absolutely boring.

An orange-yellow soup was presented next. Paavo took a sip, then looked questioningly at her. She tasted hers. "Carrots," she informed him. No spices, not even salt. No self-respecting rabbit would have touched it.

The main dish was a catastrophe called "lasagna" made without meat or cheese. Giving the name lasagna to cur-dled soy milk between layers of wide, flat pasta floating in

watery tomato sauce, a travesty of the delicious Italian
dish, stirred Angie's ethnic ire.

She looked at the others. They seemed too wrapped
up in their own worlds to care what was on their plates.
Chelsea watched Running Spirit, Running Spirit watched
Moira, and Moira stared straight ahead. Bethel watched
Martin, and Martin watched his water glass, every so
often adding to it from a silver flask kept in the inside
pocket of his sports jacket.

By the third bite of the abomination on her plate,
Angie pushed it aside. Tomorrow, she'd take over the
kitchen whether Mrs. Greer agreed or not. Meals à la
Finley were simply unacceptable. No wonder there were
ghosts at Hill Haven. They didn't serve haute cuisine
here. They served haunt cuisine.

6

Back in their room, Paavo had to shake his head, amazed. Working in Homicide in San Francisco, he thought he'd seen everything there was to see, but this bunch took the cake. He was starving on a lost weekend with the weird.

"They're not so bad," Angie said, as if reading his mind. "Just a tad eccentric."

The rain had started and was beating lightly against the many windows of the room. Someone had already placed the kindling and stacked the logs in the fireplace. All that was needed was to light it and make sure the fire caught.

"What I can't figure," Paavo said as he took the matches off the mantel, "is why these particular people invested in this inn to begin with. They don't like the food, they despise each other, and they don't look like they're rolling in dough."

"I have to admit there's nothing about the place that would seem to qualify it as a good investment," Angie added.

"The sheriff and the town were wrong about one thing, though," Paavo said as he lit the fire. "There's no cult involved here."

"That's for sure," Angie said, then chuckled. "These people don't get along well enough to form a cult."

"Their not getting along might have something to do with Finley's disappearance."

"Yes, poor Finley." She sighed then, all traces of laughter gone. "You don't think he's just gone off to meditate, do you?"

The fire was burning brightly. Still seated on the floor, he turned to face her. "No, not to meditate. He's either gone away for some strange purpose he couldn't let anyone know about, or something's happened to him. Whatever it is, it isn't right, and I don't think you should be in the middle of it."

She studied his face. "Are you saying we should leave?"

"Yes."

"Leave Finley?"

He thought it was her job, the inn, she was concerned about walking away from, not her boss. "Finley?"

"He'll need me. When he comes back."

He frowned. "If he comes back."

He could see the shudder that rippled through her. "Do you want to leave tonight, then?" she asked. She should never play poker, he thought. Everything she felt showed in her big brown eyes, as clearly as if written in neon. Right now, he saw her disappointment.

He ran his fingers through his hair, fighting off the need to console her. Every cop instinct he'd developed in over eleven years on the force told him to get Angie out of here immediately. But whenever he looked at her, all he'd learned flew right out of his head. He might as well have been a rookie.

He remembered, too, what Butz said about the rains. Well, it was raining now. "I guess it'd be more dangerous finding our way down that narrow road in the dark," he found himself saying, "than just staying here tonight."

"We'll be comfortable here," she said, her face brightening. "I mean, this room is really lovely, don't you think?"

It wasn't the room that worried him.

"It is nice," he admitted.

"This was Susannah Sempler's room," she said.

"Who?"

"Susannah Sempler. She was the daughter of Ezra Sempler, the man who built the house."

Angie walked over to the bay window and peered out at the rain. It was falling harder already, the steady beat on the windows drowning out the crash of the waves against the cliffs. Her voice grew wistful. "For over sixty years, Susannah lived here all alone. She never found anyone to love, no one to share her life with. It made me feel sorry, not only for her but also for the house. This could have been such a beautiful family home. But it's never known love. Only loneliness."

He stood. "You think a house can know feelings, Angie?"

"Absolutely. They're like living, breathing things—perhaps because so much life goes on in them. Or should. I believe houses know a lot more than we give them credit for."

As she stood at the window, her face, reflected in the dark glass, was serious and contemplative, revealing a side she rarely let anyone see. "Finley will show up soon. He has to. Tomorrow, for sure."

"Perhaps," was all he said.

At the sight of her worried face, he went to her side.

She leaned against him. "All these windows make me feel as if we're afloat in the sky." A gentle smile touched her lips. "Living in a cloud, perhaps."

His hand lightly caressed her face, her hair, her ear. He let the diamonds she wore drape over his fingertips a moment, then he cupped her face, nudging her chin toward him. He took in her dark brown eyes, serious yet filled with warmth, pleasure, and wonder. "This is how it should be with you. Not quite real, and high above the rest of the world."

She placed her hand over his large, strong one, scarcely able to believe that they were here, in this strange yet lovely room, alone. "But I am real, Paavo."

"Are you?" He bent to kiss her lightly, his eyes intent, his hand moving from her chin to the back of her head to intertwine with the curls of her hair. The mystical aura of the room, the patter of the rain, the solitude of the setting stole over him and made him think of things he didn't want to ponder—things like being together with Angie forever, like never being alone again. He tried to mentally break the spell. He needed time—cold, logical time. "There's no way a woman like you should be in my life," he said finally. "Sometimes I think you can't be any more real than the Sempler ghosts. That I'll close my eyes and you'll disappear. Or that I'm just imagining you."

"Inspector," she said, returning his kiss with one that seared, "there's no way you could imagine me."

Cold logic melted in the midst of her fire, and all his careful resolve went with it. His heart filled, and the solemnity of his expression broke. "I know," he said softly, "and that's the best part."

As his lips met hers a bolt of lightning lit their room for just a moment. Then a scream filled the darkness.

Paavo was out of Angie's arms and through the door before the scream ended.

"Stay in the room," he shouted as he ran down the hall to the stairs.

She darted after him. "No way I'm staying here alone." She hadn't gotten the first word out, though, before he'd disappeared.

Chelsea, whose room was between Angie's and the gallery, stuck her head out the door. "What was that?"

"Come on," Angie said. "Follow that cop."

Chelsea ran into the hall wearing a long, thick flannel nightgown with huge orange pansies on a bright yellow background. "What cop?" she asked, looking down the now empty hall. "Do you think that was Elise Sempler? They say she cries at night."

"Cries?" Angie stopped halfway down the stairs and looked back at Chelsea. Luckily, Chelsea wasn't close enough to barrel into her or she might have pitched Angie right over the bannister. "Elise cries?"

"Yes."

Angie shivered at the memory of the strange crying sound she had heard last night. No, she told herself, couldn't be. "That was a scream," she said. "And far too human."

As she reached the bottom step, she saw Running Spirit stepping into the living room through the French patio doors. "What's the ruckus?" he shouted.

"This way," Angie called without slowing down. She stopped abruptly, however, at the entrance to the kitchen.

Paavo and Moira were bending at the waist, facing each other. Stretched out between them was a yellow checkered tablecloth. They let it go, and Angie watched it drop down over a body and cover it from the knees up. Still showing were support-stocking-covered legs leading to black round-toed, square-heeled sensible shoes. Angie knew those shoes.

Running Spirit pushed past her. "Stay back," Paavo said.

Moira pressed her hands to her mouth as she slowly backed away. Running Spirit's hands clenched and unclenched. He was clearly torn between offering her comfort and obeying Paavo.

Chelsea grabbed Angie's arm. "Who is it?"

"The cook, Miss Greer," Paavo said. "Don't come any closer, and don't touch anything."

Angie, Chelsea, and Running Spirit nodded.

"What happened to her?" Angie asked.

"We're not sure yet," Paavo answered.

"I came in here to make sure everything was turned off for the night," Moira cried, "and found her lying there. I didn't even have to touch her to know—"

"What's going on here?" Bethel's voice rang out as she and Martin appeared in the doorway. "A party? Without us?" As she pushed her way past Chelsea and Angie into the room, she gasped and stopped short, Martin right behind her.

"Who is that?" Bethel demanded.

"Miss Greer," Angie said.

"Who?"

"The cook."

"Hey," Martin said, "the old witch must have eaten some of her own cooking—Rat Delight."

"Martin!" Bethel said.

Martin's statement, Angie knew, was on all their minds—especially after Angie had told everyone about the dead rat the night before.

Paavo turned to Moira. "Is your phone working yet? We need to get the sheriff up here right away."

"The sheriff?" Moira said with a half laugh, half cry. "No, the phone's still dead. Someone would have to try to go down the mountainside in the rain. The roads are slick, though. And it's dark. It would be too dangerous. That's why Miss Greer stayed. She'd been afraid to drive home, and now—"

"What about a four-wheel drive?" Paavo asked. "Does anyone up here have one?"

"Quint does. My gardener."

"Any chance he might make it?" Paavo asked.

"If anyone could, it'd be him. But Miss Greer had a heart condition. The doctors warned her something like this might happen when she refused to let them operate. It was just a matter of time."

Paavo had seen heart attack and stroke victims, natural deaths of all kinds. One look at the corpse when he walked into the kitchen this evening and he knew this was no natural death. Her face was a bloodless gray, her lifeless eyes a fiery red from broken blood vessels. There were no signs of a struggle near the body. Instead, she was lying there neatly. Too neatly. She was on her back, her arms at her sides, legs straight and together. Even the top button of her blouse had been fastened, and her collar rode high, completely covering her neck.

"Even if it was a natural death—" Paavo began.

"If?" Running Spirit bellowed.

"If it was, we would still need to get the sheriff up here. He needs to find out what killed her."

"What do you think did?" Angie asked.

He glanced at Moira. "Miss Tay said she had a bad heart." He counted the investors—Jeffers, the Baymans, Chelsea. "Where's your wife, Jeffers?" he asked.

"Asleep, I guess. I was out on the porch meditating."

Paavo nodded. "What about Vane? Has anyone seen him this evening?"

"His room is the only one on the third floor," Moira said slowly. "Perhaps he didn't hear anything."

"He takes some kind of strong medicine for migraines," Chelsea said.

"Can you see about getting the sheriff?" Paavo asked Moira. "If the storm continues, it might be even more difficult to get help tomorrow."

"I'll go to Quint's cottage," she replied. "I just have to get my raincoat and hat. There are a number of rain slickers in the closet just off the foyer for anyone else who might want to use them."

"Terrific," Martin Bayman said drily. "Isn't this an appetizing kitchen? Such a cozy inn we have here."

"He's right, you know," Angie said to Paavo. "Can't we move her to a bed or something? This seems so heartless."

"I should think California has laws against dead bodies in public kitchens," Bethel said.

"Why don't you ask your Eskimo friend?" Running Spirit said. "Doesn't he know everything?"

"Won't the two of you show respect for the dead and stop bickering?" Angie said, exasperated.

"It's her kitchen now," Martin said. "You two better listen to her or you might be next. I overheard you arguing with Miss Greer, Angie."

"Me?" She couldn't believe what he'd just implied. "So what?"

Martin shrugged. "Let's go, Bethel."

Bethel glared at Running Spirit, lifted her nose in the air, and flounced off, Martin behind her.

"I'll find Moira and go with her," Running Spirit said, then he, too, left.

"Do you know where they keep their sheets?" Paavo asked Angie.

"Sheets?" As understanding struck, she blanched. "Oh, yes, I'll find you one. A big one."

Chelsea looked around and saw that no one remained in the kitchen but the hard-looking detective and the corpse. "I'll come and help, Angie," she called, and ran from the room.

Outside, the wind howled and hard-driven rain lashed the house. Inside, candles instead of electric lights illuminated the library, casting an eerie glow over the somber group. Angie sat in a large wing chair watching Running Spirit pace back and forth across the room like a caged animal. His wife, Patsy, and Reginald Vane still had not been heard from, and the Baymans had retired for the night.

Paavo stayed in the kitchen, saying he'd join Angie in the library soon. As a homicide detective, he just didn't know what to do with a natural death, Angie guessed, and instinctively treated it as a murder.

At the side table, Moira poured herself a goblet of blood-red wine. Her black clothes disappeared into the darkness, and her white face, hands, and unbraided golden hair seemed to float, disembodied, in the room.

"Angie," Chelsea called from the back of the library. "Come over here. You've got to see Jack Sempler's portrait." Her gaze turned lovingly upward to the portrait that hung over the mantel.

A handsome young man stood on the cliff near Hill Haven. He wore tan riding britches and a white shirt with wide, billowing sleeves and a high stand-up collar unbuttoned at the top. His thick auburn hair was slightly tousled by the wind, and his large, intelligent hazel eyes stared off into the distance. The man looked so real, Angie's heart lurched. It seemed as if he could step from the painting and join them, full of life and telling of his adventures.

"So that's Jack Sempler," Angie said. "He's the one Elise loved, right? He went away to sea and she killed herself by jumping from the cliffs near the house."

"Yes," Chelsea said with a sigh. "It's easy to understand, isn't it? He's so handsome. So wonderful." She reached up and lightly touched the gold frame. "If only I could touch him this way," she whispered, then blinked back sudden tears.

"Who's the older man in the portrait in the dining room?"

"That was Ezra, the father. The man who built Hill Haven."

Angie couldn't stop looking at Jack. "You're right— Jack Sempler was very handsome."

"Wasn't he? This was made when he was young. About the time Elise came to live with the Semplers. He was only twenty-two, Elise eighteen, and Susannah twenty-five. You can see why Elise fell in love with him." Chelsea faced Angie. "There are no pictures of him after he returned home from sea. He was only thirty-four when he died."

Angie shivered. That was Paavo's age. "Do you know what happened to him?"

"No one knows," Chelsea said softly. "All we know is that he died in this house."

Like Miss Greer, Angie thought. And Finley? The idea had come unbidden, and she forced it away. Gazing up at the painting once more, she could almost feel Jack Sempler's presence, could almost imagine what it would be like to have those intelligent eyes meet hers.

"I'm staying in his room," Chelsea continued, "and at night I can feel his presence there with me."

"You're giving me goose bumps, Chelsea. Stop it!"

Chelsea's story wasn't all that was making Angie's skin prickle. Someone was watching her. She turned. A dark form filled the high-backed wing chair behind her. She couldn't quite make out who it was. Stepping backward, she bumped into Chelsea.

"Be careful," the man's precisely accented voice said. Angie started, then felt decidedly foolish as Reginald Vane leaned forward into the light.

"Mr. Vane, you startled me," she said, then laughed. "Too many of Chelsea's stories, I guess."

"Miss Worthington is rather taken with the boy in that portrait, isn't she? He was quite the young Romeo, I understand."

With his black suit, white shirt, black tie, and thinning hair slicked straight back, Vane looked even more like the quintessential English butler than he had the first time they met.

Angie sat once more, unsure of the propriety of a situation like this. Miss Manners never covered what one should say or do when there was a dead body in the house. Or when one's host was missing. She waited for someone else to make the first move.

"I know what," Chelsea said after a time. "Let's hold a séance. We can ask the Sempler ghosts to come and help us find Finley."

"Don't be silly," Running Spirit said. "Moira's too tired for such foolishness."

"It's not foolish," Reginald Vane said. "I like Miss Worthington's idea. Do try, Miss Tay."

"Have you ever contacted a ghost before?" Angie asked, skepticism all but dripping from her tongue.

"I may have," Moira replied, enigmatic as always. "It's hard to say if my apparent success was only because the desire for the ghosts was so powerful among those with me. They believed the ghosts were there, whether they were or not. In other words, I might have produced no more than a manifestation of the beliefs of the living, and not the dead at all."

"In that case," Running Spirit said, "given the strength of Chelsea's belief in young Sempler, you might end up with a dozen ghosts of the seafaring Jack instead of just one." He laughed.

"You can shut your mouth, Greg Jeffers," Chelsea cried. "You don't know anything about me or Jack Sempler."

He smirked. "But I know gullible when I see it."

"You are totally hateful! Why aren't you gone instead of Finley—" Chelsea clapped her hand to her mouth and, wide-eyed, looked at Moira. "I'm sorry, I didn't mean . . ."

"We will hold a séance," Moira said.

The group pulled a table away from the wall and placed chairs around it. Moira lit a candle in the center of the table while Chelsea blew out the others. Everyone joined hands.

For a long while, no sound existed but that of incessant rain and harshly blowing wind. Then Moira slowly intoned, "Jack Sempler. Elise Sempler. Susannah Sempler. Join us here, we beseech you." She waited a heartbeat or two, then began to drone the words once more.

Angie wondered what Paavo would think if he walked in now. Probably that she was as flaky as the rest of them.

Moira stared at the candle. The table didn't shake. Nothing flew across the room. The candlelight didn't even flicker. As a séance, this was a dud.

"Jack . . . Jack Sempler," Moira called. "I feel your presence. Won't you give us some sign you are here? Please. Some sign."

"He's here," Chelsea cried. "I know he's here. He'll let us know." She jumped to her feet. "*There*! Look!"

Angie's hair stood on end as she whirled around to look where Chelsea pointed. She saw nothing.

"He was there," Chelsea cried.

"I believe you," Reginald Vane said. "Please sit, Miss Worthington. Don't overexcite yourself."

"But it *is* exciting." Chelsea's eyes were shining.

"Jack," Moira called. "Come back to us, Jack."

Nothing happened.

"Elise?" Moira called. "Susannah? Tell us you are with us. Help us find my brother. Will you talk with us tonight?"

They waited. Angie held her breath, hoping to hear or see something, despite her skepticism. "Who can tell with ghosts?" she said after a while. "Maybe they had a previous commitment. You know, couldn't fit another haunting into their schedule tonight."

"That could be," Chelsea agreed, ignoring the glares directed at Angie.

Angie looked at her incredulously.

"Well," Chelsea said, not seeming to notice, "I guess I'll go up to bed. At least in my room I feel as if Jack Sempler is nearby."

The grandfather clock in the drawing room began to strike twelve.

"The witching hour," Reginald Vane said.

"On second thought," Chelsea said, "I think I'll wait until it's through striking."

They grew quiet, silently counting the strokes.

A chill went down Angie's spine. She'd seen this scene

a zillion times on TV. Old black-and-white movies, in particular, had corny scenes about ghosts at midnight. In fact, in real life it was still a corny scene.

The clock stopped. Chelsea didn't make a move to leave. What nonsense, Angie thought. There were more important things to do tonight than to sit here quaking. Things like going to bed. With Paavo. Where was he, anyway? "I think I'll say goodnight," she said and stood.

"Are you sure you don't want to wait a few minutes?" Chelsea asked, her eyes round.

Angie put a hand on one hip. "I ain't afraid o' no ghosts."

Chelsea was just beginning to join in the others' nervous laughter when a slow, dull, pounding sound reverberated through the room.

Angie sat down again, quickly. "What was that?"

No one answered.

The pounding continued. *Tha-thump. Tha-thump.* It grew louder.

Moira clasped her hands as if in prayer. Her eyes searched the ceiling and the walls.

Running Spirit grasped her wrist. "Who's doing that?" he called out. "What's up there?"

"Chelsea's room is directly above," Moira said. "I presume it's empty."

"Jack?" Chelsea cried, staring at the ceiling.

"The noise doesn't seem to be coming from there," Running Spirit said.

"It seems to be coming from the walls," Angie said.

Tha-thump. Tha-thump. Tha-thump. Tha-thump.

"It sounds like a heartbeat," Reginald Vane whispered.

"Maybe it's something evil," Chelsea cried. "We wanted the Sempler ghosts, but these are bad ones. What did you do, Moira?"

"What if Miss Greer didn't die of a heart condition?" Reginald Vane asked. "What if she died of fright?"

"Make it stop!" Chelsea cried.

Tha-thump-tha-thump. Tha-thump-tha-thump. The beat quickened.

Angie's heart raced as fast and loud as the pounding. "I'm getting out of here." She turned to run to her room.

In the doorway stood a white, unearthly figure. Elise? Susannah? Angie screamed.

"Patsy!" Running Spirit bellowed. "What the hell are you doing here?" He let go of Moira and stepped toward his wife.

"It's the ghosts," she cried, running into the room. She wore a flowing white nightgown. Her hair was frizzy and wild about her head, and her face had even less color than her gown. "They're going to kill us. We'll be dead. Like Finley."

Tha-thump-tha-thump-tha-thump-tha-thump!

"No!" Moira cried, her hands over her ears.

Suddenly, magically, the house fell quiet. No one breathed.

A moment later, Paavo casually strolled into the room, taking in each member of the little group before him.

Moira looked ready to collapse, as did Chelsea. Running Spirit appeared worried the others might think he'd lost his nerve. The previously absent Reginald Vane was devoid of expression.

Then there was Patsy Jeffers. Paavo found her most interesting, even though he suspected she was the type who had spent most of her twenty-nine or thirty years being ignored or forgotten about. Her uncombed hair was closer to dull beige than to blond or brown. Her eyebrows and lashes, if they existed, blended with her skin tone. Her flat brown eyes darted about continually, except when she looked at her husband. She gazed upon him with awe, as if in the throes of pure rapture.

They had to be one of the most unlikely couples ever.

Now, as Patsy clutched Running Spirit's arm, she searched his face, then bowed her head and pressed her forehead against his shoulder. Raising her hand to his chest, her fingers splayed over his heart. The chunky gold band on her third finger was too big for her, and her fingernails had been chewed to little half-moons.

"Paavo, thank God you're here." Angie hurried to his side. "Could you tell what that noise was? Was it as loud in the rest of the house?"

"It seemed to be coming from in here," he said.

"God, it was the ghosts!" Chelsea cried.

"I'm sure these noises have a logical explanation," Moira said. "Probably something to do with the pipes. Don't you agree, Greg?"

Running Spirit caught Paavo's eye, seeking his agreement. "Sure," he said. "It could be the pipes."

"I think we should all retire," Moira announced nervously. "The storm is terrible tonight. That's what made the noise. It was the wind through some open part of the house. Or something." She stopped, aware she was clutching at straws.

"Or maybe," Patsy said, staring at her husband, "it was Finley."

No one replied.

"It appears everyone's here but the Baymans," Paavo said, breaking the uneasy silence. "Would you get them, Miss Tay?"

Fear crossed her face momentarily before she masked it. "You want them to wait with the rest of us for the sheriff?"

"Everyone should be here."

"It might be very late before the sheriff can get through," Moira added. "Perhaps morning. Since Miss Greer's already dead, I see no reason for the sheriff to hurry. We're wasting time down here for nothing."

"The Baymans, please, Miss Tay," Paavo asked again.

She paled, but left without another word.

"You haven't met Mr. Vane yet, Paavo," Angie said. The two men shook hands as Angie introduced them. "Mr. Vane is another investor. He's from British Columbia," she explained.

Vane's grip was loose. His hands were pasty and smooth and, like the others' hands, showed no marks or scratches. "Have you been down here long?" Paavo asked.

"Miss Tay knocked on my door earlier and told me what happened to Miss Greer. I'm afraid I would have slept through all the excitement otherwise. I decided to come down to await the sheriff with the rest of you."

Paavo nodded.

"Mr. Smith's a homicide detective," Chelsea told Reginald. "It's good there was no foul play or we might all be suspects."

"You're making way too much out of this." Running Spirit's voice boomed across the room. "An old lady got sick and died. What's the problem?"

Paavo didn't want to go into just what the problem was. Until the sheriff arrived, he'd keep his own counsel.

Earlier, in the kitchen, he'd used the top of his pen to push down Miss Greer's high collar and expose her neck. Dark bruises and abrasions indicated she had been strangled. Careful examination of her hands showed the possibility of blood and skin under her fingernails, as if she had struggled with her killer.

The kitchen, however, was neat and undisturbed, with no sign of her being taken by surprise either while working or perhaps just getting a late snack. Deep scuff marks marred one portion of the otherwise immaculately waxed linoleum floor.

He suspected it had been a brief but desperate struggle with a killer she had known well enough that he or she could get close to her without arousing suspicion or fear. The killer had struck before she could even cry out.

What, though, was Miss Greer doing in the kitchen at that time of night? And why was the killer there? Could it have been a planned meeting? All of this information and speculation he'd share only with the sheriff, and perhaps Angie. Right now, in this house, there were only two people who knew how Miss Greer had died. Him and the murderer.

7

Moira led the Baymans into the library. For two people who'd retired for the night an hour or two earlier, they appeared surprisingly awake.

Paavo stood before the assembled group. "I had hoped the sheriff would have arrived by now. Since he hasn't, there's a good chance he can't get through. All of you should understand that Miss Greer's death coupled with Mr. Tay's disappearance is suspicious in itself."

"Oh, my God," Chelsea cried. Everyone faced her. "What if Finley Tay killed Miss Greer? And he disappeared to establish an alibi?"

"Why don't you stick with your horny ghosts?" Running Spirit said disgustedly. "You've got vapors for brains."

"Miss Worthington isn't the only one who will draw conclusions," Paavo said. "As a police officer at the scene, I need to ask each of you a few questions."

They grumbled loudly.

"The sheriff's investigation will go much faster if you cooperate with me now," he said. "Stay here until you're called into the living room. Miss Worthington, I'll start with you."

"Me?" Chelsea squeaked the word, her face paler than Moira's. Following him from the room, she looked like a death row inmate making that final walk.

Angie was proud of Paavo's take-charge demeanor. If she'd been wearing a shirt with buttons, she'd have popped them. If murder was afoot, he'd figure it out. Maybe even tonight.

She could see it now. After grilling them one by one, he'd gather everyone into the drawing room. Then, just like Nero Wolfe, he'd announce the name of the murderer.

But what made Paavo think there was a murderer? Miss Greer died from her heart condition, didn't she?

"He has no right to do this to us!" Bethel Bayman said, standing up. "I'm going to bed."

"That would look mighty suspicious, if you ask me." Angie spoke the words disinterestedly, as if she couldn't care less what Bethel did.

Bethel gave her a haughty glare, then with a swish of her robe, sat down again.

In the drawing room, Chelsea sat on the sofa catty-corner to the chair Paavo took. He faced her, a notebook in his hand.

"Just relax, Miss Worthington, and answer the questions as best you remember," he said.

"Yessir."

"When did you last see Finley Tay?"

"You think he's dead, don't you?"

"Let me ask the questions, Miss Worthington."

She pouted and folded her hands. "After dinner Saturday night. I saw him leave for his walk."

"Did anyone go with him?"

"I thought everyone did, Inspector. Everyone but me and Angie. Finley's nature walks were supposed to be an event."

"Did you actually see anyone go with him?"

"I guess not. I don't pay too much attention to what other people do sometimes. I'm sorry."

"It's all right, Miss Worthington. Can you tell me when you last saw Miss Greer?"

"After dinner. She was putting a dried-flower arrangement on the dining room table."

"What time was that?"

"I'm not sure. I don't pay too much attention to time."

"What did you do afterward?"

"I think I talked to Moira for a while, then maybe Angie. No, not Angie. Reginald was with me in the drawing room, but then he got a headache and I went up to my room to read. Later, I heard Moira scream."

"Did anyone else see you in the drawing room?"

"I'm not sure. I don't pay too much attention to—"

"I know. Thank you, Miss Worthington."

Reginald Vane was the next guest facing Paavo.

"What did you do after dinner?" Paavo asked.

"I missed dinner, staying up in my room. A bit later I went to the library for a new book. The only person I saw all evening that I can remember was in the library."

"And who was that?"

"Patsy Jeffers."

"I never left my wife's bedside all evening," Running Spirit told Paavo. "After all, she was feeling poorly. Oh, I did go down to dinner without her. I forgot about that."

◦　　◦　　◦

"I was at Martin's side the whole evening," Bethel said. "We're a devoted couple and Martin expects me to be with him."

"I never left Bethel," Martin said. "Marriage is, after all, a life sentence."

"After Miss Greer and I finished cleaning up the kitchen," Moira said, "I went into the drawing room to spend a few minutes with my guests, then invited everyone to the library at nine o'clock for some herbal tea or soy coffee. It's a way to sooth the nerves before going to bed. I talked for a long time with the Baymans, I believe."

Patsy lifted dull eyes to Paavo. "I was alone in my room all evening," she said. Her hands shook nervously. "I guess that means if I need an alibi I don't have any."

"Your turn, Angie," Paavo said, standing in the doorway of the library.

"Me? You've got to be joking."

Bethel snickered.

Angie marched from the library, nose in the air, and followed Paavo to the living room.

"You were here, Angie," he said when they were seated. "I wasn't. Tell me about it."

"There's not much for me to tell. The first night only Reginald, Chelsea, and I had dinner with Finley, and I went to my room before he left for his nature walk. Tonight, Miss Greer wouldn't let me help, so I didn't see her at all after dinner."

"That's all?"

"Maybe it's not much, but it's the truth. Now you just have to figure out who's lying."

Paavo quietly turned the knob on the door that led into the kitchen. There was no light, no sound at all.

He flicked on the flashlight, looked over the kitchen, and walked over to Miss Greer's sheet-covered body.

He had arranged the sheet so that it formed a tiny pleat by her left shoulder, another by her right foot. The pleats were still there. Nothing about the sheet looked as if anyone had touched it.

Proceeding to a corner, he sat on the floor and shut off his flashlight. If anyone came in here tonight, he wanted to know who. And why.

This house was filled with a looney-tunes group doing their best to scare each other away, and the man who put it all together was missing. Now the cook had been killed. It didn't make sense. But it would, in time.

Particularly if whoever killed Miss Greer came down to dispose of any evidence that might have been left behind.

His vacation with Angie would have to wait a while after all. Footsteps. He broke off his thoughts and watched the kitchen door.

The door opened. Light steps entered the room then stopped. Paavo silently got to his feet. He was just about to turn on the flashlight and find out who had snuck in here when the kitchen lights were turned on. He blinked from the sudden brightness.

"Moira," he said.

She gasped, her hand at her chest, staring at him. "What are you doing here?"

"I should ask you the same thing." He was guarded, watching her carefully.

"I couldn't sleep," Moira said, slowly walking toward him. "All of this . . . my brother missing, now Miss Greer dying. I just wanted to sit with her a while. She'd only worked with us this past month, but I feel like I've lost a friend." Tears sprang to her eyes. "I'm sorry."

"It's all right." Paavo slid his hands into his pockets. "It's been over five hours since Quint left," he commented.

She rubbed her forehead. "The road up here washes out easily, and runs so near the edge of the cliff that it can be very dangerous. They'll wait until it stops raining, or at least until the sun comes up so that they can see the road better."

"Could be."

She gave him a quizzical look. "If you're waiting for the sheriff, why do it in the dark, Inspector Smith? Do I detect something going on here?"

"Curiosity."

"Two can play at that game." She shut off the kitchen lights.

He flicked on the flashlight as she crossed the room to sit beside him on the floor.

"How did Miss Greer come to work for you?" he asked.

"Is this twenty questions?" she replied.

"You don't have to answer."

"I know." In the darkness, he could hear the resignation in her voice. "She showed up at our door one day. She lives in town and said she needed work, that if we had anything at all, she'd be interested. When my brother learned she was willing to cook whatever he told her—he has very definite ideas about food—he hired her to do that and to help me with the housecleaning."

"Did she live here or in town?"

"In town. If the inn ever got very popular, and I needed help with breakfast, we thought we might offer her a room. But for now our arrangement was that she'd arrive in time to prepare a light lunch, help with the cleaning in the afternoon, and then make dinner and do the cleanup."

"Did anyone from town come to visit her here?"

"No one."

"Do you know if she has family or friends there?"

"No family. No close friends that I could tell. But she knew almost everyone."

"Any enemies, or anyone she was afraid of?"

"Why do you ask?" Her voice, which had been mono-tone while answering his earlier questions, suddenly registered alarm.

"Just curious."

"Ah." Her relief was evident. "None that I know of."

"Did your brother like her?"

"Yes. He thought she was 'a treasure,' as he put it. He'll be very upset to learn she's passed away. Poor Finley—none of this is going as he planned."

"What about the investors? Are things going as they planned?"

"Oh, yes. Except that Finley isn't here," she said, then paused before continuing. "Up to that time, though, they were happy as clams about the inn and its prospects."

Angie stared at the ceiling while lying on the bed. Alone.

Paavo said he'd be downstairs waiting for the sheriff to arrive. What if the sheriff didn't show up all night? He didn't exactly seem like the type who'd jump out of a warm bed to traipse up to this hilltop because someone had died of natural causes.

If they were natural causes. But they must have been. Moira said she had a heart condition, that it was just a matter of time.

Things like that happened all the time. But then, with Finley missing . . .

Angie turned over. She really ought to get to sleep. Morning would come soon and she needed to help Moira with breakfast. Poor woman, between her brother disappearing and her cook dying, she had to be falling apart.

But then Angie remembered the way Moira made a big deal about holding hands with Paavo during the séance. She was certainly good at hiding her sorrow!

Maybe, Angie thought, instead of lying here thinking about Finley and Miss Greer and Moira, she should just get up and help Paavo keep his vigil for the sheriff. But she'd told Paavo she'd wait here for him, and she was always a woman of her word. For the most part.

She shut her eyes. Instead of the peacefulness of sleep, though, she again saw Moira Tay fawning over Paavo. Moira was beginning to annoy her mightily. Even more annoying: Why was Paavo being nice to Moira in return? What was it about Moira that was causing that strange reaction in him?

She didn't think the blond wraith was Paavo's type. But then, what was his type? The longer she lay alone in what was supposed to be their bed for their vacation together—their big get-to-know-each-other-better week together—the more she decided it certainly wasn't her.

She threw back the covers and sat up. There was no way she was going to get to sleep tonight. She might as well spend the time with Paavo. That's what this so-called vacation was supposed to be about, wasn't it?

She put on slippers and a robe and walked quietly downstairs. In case he'd fallen asleep, she didn't want to disturb him.

Night lights cast a faint glow in the drawing room and the foyer. To her surprise, he wasn't in the drawing room. He must be in the kitchen, she thought with a shudder. Why anyone would want to sit in a room with a corpse didn't make sense to her. But then, he was a homicide inspector. Maybe that explained it.

She went into the hall that led to the kitchen. The lights were out. He wouldn't be down there in the dark, would he? She went a couple of steps closer and was just about ready to turn back when she heard a faint chuckle.

She froze. Ghosts? But they cried, not laughed. Or so she'd been told. But who could tell with ghosts? She took another couple of very quiet steps closer to the dark kitchen.

She heard Paavo's low murmur, and with it, Moira Tay's slow, serene voice before all fell quiet again.

Shocked, she turned around and somehow found her way back up to her room.

She dreamed the house was making strange noises again. Only this time, instead of a thumping heartbeat, it was a loud, shrill cry. Elise Sempler, perhaps? The wailing ghost.

Then she dreamed an earthquake struck.

Then Paavo, shaking her shoulder, was saying, "Angie. Angie. Wake up!"

She opened her eyes. Her alarm, which she'd foolishly set for six A.M. in order to take care of breakfast, was blaring. She reached over and hit the snooze button, then shut her eyes again. Paavo put his arms around her and she rolled toward him. Her hand touched his chest. She felt clothes, a sweater. He wasn't in bed, but was lying on top of the covers. Still, he felt warm and solid. Her Paavo. She loved the feel of him, his clean, masculine scent.

He kissed her mouth, her cheek, her ear, then whispered, "Don't you need to go down to help Moira?"

She jerked awake. Everything from the night before came back to her with a resounding crash. Pushing him away, she rolled to the edge of the bed and covered her head with her pillow. She remembered seeing the clock by her bed read four A.M. before she fell asleep. Obviously he hadn't even bothered to come to bed last night. He must have spent the whole night with Moira Tay. And now his first coherent words to her were about the Other Woman. Damn him.

He pulled the pillow off her head. "Time to get up, Angie."

She stumbled out of bed and into the shower without even giving him a backward glance.

Angie stood in the drawing room, doing her best to remain balanced on one foot, her other foot pressed against her knee, her arms raised over her head with her palms touching. The room was icy cold. There was either no central heating in the old inn or it had been shut off during the night to save money.

"Take a deep breath," Running Spirit said. "Now hold. One, two, three."

If anyone had told Angie she'd be spending her first morning with Paavo this way, she would have called him insane. She'd gone to the kitchen, where she learned from Moira that Paavo and Running Spirit had moved Miss Greer down to the cellar. It had rained all night, and because it was still raining hard, everyone expected that Quint and the sheriff would be delayed even further. It was a little heartening for Angie to learn that Running Spirit had been there with them last night—part of the time, at least.

Instead of cooking right then, Moira invited Angie to
take part in the morning exercises. "We never eat until
about eight o'clock. The early morning is for exercising—
best done on an empty stomach, of course."

"Of course," Angie had replied. Not eating breakfast
until eight A.M. was one of the sanest things she'd heard
from this crowd. Now she could get another hour's sleep.
Normally, her day never began before eight anyway.

Moira went on to explain that Finley had always
directed his own special blend of tai chi chuan and yoga,
saying they helped a person awaken spiritually as well as
physically. Usually, the exercises were held outdoors, no
matter how cold, but the rain made that impossible.

Running Spirit volunteered to direct the morning
exercises. He planned to create an energizing force to
draw Finley back home. "Whatever it takes," Angie said,
as they walked toward the drawing room. All she wanted
to do was go back up to bed. Staying up all night confused about some man hadn't exactly left her feeling
great this morning.

Angie was about to tell Moira she'd exercise some
other time when she spotted Paavo among the group of
exercisers. The man looked disgustingly awake.

Moira then removed her bulky sweats to reveal skin-
hugging spandex leggings and a tummy-baring sports bra.
She moved in a slow, trancelike walk to Paavo's side and
smiled. It was a wan, typically Moira smile, but a smile
nonetheless. Paavo didn't smile back. Angie would have
passed out if he had. But he didn't give Moira one of his
usual icy, cut-to-the-quick glances, either.ƒS

Angie went to his other side. Even though her eyes
never left Running Spirit's half-clothed form at the
head of the group, she noticed that Paavo's brows rose
in surprise at seeing her there. Archly, she nodded in

acknowledgment. What was so difficult about a little predawn yoga, anyway?

Now, after a half hour of exercising, her ability to stay upright on one leg seemed about as shaky as her relationship with Paavo. Her whole sense of which end was up went haywire. She put her foot down before she fell over—ready to put her foot down in more ways than one. Visions filled her head of going back to her room to crawl under a toasty-warm electric blanket and thaw out. From there, she could contemplate which was worse about this place: the cold, her hunger, the dead woman in the cellar—or Paavo and Moira making goo-goo eyes at each other. This was surely the vacation from hell. Finley or no. Inspector Paavo Smith could decide if he was leaving with her.

She turned to tell Paavo she was going back to the room when Running Spirit handed out blankets to spread on the floor.

This was more to her liking. She spread her blanket beside Paavo's, then stretched out on her back. Her eyes closed and she yawned. At home she'd never attempt anything strenuous before having at least one cup of coffee. But the thought of the crushed and boiled seeds that had passed for coffee last night made her mouth pucker.

She tried hard to pull her thoughts and taste buds away from dreaming of a cup of rich, dark, fresh-brewed, eye-opening, caffeine-laden coffee and back to Running Spirit's instruction.

When she opened her eyes she saw she'd missed something crucial. The man sat on the ground, coiled into a ball, his back twisted, and his arms circling his knees . . . backward. Angie sat up quickly, then stared at the jumble of limbs. She couldn't begin to fathom how to do that to herself. Or if she even wanted to.

Paavo was making a valiant attempt; he kept in good physical form because of his police work. A form she should be snuggling against.

On the other side of him, Moira's supple body was so long and thin, she looked as if she could wrap her arms around herself twice over if she wanted to. Nothing about Angie was long, not even her hair, and thin was only attained by vigilant, continuous dieting.

Reginald Vane simply sat with his hands on his knees and his eyes shut. He wore a white shirt. At least he'd left off his bow tie.

Patsy wasn't there. But then, even when Patsy *was* there, she wasn't.

Also absent were Martin and Bethel. Martin was probably sleeping off last night's bout of drinking. Bethel? Who knew? Maybe channelers didn't need to do all this mundane physical stuff. But where were the two of them last night during all the noise? It had been loud enough to get through even to Patsy.

Chelsea was probably sitting in her room hoping that Jack Sempler would materialize.

With that thought, Angie realized that if she were to stay at this inn any length of time—which wasn't in the least bit likely—she'd need to come up with a transcendental excuse of her own to duck Hill Haven Inn's activities.

"Breathe deeply," Running Spirit said, as Angie tried in vain to get her arms and legs into a position that had some semblance of his. "Now hold it, one, two . . ."

Finally the session ended, with everyone in a lotus position. Angie tried a modified one, sitting upright, legs crossed, knees outward, bracing a hand on each knee with her thumbs and middle fingers touching. Angie listened to Running Spirit's deep voice grow surprisingly soft and soothing, telling the group over and over to breathe deeply and to clear their minds of worldly worries and thoughts. . . .

A short while later, for the second time that same morning, Paavo woke her up and told her it was time to help Moira cook breakfast.

8

Paavo opened his eyes, then turned quickly toward the alarm clock. Ten o'clock. He sat up. After exercising he'd lain on the bed for a minute and must have dozed off. Where was Angie?

He stood and went to the windows to see if Quint's truck was out there. Instead, he saw Chelsea and Angie climbing into the back of Finley's old van. What the hell?

He ran down the stairs two at a time and out the door. Rain was falling lightly. "Angie, where are you going?"

In the van with her and Chelsea were Running Spirit, at the wheel, and Moira, beside him.

"I didn't want to wake you," she said.

"We're going to the sheriff, since the sheriff won't come to us," Chelsea said.

Paavo turned to Moira. "I thought you said it was almost impossible to get through with a four-wheel drive; how do you expect this old van to make it?"

"Running Spirit said he could do it," she said.

"Get in or get out of the way, Smith," Running Spirit said.

Paavo climbed in beside Angie. He guessed it was worth a try. But if this old van could get through, why weren't Quint and the sheriff here already?

Running Spirit drove slowly, with all the caution he could muster. It was difficult to even see the road, so much mud and water had puddled on the ground. The road began a sharp descent winding along the side of the steep cliff, and the van nosed downward. Angie's heart was in her throat.

The van began to slip on the mud and Running Spirit hit the brakes, causing it to fishtail for what felt like forever.

"I thought you knew how to drive in these conditions," Chelsea said accusingly.

"Shut up!" Running Spirit said, his knuckles white.

"Maybe we should turn around," Angie said. "So what if it takes another day or two for the sheriff to make it up to the inn. It's not as if Miss Greer is going anywhere."

"I can do it." Running Spirit's voice didn't sound nearly as convincing as he might have hoped.

"You're doing fine, Greg," Moira said. "Let's go on."

Paavo leaned forward. He saw Angie shut her eyes each time the road made a sharp turn along the edge of the cliff. She was turning paler by the minute. He could sense the tires becoming clogged with the wet, sandy earth and losing traction. "Time to stop," he said.

"What?" Running Spirit did as he was told. "Why?"

Paavo pointed at a spot ahead. What had once been the roadway, cut into the side of a cliff, was now covered by a thick mudslide.

"Oh, my God." Angie leaned over Chelsea to peer out the window at the cliff beside them. "If that much mud could slide down and cover the road up there, is it possible that a slide could happen here as well?"

No one wanted to answer that.

"What in the hell's going on?" Running Spirit demanded. "Your brother never said anything about the inn being cut off whenever there's a little rain. Did you know about this?"

"Apparently there was a fire last fall," Moira said weakly, "that stripped the area of the trees and foliage that held the earth in place. The loss in value that fire caused was one of the reasons Finley was able to afford the property."

"Well, that's just bloody great!" Running Spirit leaned back in his seat, drumming his fingers rapidly on the seat. "He could afford the place because no one would be able to come here half the year! How am I supposed to run an ashram like that?"

"The trees will grow back," Moira said softly.

Running Spirit sulked.

But soon they had a bigger problem. There was no room to turn the van around. Running Spirit would have to back out of there.

Paavo got out of the van to direct him. The rain was falling in heavy sheets now. Running Spirit put the stick shift in reverse and gave it some gas, easing off the clutch. The tires spun, but the van didn't move.

Moira, Angie, and Chelsea also got out, and they all tried pushing. Angie stopped to spit out a mouthful of rainwater and mud that had splattered up from the spinning tires of the van. Could it get any worse than this?

It did, when they realized they'd have to push the van a long way up the narrow road before they could find a spot to turn it. The heavy rains made the danger of another mud slide even greater. They had no choice but to walk as fast as they could back to the inn.

"At least we learned one thing," Angie said as they trudged along, Paavo holding her hand and helping her up the hill. "Even if Finley was out there somewhere and was trying to come back to Hill Haven Inn, there's no way he could do it."

Back at the inn, the phones still weren't working. Angie vowed to get a cellular phone for her car the instant she got away from here. She never wanted to be stranded this way again.

Like the others, she spent the rest of the day watching the rain and wishing she were anywhere else but here. Paavo, Reginald Vane, Moira, and Running Spirit decided to go out in the rain to look around some more for Finley. While Moira told them he'd probably left the hilltop and was somewhere else alive and well, there was enough of a nagging doubt in all their minds that searching a bit would help put them at ease. Moira went along to show them some of Finley's favorite nature walk areas.

Angie decided not to go. She'd had enough of walking around in the rain on the trek back from the van to last her all the way to next winter. Instead, she went into the kitchen and made a list of all the ingredients that were already there and the quantities, so that she could figure out what kinds of meals she could cook with them.

There were so many sacks of soybeans that if they ever got wet and the beans began to swell, they'd all be in danger of smothering—if the house didn't explode first.

Patsy Jeffers stepped into the kitchen. Her face was pale, her hands shook, and her eyes were red-rimmed.

"Are you all right?" Angie asked.

She nodded, her eyes darting nervously. "Have you seen Greg? I mean, Running Spirit?"

"He's gone off to look for Finley, in case Finley's out there hurt or something. I'm not sure which direction he went in."

"I suppose Moira Tay's out there, too." She tugged at her lower lip as she gazed out the window to the forest.

"I believe so," Angie replied. Running Spirit's interest in Moira hadn't been lost on any of them, and particularly not on his wife. "Have you and the Tays been friends for long?"

"Greg—I mean, Running Spirit—apparently met them years ago while they were all living in San Francisco, in the Haight-Ashbury. He's been friends with . . . with Finley . . . ever since."

"Oh, how nice." Angie needed to change the subject. "How long have you two been married?" She found herself more and more interested in the concept of marriage with every passing day, despite the last twenty-four hours' slight reversal.

"Six months."

"Really? You're practically newlyweds."

"I still can't believe he's my husband." Patsy chewed on her thumbnail as she spoke. "I'd do anything at all for him. I think that's what love is all about. Do you agree, Angie?"

"It's nice the two of you share an interest in this inn. Sometimes it's hard to find something to be in agreement about, no matter how attracted you might be to each other." Just like me and Paavo, she felt like adding.

"This is the only place in the world where everything is natural and fresh and alive," Patsy said.

Tell that to Miss Greer, Angie thought. "I didn't realize how special this inn is," she said.

"Oh, yes," Patsy exclaimed. "Finley explained it to me and Running Spirit before we invested. Growing their own food is part of Finley's food philosophy, you know, along with the value of the soya bean." Patsy took an apple from the refrigerator and picked up a paring knife.

Angie watched the knife in Patsy's shaking hands with apprehension.

"No. I had no idea."

Patsy hacked the apple in two. "He told us he used to have two milk cows and gave them all the best care and the best food, but despite that, they became sick and died. He figured if his cows could get diseased, any cow could, so he won't use milk or butter." She cut the apple halves into fourths. "He also used to raise chickens, but then they became diseased, so he stopped using eggs. After he learned that some fish get worms, he stopped eating fish or having anything to do with products from the ocean." She cut the apple into even smaller pieces. "Everything he prepares here is absolutely fresh, clean and natural."

As much as Angie enjoyed cooking, she couldn't imagine being that preoccupied with the state of her food. "How does he keep birds from flying over his garden?"

"How does he what?"

"Nothing."

"There's only one thing that would make this place even better," Patsy said. The apple was quickly approaching apple sauce.

"What's that?" Angie asked.

Patsy scooped up the apple pieces and threw them in the trash. "If it belonged to Running Spirit. Then, along with physical cleanliness, he could lead all the guests to a spiritual cleanliness as well."

"Maybe he could add a lesson called Waste Not, Want Not."

Patsy Jeffers wandered off and soon Moira came into the kitchen to prepare dinner. Angie stood to the side and watched. It gave her something to do, took her mind off

Finley and Miss Greer, and let her see what Finley's cooking style was all about. No matter what the investors wanted, she knew Finley wouldn't back off completely from his food philosophy, and she needed to know as much about it as possible so that she could incorporate it into food that was tasty.

After a few minutes, she decided she knew enough. Moira whipped up what should have been a delicious barley casserole baked with almonds, mushrooms, and onions, and then covered it with a layer of soy cottage cheese. She also cooked cabbage and bread crumbs covered with soy milk and made to resemble, but not taste like, scalloped potatoes; soy patties; cream of eggplant soup (made with soy milk, what else?); and a spinach salad with an oil-free dressing. If Finley insisted on sticking very closely to this style of cooking, the investors should demand their money back.

Moira had Angie follow, on her own, the recipe for soy patties:

> *one pound soybean pulp*
> *one pound of cooked natural brown rice*
> *three tablespoons canola oil*
> *one minced onion*
> *two tablespoons soy sauce*
> *sage to taste* (Whose taste? Angie wondered)

> *Mix the ingredients, form them into patties, roll in whole-wheat bread crumbs, and bake at 325° until browned.*

Angie would add it to her recipes-to-never-use file.

They talked as they cooked. Angie found it bizarre that Moira seemed so sure Finley would show up at the inn once the road was open again, as if nothing had happened to him.

From all she'd learned of Finley Tay, and after her one day with him, she believed Tay to be a man obsessed with his own importance and power. He wasn't the type to walk away from a place he'd planned for so long, or the type to go riding off with a bunch of hot tub installers, no matter what Running Spirit said.

Something must have happened to Finley right on this property. As far as Angie was concerned, the chances of his still being alive dwindled with each passing hour. She was pretty sure Paavo would feel the same way—if she could have the time with him to discuss it.

On the other hand, she also realized that Finley had to be angry at the investors' challenge to his mastery of the kitchen when they insisted he hire her to make his menu more palatable.

Maybe his disappearance had, in fact, been based on no more than a mammoth-sized snit.

Someone in the inn probably knew. But no one was saying.

Angie stepped out of the shower, wrapped herself in the big terry cloth towel, then stepped into the dressing room to figure out what to wear to dinner. The door to the bedroom was open and she saw Paavo in there unbuttoning his shirt.

His gaze slowly drifted over her. She need not have bothered drying herself earlier; she could feel steam rising off her skin like it was dry ice.

"I'm next," he said.

Her heart leaped, until she realized he was just talking about the shower. "Okay, let me get out of your way." She found a simple blue dress and carried it into the bedroom, holding the dress with one hand and the towel closed with her other.

"Wait." He caught her arm. "I'm sorry I was busy all last night. If the sheriff had shown up, things would have been different."

"It's all right," she said, freeing her arm. "I understand."

"Good." He looked relieved.

"At least you had company to keep your vigil."

His gaze followed her as she returned to the dressing room to find nylons and underwear, and stayed with her as she carried them back into the bedroom. "You little snoop," he said finally.

"What's the matter, Inspector, surprised that others around here know how to investigate?"

"So that's what's wrong." He walked to her side and turned her around to face him. She spun away and walked to the vanity, picked up her hairbrush and brushed her wet hair back off her face.

He stepped up behind her and put his hand on her shoulder. "You know there was nothing to Moira's visit last night." Her skin was creamy smooth. He loved the feel of it. He moved closer, bending over to kiss her neck, but she again walked away.

"I know. You explained to me how you needed to be alone. I didn't understand that there's alone, and alone-with-Moira. Silly me."

He followed her. She stopped near the fireplace and looked at the dead embers. "I was asking her questions," he said.

"I'm sure she had lots of answers."

"She did."

He stepped up behind her and cupped her elbow. When she didn't run, he moved closer and ran his hand lightly along her arm, barely touching her, up to her wrist, to the hand that held the towel together above her breasts. He slid his hand to the edge of the towel, to her skin.

She could feel his breath against her ear. Heavier now, deeper, fuller as his finger began to dip under the terry cloth.

"Excuse me," she said, walking away. "I've got to help Moira serve dinner."

His bleak gaze followed her. "Fine," he said finally. "She'll appreciate it."

To Angie's surprise, Paavo waited for her to dress, then helped her and Moira put the dinner on the table and call the investors. A number of unlit candles had been placed around the room, on the table, the mantel and the side buffet. The lights had flickered a couple of times from the storm, and at any time the power might be lost.

"I wonder," Chelsea said to no one in particular, "if the sheriff's found out anything about Finley. I'll bet Finley's sitting in town right now, furious he can't get here."

"I doubt the sheriff's even looking," Martin Bayman said. "The townspeople aren't too fond of an inn being here. They seem to think it's strange, for some reason."

"They're afraid of the ghosts," Patsy said. "Afraid of Susannah. This is her house, you know. Finley told me all about her and Jack and Elise. Susannah doesn't want anyone else to live here. Not even us."

"They don't care about ghosts." Bethel sniffed. "People are simply intolerant of things they don't understand."

"I believe," Reginald Vane said, his bow tie bobbing as he swallowed, "we need to listen to what the sheriff has said about the townspeople. Maybe we should leave—as soon as we're able—and forget this inn business."

"That's the first sensible statement I've heard all evening," Bethel cried. "Allakaket has been warning you, but you won't listen. None of you! Something is very wrong here." She tilted her head heavenward, her arms raised outward, causing the long kimono-style sleeves of her tunic to dip into the barley casserole on her plate. "Will no prophet be honored in his or her own time?"

"Bethel," Martin said, pulling out a whiskey flask and pouring some into his water glass. "Pipe down."

Everyone turned to their dinners, took a few bites, then pushed the plates away.

"You can try to ignore it," Vane said, giving a tug to his bow tie, "but he who mocks the spirit world always pays a terrible price. Almost as heavy a price as the fool who doesn't listen to warnings."

Bethel stood and in a hushed voice cried, "The spirits are uneasy."

Just then a flash of lightning filled the window, followed by a loud booming roll of thunder.

Nine pairs of wide, very round eyes glanced at each other. At that moment, Angie wouldn't have been surprised if Boris Karloff walked into the room.

After dinner Angie helped Moira clean up the kitchen. They were discussing tomorrow's breakfast—Angie felt obligated to try to convince her that they should make something besides the steady diet of cold granola cereal and oat bran muffins—when Patsy entered the room.

"Where's Greg?" she demanded.

Angie and Moira exchanged glances. "I haven't seen him," Moira said.

"Yes, you have. I know you have. He's here!" She opened a cabinet under the sink.

"Patsy." Angie touched her arm. "He's not hiding. He's probably upstairs."

"He's here. No one believed Susannah either about Jack and Elise. But she knew. Just like I know!"

Angie swallowed hard. "Maybe I can get you some aspirin?" She wished she had something a lot stronger. Her second sister, Caterina, was a walking pharmacy, but not Angie.

"I don't need aspirin. I need Greg!"

Moira stepped nose to nose with Patsy. "No one knows—or cares—where he is."

Angie wondered if she'd brought her Midol. That was the strongest medicine she ever took. Her mother insisted she wouldn't need it if she'd get married and have babies, but that seemed a pretty extreme way to avoid having to take a pill or two.

"I'll find him!" Patsy ran out of the kitchen.

Angie took a deep breath of relief.

"That woman needs aromatherapy to soothe her nerves," Moira said. "Maybe when Finley gets back."

Angie looked at the teaspoon she'd been wiping when Patsy burst in on them. It was bent nearly in two. "Do you think the inn might have a place for a new Uri Geller?" she asked.

After finishing with the dishes, Angie went in search of Paavo. She found him standing just outside the French doors to the garden, under the porch roof. The rain had stopped for the moment. Angie paused. She'd rarely thought of how air smelled before, but now she smelled its cleanliness, free of exhaust and diesel fumes, free of the dirt, garbage, and even cooking smells that were part of life in the big city. Also free of the ever-present smell of decay of the old inn.

"All done?" Paavo asked.

"Yes."

He held out his hand to her, his gaze questioning. She took it.

"Look." Pointing at the sky, he drew her closer.

The full moon was high. Across the face of it dark rain clouds drifted, making the moon look eerie. Bewitched. "It looks like a werewolf moon," she said.

Blue eyes caught hers, and she saw them crinkle into a smile. "Aren't the Sempler ghosts enough for you?" he asked.

"Oh, I don't know. I could imagine Running Spirit turning into a werewolf. He's big and hulking. Reginald Vane would make a great vampire, like Dracula, so stiff and proper, always wearing a suit. Actually, he'd make an even better Bela Lugosi. I can see him going around crying 'Bevare! Bevare!' in a Transylvanian accent."

"What about Martin?" Paavo asked.

"Martin?" Angie thought a moment. "Martin couldn't be anything but a ghost. He seems like no more than a faded image of the man that once was. I can't help but think he drinks so much because of some deep unhappiness."

"And me?" he asked.

He was so many things to her. Quiet, intense loner; warm, gentle lover. A man with integrity and responsibility enough to make her proud, yet who denied having a surfeit of either. A man who gave her everything he could, yet refused to accept anything in return. "You're Dr. Van Helsing," she said, "victor over Dracula. A brave man, always ready to fight the powers of darkness, no matter what the cost."

"You're such a romantic, Angie. Be careful. Romantics are easily hurt."

"And you're not?" she asked.

"Me?" He sounded truly shocked. "I'm as cynical as they come."

You don't know yourself well, Inspector, she wanted to say. Instead, she turned back to the moon. "Do you ever wish that there were things like ghosts?" she asked.

"Something to latch onto when you want to believe that there's more to life than just what we see here and now?"

He turned her toward him, taking her hands. "The best part of my life is very much alive."

Angie's heart flip-flopped.

"Hello, you two!" Bethel called. She and Martin stepped onto the porch. "I'm so glad you're here, Inspector Smith. I feel much safer knowing a policeman is with us. Allakaket feels something bad has happened to poor Finley."

"He does?" Angie asked.

Bethel gave a loud sigh. "I can't begin to tell you how horrible it's been."

"Nanook's been going nonstop," Martin said. "And Bethel won't keep his pronouncements to herself."

Bethel wrinkled her mouth in disgust, then turned to Paavo with a smile as she patted the few strands of curly gray hair peeking out from under her gold turban. "Tell me more about what the sheriff said to you yesterday. Does he suspect foul play, do you think?"

"He didn't," Paavo said. "At least not then."

"That's a relief." Bethel smiled again.

Martin slid his hands into his pockets. As he glanced up at the moon, he walked down the porch steps onto the brick patio. "That's a spooky moon tonight," he said. "As befits this house—

'A savage place! as holy and enchanted
As e'er beneath a waning moon was haunted
By woman wailing for her demon-lover!'"

he quoted.

"Very good," Angie said. "But are you referring to the ghostly Elise, or just Chelsea?"

Martin laughed.

"Don't encourage him, dear," Bethel advised.

"But that is a most interesting question," Martin said.

"On the other hand," Angie added, "we might all simply be feeling what Milton called 'moon-struck madness.'"

Martin smiled, Paavo looked surprised, and Bethel annoyed.

"An apt thought," Martin said as he came back under the shelter of the porch roof. He faced Paavo. "Moon-struck madness could be an excuse for many things. Including criminal things."

"Anything can be an excuse," Paavo said. "Or nothing. But the question is usually one of motive."

Bethel jumped to her feet. Her eyes rolled back in her head and her fists were clenched as her arms crossed over her breasts. In a deep baritone, she said, "The motive lies in the house."

Angie was so shocked that she jumped back about five feet.

Bethel's arms fell, her body sagged, and she looked from Angie to Paavo. "See? What did I tell you? Allakaket's constantly tuned in to this problem. At the drop of a hat he takes over and speaks! He's never been so out of control before, never had so much to say. Even I don't know what it all means."

She took several deep breaths while Martin came to her side and patted her shoulder.

"The motive for what?" Angie asked.

"I find Allakaket's behavior absolutely fascinating," Bethel continued, ignoring Angie. "But this jerk I'm married to won't even write these things down. He expects me to, I suppose. Jane Roberts's husband wrote down every time Seth burped and look at how rich and famous it got them."

"Who's Seth?" Paavo whispered to Angie.

"As you can see," Bethel continued, "when Allakaket takes over my body, I can't just tell him to wait a minute while I grab a pen and paper."

"Why don't you carry a tape recorder?" Angie asked. "Then you could ask him what motive he's talking about."

"Allakaket wouldn't know what a tape recorder was. He'd never turn it on. I don't know what to do."

"I'd look for a twentieth-century spirit for starters," Angie said.

"I give up," Bethel cried. "Let's go, Martin. I think we're disturbing these young people. They probably don't want us hanging around while they're out here under the light of the silvery moon. It is romantic, Martin." She hooked her arm in his and gave him a coy look. "Don't you think?"

"Real romantic. You, me, and Allakazam. If I try to get fresh and he takes over your body, he might deck me." Martin looked back at Angie and Paavo and winked, then opened the door for Bethel to enter the inn.

Bethel glanced at the sky. "The storm will be even bigger tonight."

Martin pulled the door shut as they went inside.

"Now," Angie said, sauntering close to Paavo. "I think you were telling me something about liking being with little old live me, as opposed to—"

She saw Chelsea's silhouette through the French doors. "Excuse me one minute." She hurried to the doors. "Chelsea, come here!"

Chelsea stepped outside with her.

"Have you seen Patsy?" Angie asked.

"No." Chelsea glanced from Angie to Paavo, confused.

"I'm worried about her," Angie said. "She's so jealous of Moira and Running Spirit she's ready to snap." It would seem she glanced quickly at Paavo to see if he had any reaction to her statement about Moira and Running Spirit. He looked unconcerned. Good. She had been mistaken about his interest in Moira.

"Poor Patsy," Chelsea said. "Did you know she wants to buy this inn for Running Spirit?"

"I think what she really wants is to buy it so she can get Moira out of her life," Angie suggested. "Do you think she's serious about it?"

"From what I've heard," Chelsea continued, "she made an offer to Finley. Apparently he was considering it. But now he's gone. If he doesn't come back soon, she seems to think Running Spirit and Moira will fall in love."

"She did say something about no one believing Susannah about Jack and Elise, just like no one believes her about Running Spirit and Moira," Angie said. "Do you think she sees them all as being like the ghosts? Reincarnations or something?"

"Wait," Paavo said. "I thought Susannah and Jack were brother and sister, just like Moira and Finley. Doesn't Patsy have everything mixed up?"

"That's true," Chelsea said thoughtfully.

"Oh, well," Angie said, "who's to know about reincarnation?"

"Shirley MacLaine does," Chelsea offered.

"I think I'd rather have it explained by her brother, Warren Beatty."

"I hate to break up these lofty supernatural musings," Paavo said, "but it's raining hard again."

9

"*Misery. Shame. Sorrow.*" Moira pointed to the nine of swords lying on the table between her and Chelsea. Angie and Paavo sat behind Chelsea, while Martin leaned against Bethel's chair and sipped a bourbon and water. Reginald Vane sat alone in a dark corner.

"Oh, no!" Chelsea looked stricken.

"But don't worry," Moira said.

"No?"

"The next card, the queen of cups, is the ideal wife and mother."

"Who, me?"

"Hmm, interesting."

"What is?"

"This card." Moira tapped the jester. "The fool. The fool is no man. He aims aimlessly for nothing, knowing only that he knows nothing."

"I hope I haven't missed anything," boomed Running Spirit, stepping into the library.

"We were just talking about you," Martin said.

"Here," Moira continued, ignoring the others, "is the culmination, the tenth card, the star."

Angie looked at the card showing a naked woman with two jugs of water, pouring one on the ground and one into a stream. It didn't make any sense.

"I'm afraid to ask what it means," Chelsea said. "I haven't heard one word about Jack."

Moira shut her eyes and, placing her fingertips on the edge of the card, said, "This card is a promise of renewal and recovery. With the others, it tells me that a person of significance will enter your life. You will see things in a new way, and you will be improved by it."

Chelsea looked at her blankly; then slowly a broad smile filled her face. "Jack. I should have known!" She stood and looked around the room, then crossed her arms over her breasts and twirled around and around. "Jack will enter my life. My tarot said so."

Running Spirit smirked. "Good job, Moira."

Angie was horrified that Chelsea would fall even deeper into her fantasy I-love-a-ghost way of hiding from the world.

Reginald Vane shook his head in disgust. "We need to stop playing games here and take stock of our situation. Finley's been gone for forty-eight hours, and now his cook is dead. While it's possible he might return, we must consider that he might not."

"Here, here," Martin said. "A man with logic. Practical. A man of science, in fact. I can see, Vane, you don't belong among these psychics and seers."

"What's that supposed to mean?" Bethel asked, frowning.

Vane faced the group. "Since we can't expect Moira to run all this alone, I propose we immediately stop any thought of an inn and put the property up for sale."

"But I like it here," Chelsea protested.

"Despite Finley and Miss Greer?" Vane asked.

"I thought Miss Greer just had a heart attack or something. That can happen to anybody. And I think Finley's just stuck in town. I'm not worried," Chelsea said, jutting her chin out.

"That's either brave or very gullible of you," Vane said.

Could Vane know, Paavo wondered, the truth about Greer's death? Supposedly Vane was asleep in his room when she was killed.

"Bethel and I could take the inn over if the rest of you want to sell your shares," Martin suggested. "Not at a profit, mind you. But we're willing to take the risk that people will come from miles away to see a channeler."

"They'll come from all over the world," Bethel said. "I can see it now."

"Not when they hear about ghosts and unexplained deaths," Vane replied. "Even the curious have standards."

"Finley will come back," Moira said. "He always does."

"Like a bad penny?" Martin asked.

"Like the owner of this inn." Moira turned her back on Martin and eyed Paavo a long moment. "Would you like your tarot read, Inspector Smith?" she asked, leaning toward him.

"What does it take to get you people to listen to reason?" Vane demanded.

Moira kept her attention on Paavo. "Reading tarot is quite interesting. I become the vehicle between you and the cards. By delving deeply, I can reach your subconscious. I would become as one with you, Inspector, to find the mysteries you have hidden so well."

Angie held her breath. As much as she'd like to delve deeply into Paavo's hidden thoughts, she wanted to be the delver, not Moira Tay.

"He doesn't want to be bothered," Running Spirit said, pulling up a chair and sitting catty-corner from her at the table. "Unless it tells him who's behind the deaths around here. But you can read my tarot."

"Do you mind?" Moira asked Paavo.

"I give up!" Vane stomped out of the room.

The only thing Paavo minded was that Vane and Jeffers both implied that multiple, unnatural deaths had taken place here. How did they know? What did they know? "I don't mind," he said.

"Didn't I tell you?" Running Spirit's cocky tone carried over the sound of the rain that pummeled the library windows and the wind that howled through the fireplace.

Paavo watched as Moira sat, her back straight, gazing steadily at Running Spirit. "Wouldn't it be said I had an unfair advantage?" she asked. "After all, we were once close friends."

"There's more to me than you ever imagined, Moira," Running Spirit said. "More than you've ever let me tell you."

The soft sound of crying suddenly touched the air. The same sound Angie had heard the first night she was at Hill Haven.

"Elise?" Angie asked Moira.

"I don't . . . know what you're talking about," Moira insisted.

Then, as quickly as it began, the sound stopped.

Moira placed the tarot cards in the middle of the table and stood. "I'm going to brew some tea; excuse me."

"I'm not letting it go, Moira," Running Spirit said.

She picked up a candlestick, but as she stepped past Running Spirit on her way to the door, he reached for her hand. Holding it, he looked into her eyes. She returned his gaze. No one breathed. Then Moira jerked her hand free and hurried away.

Angie touched Paavo's arm. "It seems there's more to the past than ghosts around here."

"I'm feeling very tense vibrations," Bethel cried. "I don't think I like this."

"Moira's just tired. It's been a long day," Running Spirit said testily. "Everyone who wants to join me in our journey to the astral plane must meet at dawn tomorrow."

"This *is* the astral plane, *dumbkoff*," Martin said.

Running Spirit glared at him.

"What do you mean?" Angie asked.

"If it's not raining too hard," Running Spirit began, "we'll walk under the trees at dawn, lie down, and project ourselves—out of body—onto the astral plane. On my last trip, I was up in the ozone layer watching the hole grow larger and larger. It was like . . . manifest."

Chelsea let out a sigh. "I wonder if I'd be closer to Jack there. That's so very sensitive."

"That's so very full of it, you mean!" Bethel peered down her nose at Running Spirit. "Nobody does OBE's anymore. They're so eighties."

"Listen, you old fraud—"

"So, tell me, Running Spirit," Angie said, not wanting to hear another argument between those two. "You get up at dawn to do that?"

"That's right. We'll do it in the living room if we can't go outdoors."

Angie stood. "Dawn will be here before we know it. It's been a long day. Are you ready to go, Paavo?"

He glanced up at her, then at the others still comfortably seated. How much did they know? What would Running Spirit bring up when Moira came back, since he'd warned her he wasn't going to let it go. Not let what go? But first Paavo had to get Angie out of here. If she had the slightest suspicion there was more than meets the eye going on here and began snooping around, she could be next on the hit list. "I'm going to have some tea first."

Angie felt rocked by his words. "Tea?" He never drank tea. Especially not herbal tea, which she was sure was the only kind Moira Tay would bring herself to make.

"You go upstairs, Angie. Chelsea's probably ready to go up, too. Right, Chelsea?" he asked.

Chelsea looked from him to Angie. "Well, yes. I am tired."

"Take a candle," Paavo said to Angie. "I'll be up later."

He couldn't have been plainer if he'd carried her out of the library and deposited her in the hallway. So that was the way it was? Steeling herself, when no strange thumps or bumps in the night began, she bade the others an abrupt good night and stalked regally from the room, Chelsea following. Then, when they were both in the hallway, they ran up the stairs and into their rooms, locking the doors behind them.

10

Paavo hated seeing the hurt look on Angie's face as she went upstairs alone. But there was too much about this crew that made him suspicious. They knew or at least suspected a lot more than they'd admit to. He wanted to see what would happen when Moira came back—if she and Running Spirit would get into it like they had earlier, maybe say more than they would otherwise.

Moira carried a teapot and cups into the room and set them on a table. She, Martin, Bethel, and Running Spirit were the only ones besides Paavo remaining in the room.

They were night people, people who lived and thrived in shadows. At night, men and women like them opened up, put aside the wary alertness of the day, and relaxed in the company of like beings. The sunny daytime people like Angie wouldn't begin to understand them or the dark side that made up their world. He did. He worked in it. At times, he lived it. He knew how interesting, and how ugly, it could be.

As much as he could, he would keep Angie away from it.

"So what do you think has become of our Finley, Inspector?" Bethel asked.

"You tell me. I've never even met the man."

Bethel laughed. "That's right. Aren't you the lucky one? Allakaket said I shouldn't trust him. But Martin wouldn't listen to me. Isn't that right, dear?"

"Oh, now this is all my fault, is it?" Martin asked. "Wasn't it you who kept saying something about your big chance for a comeback?"

"Comeback? I never *left*."

Martin stood. "I'm going to bed."

"It's too early." Bethel turned her back on him. "Moira, do you have any rune stones?"

"She'll read my tarot or nothing," Running Spirit said.

"Who made you lord and master?" Bethel asked indignantly.

Running Spirit put on a CD of Yanni. "Moira, why don't you bring out something to help us enjoy the music?"

She glanced at Paavo. "I don't do that stuff anymore, Greg. I gave it up years ago."

He laughed. "What do you mean? Are you worried about him?" He pointed at Paavo. "He's your cook's boyfriend. He's not going to turn us in. I'm not talking heavy stuff. A little pot. A little hash. That's all. Hey, I know plenty of cops who are real cool about that."

"I meant what I said. No more, Greg."

"The name's Running Spirit."

Martin placed a bottle of whiskey on the table. "Looks like this'll have to do. It sure as hell's been good to me all these years."

Moira put out glasses along with soda, ice, and Stolichnaya straight from the freezer. Somehow they all ended up talking about the nature of magic—black magic as well as white. Each had delved to some degree into the black side of it. Paavo wasn't surprised.

He didn't talk much. Instead, he listened and asked questions. But whenever the talk veered toward the inn or the strange occurrences here, someone artfully turned it away again. It was always a different one, nothing Paavo could put his finger on.

Moira sat between him and Running Spirit, but she faced Paavo. She spoke of her belief that spirits, good and evil, coexist in this world. She had nothing new to say, but then, what did he expect? It wasn't as if she could present him with proof.

Running Spirit interrupted, telling Moira why she was wrong in everything she said. He bored Paavo. The man was like a barking dog, so pleased with the sound of his own voice he'd cock his head to listen, not realizing it was nothing more than noise.

Paavo put down his empty glass. There'd be no more tarot tonight. He was wasting time here. They were all too aware of his being a cop to open up any.

When he reached the stairs, instead of going up to bed, he crossed the dark living room and stepped out onto the porch. Standing under the shelter of the roof, he watched the rain. There was no breeze and the crisp air felt good after the stuffiness of the library.

He enjoyed the soothing sound the rain made and tried hard to let the peace it offered wash over him.

But the jolt that had hit him when he first arrived at the inn and saw Moira still prickled whenever he looked at her. Not because of her, but someone else. It'd been years since Sybil's name or anything about her had crossed his mind.

Seeing Moira, though, brought it all back again.

Sybil. A strange name for one of his generation. But

then Sybil wasn't like others of his generation. Maybe that was why he'd been so taken with her.

They'd met after his discharge from the army. He'd gone back to San Francisco to look for a job and an apartment, and was staying with Aulis Kokkonen, the elderly Finnish man who took him and his sister in after their mother abandoned them.

Sybil was a couple of years older than he. Tall like Moira, with long, straight blond hair and gray eyes that looked into your soul and beyond, her features were beautiful, delicate, and her body close to perfection. She was interested in the occult and spirits, and fascinated him, especially since she was more than a little fey. She seemed to always call just a second after he thought of her, or to show up at his house whenever he felt the need to see her. They were young and, he thought, in love.

Then he decided to join the police force. Something about the rough time he'd had as a youth, and the discipline and order he'd enjoyed in the army, made the police attractive to him. He liked what the force stood for and what it meant to do the job well.

Sybil said she understood, that she approved. But she moved deeper into the occult, to the dark side, while his days and nights were taken up by the police academy and his studies. He tried to convince her that many of the people she was spending time with could be dangerous. She didn't listen.

He grew tired of their arguments and stopped calling. Twice she tried to see him, but he was too busy for her and her problems.

Eventually there was no more contact between them. He'd heard she fell in with a group that called themselves witches and warlocks, but in fact were no more than street people, wandering the city slums. He saw her once, about four years later. She was on a street corner begging for money as he rode by, a uniform in a squad car. Her beautiful hair had been shaved off and she wore a ring through one eyebrow and another through her bottom lip. Her skin had a sickly pallor and she'd aged so much it was frightening.

He didn't even stop.

Some months later he went back to that area a few times and cruised around trying to find her, but he never saw her again.

Over the years, he often thought that if he had spent time with her when she had tried to contact him, or had stopped and spoken to her on the street that night, he might have made a difference. He might have been able to help her.

Guilt . . . that was the feeling he carried over Sybil, and that was the feeling that struck him when he looked at Moira. He'd turned his back on Sybil, but he'd been close enough to her, close enough to her type, that he could see and understand that Moira Tay was also a woman who was hurting and alone.

He wouldn't turn his back on her. If she needed help, he'd do what he could. As a cop. No more—but also, no less.

Paavo stood over the bed and watched Angie sleep. He'd gone out with a number of women after Sybil and before he met Angie, but not for very long, and never with much emotional involvement.

Why should he? After a mother who left him, a sister who died, and a girlfriend who decided she was a witch, he'd written off women in his life. His was not a sterling track record.

Angelina was clearly too young and too naïve to know what a bad bargain she'd made with him. Not that he hadn't told her often enough. But she was too stubborn to listen. Someday she'd figure it out. Of that he had no doubt.

In the meantime, though, to be able to simply stand here and watch someone as beautiful and good-natured as she sleep in his bed was a kind of wholesome pleasure he never expected to have in his life. To know that, if he'd ask her, she'd say she loved him, and would open her arms to him, was more than he'd ever believed could be his.

If he lived to be a hundred—although he often doubted he'd make it to forty—he'd hold these few months with Angie forever in his memory. These few months when Angie loved him.

He sat on the bed and lightly touched her hand. "Time for you to get up, Angel."

She opened her eyes.

"Time for breakfast. We already did our morning exercises."

"What time is it?" She sat up. The alarm clock read 7:30. "Haven't you been to bed?"

"Not yet."

"You stayed up all night with those people?"

"So it seems."

She threw back the covers, got up, marched to the dressing room, grabbed an armful of his clothes, then went to the door to their room and threw the clothes out into the hallway. He followed her from one place to the other. "What are you doing?" he asked.

At that point, she grabbed him and shoved him out the door as well. "Angie!"

"You like being with Moira Tay so much, you can just

room with her!" As he took a step toward her, she slammed the door in his face.

So much for his gentle, good-natured Angie, he thought.

Angie cooked soy cheese omelets. She was too irritated with Paavo and with being here to take the trouble to come up with anything more imaginative. She served light, airy muffins on the side.

Breakfast was a snap. Moira and Reginald Vane were the only ones who showed up. Did the woman ever sleep? Angie wondered. She wasn't surprised that Martin wasn't there. He must have been nursing a hangover. Bethel, she learned, rarely rose before ten each day. She figured Running Spirit and Patsy were out having their OBE, rain or no. And Chelsea, after last night's tarot session, was probably sitting in her room waiting for Jack Sempler to show up.

Since breakfast was so lightly attended, Angie decided to prepare a good-sized lunch.

Quickly she searched through the cupboard and shelves of the kitchen and pantry, trying to figure out what to cook.

Finley's larder was running low. For sure, he hadn't planned on eight guests being stranded on this hilltop.

Behind a door in the kitchen a staircase led to the cellar where Paavo had moved Miss Greer's body. The last thing Angie wanted to do was go down there—she'd read too many mysteries with gory descriptions of days-old dead bodies not to know the horror that must be down in that cellar. But she also knew that many people put preserves or other foodstuffs in cellars.

She opened the cellar door, then flicked on the light

over the stairs. "Hello, down there," she called, feeling foolish. If Miss Greer had answered, she would have fainted dead away.

She tiptoed down the long, straight flight, expecting to see the sheet-covered body lying on the floor. Cold chills raced up and down her back. She wouldn't look at it. One glance, that's all. But if that sheet started to move . . . She never did like Casper the Friendly Ghost.

The body wasn't there. What was there, back in a corner, was a big freezer chest. Had Paavo and Running Spirit folded Miss Greer up and put her in there? How horrible! She guessed it was better than having the body liquefying on the floor . . . but not by much.

A small, ancient refrigerator stood against a wall near the stairs. She could tell by the hum that it was plugged in and running. Curious, she opened it. Inside were cheeses—cheddar, jack, provolone, even a wedge of Brie. Most packages had been opened, but some weren't. There was a cube of real butter, a quart of plain old-fashioned fattening milk, and in the tiny freezer compartment, a pound each of bacon and hamburger and a half-gallon of Dreyers Chocolate Chip Cookie Dough ice cream. "Finley Tay, you old fraud," she whispered.

She piled all the food she could hold into her arms—she didn't want to come down here again—and ran back up the stairs as fast as her quivering legs would carry her. Her one regret was leaving behind the ice cream.

The thought of Miss Greer down there was too creepy to deal with, and she didn't want to stay another minute alone in the kitchen. After stuffing the food in the upstairs refrigerator, she grabbed a yellow rain slicker and went outdoors to the garden.

She took deep breaths of the crisp air, trying to concentrate on the one thing she could understand in this wretched inn with these strange people—food and its preparation.

In the garden she found ripe artichokes and asparagus. Some old places like this had root cellars where dried vegetables and such were kept. She'd have to ask Moira.

She picked some vegetables and carried them into the kitchen, concentrating hard on what to do with them instead of thinking about death.

From her studies of vegetarian cooking, she knew that, for the most part, it was simply a matter of substituting something for meat. The biggest problem was that there were so many different levels of sensitivity. Some vegetarians would eat almost anything short of a T-bone, rare, while others wouldn't even eat a cheese pizza since cheese was a dairy product. Some ate fish, some didn't.

Dead fish, each with one eye staring upward from an ice-filled chest . . . much like the one downstairs . . . came to mind.

Vegetarianism, she told herself firmly, could stem from religious, moral, or health convictions, and lectures for the unenlightened carnivores differed accordingly. As far as this group went, she had no idea where their sensitivities lay. But something told her they probably weren't very deep or profound.

And if one of the vegetarians was a murderer . . . the thought boggled.

Eventually she managed to concentrate on food long enough to hit upon a good luncheon item—crêpes. She would make a stack of thin pancakes and two kinds of fillings. Then it'd be a simple matter to ask each person their choice, and while they were eating their salads, she could assemble the crêpes. If anyone objected to the eggs in the thin pancake batter, they could eat the filling without the crêpes.

She began by figuring out a Finley-fanatic filling, mixing together soy cottage cheese, minced mushrooms, peppers, green onion, thyme, and marjoram. For the sauce she used flour, soy butter, soy milk, pepper, and—she couldn't resist—a dash of nutmeg.

For the others, she combined jack cheese, chopped spinach, and sliced mushrooms with an egg, green onions, salt, and pepper. To go with this, she decided on a Mornay sauce of flour, butter, milk, grated parmesan, and more jack cheese, since there was no Gruyère. As she cooked it, she added salt and a dash of cayenne.

She had picked an artichoke for each person. She put them on to boil. Instead of salad, she'd serve artichokes with a variation of a *sauce moutarde*, made with Dijon mustard, mayonnaise, a dash of olive oil, lemon juice, parsley, and her own addition, a hint of curry.

This should make everyone happy, she thought. If not, they were welcome to take over the kitchen anytime.

Chelsea was the first to come into the dining room for lunch. Reginald Vane followed and sat beside her. They were soon lost in a conversation about the existence of angels. Moira and Running Spirit were next, followed by Martin and Bethel. Last, Paavo entered the dining room. Angie felt as if her heart would stop when he sat beside Moira.

Patsy didn't join the others for lunch.

Angie took their requests for the crêpes. Everyone wanted her recipe, not Finley's. She went into the kitchen, rolled the crêpes, put sauce over them, and placed them under a moderate broiler just long enough for the top of the crêpes to brown lightly—not quite ten minutes.

When she brought the crêpes out to be served, she discovered the group in a heated discussion over Patsy. Apparently, it had required a lot of questioning before Running Spirit admitted that he hadn't seen her all morning.

"There's nothing to worry about," he said. "She'll turn up."

Angie had stopped in the doorway when she first heard this bickering, but given Jeffers's assurances, she proceeded to give out the platters of hot crêpes, then stood back to watch the expressions of pleasant surprise and receive words of admiration as the group tasted some good food for once.

Bethel picked up her fork, then put it down again. "Do I have to remind you, Greg Jeffers," she said, "that Finley is still missing? If Patsy's gone too, doesn't that feeble brain of yours tell you we should know it, and we should worry about it?"

"She's around." Running Spirit didn't even try to hide his exasperation. "Patsy never goes far enough away from me to have anything happen to her. She's sulking somewhere. That's all."

"Sulking?" Bethel said. "Whatever would she be doing that for?"

Running Spirit's eyes narrowed. "Why don't you tell me?" He spoke through gritted teeth. "Or maybe Allakaket can do it? In fact, since you're such a know-it-all bitch, why don't you clue us all in on where she is?"

"Martin, are you going to let him talk to me like that?"

Martin had taken a bite, but had to quickly swallow it in order to answer. "He's got a point, you know."

Bethel turned to Paavo. "Inspector Smith, don't you think we should be worried about Patsy?"

Paavo glanced at Running Spirit. "If Jeffers really has

no idea where she is, then yes, I think we should go out
and look for her immediately."

"Go out?" Running Spirit stood. "Patsy's in the house,
I tell you. She wouldn't set foot out in nature alone.
There's no way she's gone off and gotten herself lost.
She's hiding. She just wants to make trouble."

"A commendable pastime, I'm sure," Martin said, raising his glass to Running Spirit.

Moira half stood, leaning over the table, her face absolutely devoid of color. Her body shook as she faced
Running Spirit. "Tell me you're sure she's hiding somewhere in this house. Tell me she hasn't disappeared like
my brother."

He grabbed her wrist. "She's all right."

"Let's find her so we can be sure." Moira turned and
glided from the room. Running Spirit leaped from his
chair and hurried after her.

Martin and Bethel got up to follow, as did Reginald
Vane. Chelsea cut the crêpe in half with her fork, picked
it up with her fingers, and crammed it into her mouth
before running after the others.

Angie slowly walked toward the table. Paavo still sat
there watching her. She noticed that he hadn't taken a
bite of his lunch, either.

Disappearing owners, constant bickering, occult
noises, Paavo spending his nights with another woman . . .

She sat down across from him, looked at the crêpes
and artichokes she'd so carefully and proudly prepared,
then burst into tears.

11

"*One of these must be the cliff* Elise Sempler jumped off," Angie said to Paavo as she peeked over the edge of the cliffs near Hill Haven Inn. Jagged rocks, separated by frothy, swirling ocean waves, dotted the cove at the bottom of a long, sheer drop. She stepped away, struck by the image of Elise hurtling three hundred feet to her death, and directed her gaze outward.

Despite the constant fall of rain, the scene before her was beautiful, perhaps made even more so by the dark swirling grays of the sky, the stark gloom that surrounded them. Tall, rough monoliths of dark brown and tan jutted through the surface of the ocean, taking the full brunt of the incoming waves and shooting sprays of mist high into the sky. Up and down the coast, craggy rock formations tumbled into the Pacific.

Paavo held his hand out to her. She took it, knowing he'd asked her along more as a peace offering than because he needed her assistance in searching for Patsy. He had quietly and gently comforted her after her disappointment at lunch, going around the table to sit by her side and wrap her in his arms. She dampened his shoulder

as he told her she was the only one who seemed to be trying to do anything special at the inn. That if the others
didn't appreciate her, it was only because they were too
wrapped up in themselves to appreciate anyone else. He
appreciated her.

How could she stay angry with a man who said that?

She hadn't thought of the others that way, but Paavo's
words made sense. Sometime they needed to have a long
talk about this place and the strange things happening
here, but not now. Not in this quiet, beautiful setting,
where she wanted nothing more than to enjoy his near-
ness and their truce.

They journeyed southward along the edge of the land,
searching as they went for any sign of Patsy. Or Finley.
Above the cliffs, redwoods stood like sentries protecting
the coast.

"What do you think of the Sempler ghost stories?"
Paavo asked after a while.

"I love old ghost stories; most are so romantic and
thrilling, not scary at all. But I've never been able to
believe them, not even when I wanted to," she replied. "I
worry about Chelsea's fascination with the ghost of Jack
Sempler. I guess she's seen *Ghost* one time too many.
Jack Sempler doesn't exactly have the Patrick Swayze
look, though. He's more *The Ghost and Mrs. Muir*
type, if you ask me."

"Meaning?"

"Old and black-and-white."

"But still a romantic figure?"

"Most definitely."

"From what I've heard about the Semplers, they
should be the last people any young woman would
romanticize."

"Oh, I don't know." Angie glanced his way. "I think a

lot of women are fascinated by mysterious men—the quiet, hard-to-be-sure-about, dangerous sort."

He looked puzzled. "I don't understand it."

She couldn't stop the grin that played on her lips. "I know."

They continued in silence, poking under the few bushes and brush on the wind-swept coast, searching the landscape and ground for any footprints, any sign someone had been here recently.

"The brother–sister connection—Jack and Susannah, and now Finley and Moira—is an interesting twist," Angie said. "Don't you think?"

He stopped and picked up a coral-pink pebble, rubbed it clean with his fingers, and gave it to her. "It means no more than that families usually live together. Don't let these people get to you, Angie. It can be dangerous."

Angie held the pebble, warmed by his touch, tight in her hand a moment, then put it deep into her pocket. "You may be right. But there seems to be something peculiarly sad and lonely about this house and the lives of both the Semplers and the Tays, and now, Patsy Jeffers. Patsy was likening herself to Susannah the other day. I hope she never sees herself as Elise, the outsider who loves, but then is abandoned, and kills herself by jumping off these cliffs."

"If she did, with these tides we may never find her body."

Angie watched the tide pound the huge rocks offshore and shivered. "Don't say that. I'm sorry I mentioned it."

Paavo put his arm around her shoulders. Her arm circled his waist, and they held each other as close as their cumbersome rain slickers would allow as they walked along.

After a while, he said, "I think we should climb down

to the beach to see what we can find or observe from that angle."

"What beach? All I saw were rocks. Judging from the waterlines, they're probably underwater when the tide comes in."

"Come on."

Continuing along the cliff tops, they came to a spot where the land was less formidable, and where rolling hillsides led down to the water. "Here's a path," Paavo said, starting down.

She didn't relish trying to climb down hillsides on bright, sunny days; in the rain it seemed impossible. "It might not be a cliff, but it still looks plenty steep and much too slippery," Angie said. "I don't think this is such a good idea."

He glanced down at her shoes. Colorful Nike pump-up sneakers. At least they weren't her green clogs. "Don't worry," he said. "If you get stuck, pump up your shoes and pretend you're Michael Jordan doing an alley-oop. You'll spring right up the hill."

"Michael Jordan doing a what?"

He took her hand. "Let's go."

She had to admit Paavo was a good person to hike with. Whenever she started to slip, his grip would tighten and she'd steady herself. He never let her fall once.

When they reached the beach, Paavo climbed out on a jumble of boulders jutting far into the ocean. He stood on the farthest point, staring out at the ocean like some old-time sea captain. Seeing him out there, alone on the slick rocks, made her more than a little nervous. The breeze from the ocean was strong and chilly.

"Be careful!" she called.

He glanced over his shoulder at her. "What?"

"I said, be careful. You scare me way out there. She

felt foolish the moment she said it, considering the dangers inherent in his job. But her ever-present fear of losing him was even with her on this beach. It was, she supposed, the ghost she carried.

He was walking back to her, surefooted as he clamored over the rocks.

"I'm sorry," she began, holding her hands out to his. "I don't mean to be such a pest about—"

He kissed her. He'd taken her hands, leaned forward and astonished her in midsentence. "Don't be sorry," he said.

His words, his actions, told her how new it was for him to have someone worry and call out a simple warning, the kind mothers and wives and families say all the time. But he had had none in his life. She nodded, not trusting her voice just then.

She took his hand, and they continued along the beach.

At the end of the small beach area, they had to climb over some large boulders, then found another small, sandy cove. This series of coves and boulders continued until the shore suddenly became a long, sandy beach.

"This is beautiful!" Angie gasped.

"What a great place," Paavo said. "A place to lose yourself, to lose all notion of time."

His words surprised her. Despite her hope that he could come to Hill Haven Inn and do nothing but rest, the strange disappearances, Miss Greer's death, and, she feared, the peculiar people staying with them, didn't allow him to relax. The lines of tension and weariness that so often marred his expression because of the constant, often heart-wrenching pressures of his job had eased little.

The first time she met him, his eyes had been hard as

granite, cold as the north Pacific. But later, when he turned them on her with warmth, she'd lost her heart. The more she came to know him, the stronger and deeper the feeling grew. If she had to stay on an isolated beach on a rainy, gloomy day like this with him forever, she'd be happy.

They reached the end of the beach and faced a pile of rocks higher and larger than previous ones, separating this beach area from the next cove.

"Stop," she said. "Let me catch my breath."

"You need to exercise more," he offered.

"Thank you, Richard Simmons. Look how far we've come . . . and how high up those rocks are."

"They're too high for you. Wait here. I want to go over one or two more of these rock faces before we turn back."

She couldn't imagine the need for that. "Why?"

"We've already come this far."

"True, but Patsy's a lot more delicate than I am. There's no way she would have walked this far. Especially alone."

"I know."

"So why are you going farther to search for her?"

"Remember, she's not the only one missing."

He was right.

"This won't take long," he said. "Stay here."

As she watched Paavo climb quickly over the tall, slick rocks, Angie knew there was no way she could have kept up with him. Hard as it was going up the rocks, she hated to think of how dangerous it would be going down the other side.

So she waited.

And waited.

She walked along the beach, back in the direction

they'd come from. The cliffs loomed high above her, shrouded in fog and mist. She couldn't remember ever feeling so alone. She was from a big family—four older sisters, a mother and father who were still married after forty-two years, a multitude of aunts, uncles and cousins up to four times removed. Whenever she went to do anything, there were always at minimum ten people there to do it with her. Being alone was a concept quite foreign to her. Looking around the quiet beach—without relatives, neighbors, cars, phones, or shops filled with people surrounding her—rather than seeing the beauty of it, she saw only the vulnerability of her isolation. Times like this, she found the city a much less frightening place than the country.

But then, she knew the city. Here life was alien.

She hadn't thought much before about how narrow the beach was. She preferred the wide beaches of the Riviera and Tahiti. The ones you could get to by stepping out of your hotel room and walking a few feet. Those were proper beaches. She moved closer to the cliffs. Not these skinny, narrow . . .

She saw water in a crevice of the cliff about three feet up from the beach. Her mouth went dry. Surely it was rainwater. Wasn't it? She watched a tall wave breaking on a boulder not far from shore. The spray shot high into the air, and when the wave hit the shore it flowed a lot closer to Angie than the last one had.

Oh, God, she thought. Was this low tide or high tide? She might not know much about nature, but she knew that when the tide came in, some of these coves were underwater. Well underwater. So if it was now low tide, how high would the water reach once it came in?

She looked at the water in the crevice. Did she want to stick around here to find out?

Paavo had told her to stay put because he thought it would be too dangerous for her to climb over the rock face with him. Compared to a tide coming in and drowning her, not to mention sweeping her off her feet and dragging her into the undertow or smashing her up against the rocks before it drowned her, that rock face didn't look very dangerous at all.

She ran back to the rocks Paavo had climbed over, shouting his name the whole time. She got no answer.

She climbed up onto the rocks a little way, but soon the rock became so slick and smooth she couldn't go any higher.

She watched another wave hit the shore. How fast did the tide come in, anyway? She remembered something about six hours, but was that one way or round trip?

Why hadn't she paid more attention to these things about life? What had she wasted her time on instead?

She noticed that closer to the cliffs the rock ledge was higher, but also a lot more jagged. She could probably find a better toehold there. Once at the top, she might even be able to see Paavo. How far could he have gone?

She glanced over her shoulder, then down. Then up. The silence was eerie.

She worked herself sideways, able to climb a bit higher on the rocks before, once again, the boulder turned smooth and steep. She clung to the rock, halfway up and halfway down.

Maybe if she turned around and sat on the rocks she could sort of scoot upward? She tried it, feeling like a klutz; but at least she was making progress. All of a sudden, the ground beneath her bottom began to slide. Wet earth, sand, and small rocks turned into an oozing mud that whooshed her along right to a ledge near the foot of the cliff.

There she sat, her heart still up on the rock face while she thanked God that she was alive and, from all she could tell, hadn't even bloodied herself.

Looking up, she realized she'd slid only about six or seven feet. No wonder nothing was broken. It had only felt like a plunge off the Empire State Building.

She crawled forward. She was on a kind of ledge, like a horizontal tuck in the hillside. The beach was still a few feet below her—straight down. She looked upward. The top of the cliff was so high, she could scarcely see it.

Well, she couldn't sit here forever. She had to go up and over the rocks Paavo had climbed, or back down to the beach. Since down meant the tide, one way or another she had to go up.

To stand up, she put her hand down a little behind her to brace herself. But the loose, wet sand crumbled beneath her fingers and slid away. She moved her hand back a bit more and tried again, but this time the ground felt smooth, and soft, and mushy. Yanking her hand away, she turned and looked at what she'd touched.

A creeping horror filled her for a long moment before she turned and scrambled up the rock face, screaming Paavo's name and climbing so fast she didn't have time to worry about falling or how steep the rocks were or anything else but how to get far, far away from the rotting mass that Finley Tay's face had become.

12

Reaching the top of the ledge, she looked at the long drop to the next beach and stopped. "Paavo!" She called his name over and over.

Silence.

She didn't have to be a medical examiner to know Tay was dead, and had been for several days. It was good, in retrospect, that she hadn't eaten lunch. She'd never have been able to hold it down.

Slowly, she rose to her feet. How had she gotten up here, anyway? Maybe she could make it down to the beach to find Paavo. Or she might be better off going upward to the top of the cliff. All she needed was a rope or a hanging vine. Of course there were no hanging vines in California, and no one had left a rope hanging around, either. But even thoughts of playing Tarzan couldn't shake the memory of Finley's face. She shuddered. She could still feel the spongy mass under her palm, between her fingers.

Making the sign of the cross, she took a tentative step

down the far side of the rock face. A loose rock bounced all the way down to the beach. With shaking legs, she sat again. Just as she mustered the courage to try once more, she saw Paavo ambling over some rocks and heading toward her.

She waved her arms, calling his name as loudly as she could.

He ran over and stood on the beach, looking up at her on the ledge. "What are you doing?" he demanded, his face pale and tight, his breath coming in quick, short spurts.

She started to stand, but couldn't.

"Don't move!" He began to climb up the rocks.

"I found Finley Tay." May as well sound like I planned it, she thought.

He stopped. "You found Tay?"

"He's dead."

"Wait."

As if I have a choice, she thought. In no time, he was by her side, his intense gaze reflecting his concern for her and her finding. She reached up and lightly touched his shoulder, his wet hair, not realizing until he was with her how badly shaken she was by her gruesome discovery.

His hands gripped hers. "Are you all right?" His deep voice was like music to her.

"Yes."

"Your hands are cold." As if not trusting his eyes or her answers, he swept his hands urgently over her.

"I'm all right." She stilled his hands, and her voice grew soft, hushed. "He's down there."

Paavo left her to climb down to Finley's body alone.

Finley lay on his stomach, his face turned sideways, facing outward. Paavo carefully brushed aside some of the sand.

Finley's thin, angular face was bloated. Maggots and beetles crawled amid the dirt-filled orifices.

Paavo stared at the matted blood on the back of Finley's head, and at its peculiar concave shape. The skull had been crushed. He'd never seen an accident or a fall do anything like that. Unless something fell on him from a high distance—a tree limb, or large rock from a rock slide—whatever hit him had been hurled down with a great deal of force. The kind of force that means murder.

"Do you think he fell and the fall killed him?" Angie called from above.

"I'm not sure what the exact cause of death was, but it was more than a fall. Given the lack of blood here, I'd say he was killed elsewhere, then most likely pushed over the cliff to this ledge and covered with sand. In this spot, his body was impossible to see from the top of the cliff or from the beach."

"Can we get away from here, Paavo?" Angie asked in a tremulous voice. "This gives me the willies."

Paavo climbed back up to her side. "Just one question."

"Yes?" She took hold of his hand, feeling secure now only when holding onto him.

"What made you climb up here in the first place?"

"I grew worried about the tide coming in. That beach is awfully narrow."

"That's because the tide *is* in."

"Oh."

Angie went with Paavo to tell Moira that they had found her brother. As a cop, Paavo had given bad news like this to people before, but Angie had never needed to. It wasn't a duty she ever wanted to repeat.

They left Moira alone with her sorrow. Paavo needed to find a tarp or something similar to cover Tay's body. He planned to do as thorough a review of the surroundings as possible before anyone else went out there. No way would he allow Finley's body to be moved the way Miss Greer's had been. He'd keep the crime scene as secure as possible until the sheriff could reopen the road and get some of his own men up here.

Before leaving, Paavo walked with Angie up to their room.

"I want you to stay here," he said, "and keep the door locked. I'll leave my gun with you on this nightstand."

"I can't imagine I'm in danger. It had to have been a personal thing against Finley. He had enough enemies. In town as well as among these investors."

He thought of Miss Greer's body. "Until we know why Finley and Miss Greer are dead, any of us could be in danger. Including you."

"Miss Greer? I thought she had a heart attack?"

"No. I suspect she was murdered. And she was the cook here. Now you are. Or were."

"I still am. It's my job—"

"Humor me."

"Yes, Inspector. Anything you say, Inspector."

He knew that tone only too well. Frowning, he left.

Alone once more, Angie took a hot shower to rid herself of the chill from the outdoors as well as the smell and spongy feeling of Finley Tay's face. No amount of soap seemed to help, though. And the chill she felt was from a lot more than a cold rain.

Frightening memories of the beach kept flashing before her. Finally, unable to bear it any longer, she went to Chelsea's room and knocked on the door.

Chelsea opened it, a bright, expectant smile on her

face. She wore a cherry-colored velvet housecoat and a large black plastic butterfly barrette in her hair. Despite her outfit and her smudged eyeliner, Angie thought the woman's smile made her look almost pretty. But her smile faded when she saw Angie. "Yes?"

"I'm sorry to bother you," Angie said, realizing that Chelsea must have been expecting Jack Sempler to knock at her door. All the ghosts Angie had ever heard about would have just walked through it. "I wanted to tell you we found Finley Tay. He's dead."

Chelsea looked horrified. "Oh, my God! Come inside. Where was he?"

Angie walked into the room and sat down on the bed. "At the foot of some cliffs. Paavo and I were looking for Patsy, and instead found him. I put my hand on some sand. It slid away and there he was." She shivered.

"You poor thing! And poor Finley. Did he fall?"

"We don't know. Paavo doesn't think so, though."

Now it was Chelsea's turn to tremble. "Let's talk about something else. This is too horrible for me."

"Was Finley a good friend of yours?" Angie asked.

"No. I scarcely knew him." She bit her bottom lip. "I don't mean to speak badly of the dead, but he used to scare me. Just a little."

"Really? Yet you invested in his inn?"

Chelsea played with a button on her housecoat. "It was all because of Jack Sempler," she said quietly.

"Sempler?"

She looked ready to cry. "Finley and Moira said Jack Sempler was here. Then last night the cards told me he would come to me. I've been waiting, but he hasn't shown up yet."

Seeing Chelsea's forlorn face, Angie wanted nothing more than to give this whole crowd a piece of her mind.

It was wrong of Moira to have given the tarot cards the spin she did, and to have allowed Chelsea to think that a ghost was going to visit her.

"Is that why you didn't come to breakfast or lunch today?" Angie asked.

"I didn't want to take the chance that he'd come here while I was out." Chelsea wiped away her tears.

"Would you like me to bring you something to eat?" Angie asked.

"No. For once, I've decided food will come second for me." She glanced down at her girth and gave a wry smile. "I'm going to fast until he appears."

"That'll make him appear for sure."

"Do you think so?"

Angie bit her tongue. The words Moira once spoke, saying that Chelsea's wealthy parents had thought the inn a good investment for Chelsea, made Angie wonder if part of their willingness to pay wasn't because they wanted to keep Chelsea away from them. But dealing with Chelsea's naïveté by shunting her away like this was no solution. And for Finley Tay to have taken advantage of the situation was reprehensible. "You have to remember one thing, Chelsea. It's possible that ghosts—well, those on the 'other side' as they call it—don't exist in the same time zone as we do. His 'tomorrow' might not be exactly the same as your tomorrow. So if he doesn't show up today, I don't want you to be too disappointed. Promise?"

"I was worried about that myself." Chelsea sighed. "But then I decided he would translate into my time frame. He'll be here. He won't disappoint me."

"Chelsea, you can't count on ghosts."

"You can't? How do you know?"

Good question. "My Italian grandmother told me. She knows all about ghosts and spirits and the evil eye."

"The evil eye? What's that?"

"It's when someone puts a hex on you. Salt helps ward it off, if I remember right."

"Salt? Well, that's good." Chelsea pulled a big bag of Ruffles out of the armoire and opened it. "Have some. Then we won't have to worry about evil eyes, at least."

Angie's eyes lit up and she grabbed a handful of salty, fat-laden, fried potato chips.

"Here," Chelsea said, handing her a Pepsi-Cola from under the bed. "Something to wash them down with."

It was the real thing, not the caffeine-free, diet variety.

"Where'd you get all this?"

"I stocked up before I came. Not that I don't love the food here. This is just in case I feel stressed."

"I know what you mean." Angie popped open the can and drank. Warm, but tasty nonetheless. "I often turn to chocolate, myself."

Chelsea giggled. "Me, too." She opened the top drawer of her nightstand. Snickers. Mounds. Butterfingers. Oh! Henrys. A bag full of Reese's, another of Hershey's Kisses, and two packages of Oreos. "Have some."

It was too much to resist. Angie reached for a Snickers. "I like your kind of fasting."

Chelsea kicked her shoes off, then arranged herself Indian style at the foot of the big double bed. Angie did the same. "Finley always said lunch should be no more than a single piece of fruit or a raw vegetable," Chelsea said. "Light and healthy."

The Snickers tasted better than ever. Angie was close to heaven. "This would be perfect if we had some real coffee," she said.

"No problem. I keep a little electric Krups in the bathroom, and I brought some French roast from home. I'll put it right on."

"Chelsea, I love you!" Angie called into the bathroom where Chelsea had gone with her bag of coffee.

"I knew I'd hear those words today," Chelsea called back over the whir of her coffee grinder. "Only I'd hoped it would be Jack Sempler who'd say them to me." In a minute, she came out and took her place on the bed.

"What makes you so interested in Jack Sempler?" Angie asked. "Where did you first hear about him?"

"Have you ever experienced déjà vu, Angie?"

"Hasn't everyone?"

"I mean the real thing. Like you know you've been somewhere or known someone before. In a past life, for instance."

"No, I guess not."

"Well, I did. I was at a paranormal convention in Anaheim, looking at materials about ghosts. Finley was there telling people about the inn he'd be opening in a few months and inviting them to it. He talked about the healthful regimen he'd have, but also about the Sempler ghosts. He handed out pictures.

"One of them was of Jack Sempler. The one over the mantel in the library. When I saw him, I knew him. I really did. I looked at those sad eyes searching the horizon and I knew he was searching for me. I've felt the same way." She twisted her pearl ring.

Angie leaned forward. "What do you mean? What way?"

"Like . . . like there should be someone out there for me, but I don't know how to find him. And if I don't find him, then I'll have to go through this life, through my whole life, all alone. Just like Jack did." Chelsea took a bite out of a Mounds and didn't say any more until she swallowed it. "You'll probably think it's silly, but I used to visualize myself with the man I love. I used to think he was Elvis."

Angie swallowed an unchewed bite of Snickers and nearly choked on it.

"But I was wrong," Chelsea continued.

Angie nodded, her eyes watering.

"I now realize that the man looked like Jack."

"This was before you ever saw Jack Sempler's picture?" Angie asked.

"That's right."

"Wow." Angie put her chin in her hands. She couldn't imagine visualizing the love of her life wearing a high stand-up collar and riding britches. But she could imagine someone like that before she'd ever imagine Elvis. Imagining a homicide cop was probably somewhere in between.

"Spooky, isn't it? They say that if you visualize something enough, it'll come true. I've visualized Jack Sempler until I nearly wore out my eyeballs! Now I just, well, I love him. I don't know what else to say. And I have to see him again."

"Again?"

"I believe in reincarnation. I believe we knew each other in a past life."

Speechless, Angie nodded. Chelsea sighed, then poured them each a cup of coffee.

"And so that's why you became an investor in the inn?" Angie asked.

"Yes. This way, I can come here whenever I want and stay in this very room. Jack's room. It's really much cheaper in the long run, as Finley explained to me before I gave him my money."

"I'm sure," Angie said, taking a deep, satisfying swallow of the steaming brew. She felt nerve endings and capillaries throughout her body crying in unison: caffeine, yes!

"Since Jack died here, his ghost is here." Chelsea stuffed a couple Reese's Pieces in her mouth.

"It's strange no one knows how he died."

"I think it was because he never found the woman he was destined to love." Chelsea hesitated, then as if floodgates opened, words gushed out. "I understand him, Angie. I've never found the man in this life that I should love. But there's got to be someone for me. I can feel it in my heart. I'm filled with love to give. But I can't find anyone to love me in return."

Angie's eyes stung, but it wasn't from the candy this time. "You will, Chelsea," she said softly.

Chelsea shook her head. "No. I've tried hard. Nothing's worked. I'm not very good-looking."

"There's nothing wrong with your looks."

Chelsea didn't appear convinced. "That's easy for you to say. You're *thin*, not to mention pretty."

"That doesn't mean I can get the right man to love me the way I'd like," Angie said, and sighed. "Not at all."

They pondered this a moment, then each took another candy bar.

"You think, then, that Jack's true love wasn't Elise?" Angie asked after a while. Her head was beginning to spin from so much chocolate.

"No, not Elise. He never really loved her. If he had, he wouldn't have left. No one knows the name of his true love. But I've heard she had long red hair and big green eyes."

Looking at the red hair and green eyes of the woman before her, Angie felt a chill. "Finley told you all that?"

"Moira and Finley did. Now that Finley's gone, though, I don't know what'll happen to the inn, or my investment. All I know is that Reginald Vane will be happy." Chelsea munched on her Oh! Henry.

"Reginald? Why?"

"His main interest in the inn is to see that it doesn't open. He thinks it's wrong to disturb the ghosts who live here."

"So he became an investor? He wants to lose money?"

"That doesn't make sense, does it?" Chelsea admitted.

Angie stood. "Promise me you'll at least come down to have dinner with us."

"I can't. Give my best to Moira, though. I don't think I want to see her quite yet."

"Okay."

"Angie, thanks for coming here. You're the first one who's listened to me. The first one who's tried to understand."

"I'm glad we had this chance to talk," Angie said. "I'll bring you up a dinner plate later." She quietly closed the door as she left.

13

With the discovery of Finley's body, the desire to find Patsy alive and well had whipped everyone but Moira into a frenzy of activity. No one wanted to consider that what had happened to Finley could have happened to Patsy as well.

They'd find her.

Angie made a big pot of vegetable minestrone, served with lots of grated parmesan on top, along with bread, cheese, and a big vegetable salad. The lack of meat bothered her, but since the storm hadn't let up, she realized she had to be frugal with the food. What if it wasn't as easy as everyone thought to dig their way out of here? She was afraid of using too many of their supplies in case they'd need them later. She hadn't grown up with stories of the Donner party starving while crossing into California for nothing.

As those who went outdoors to search for Patsy grew tired, cold, or hungry, they would come inside and eat a bowl of hot soup before going out to look for her once more. But as night fell, an icy wind from the north hit, along with the constant rain. More and more of the group found themselves indoors and hesitant to go out again.

By midnight, Angie sat alone, half-asleep on the velvet settee in the drawing room, listening for Paavo's footstep. Everyone else had gone to bed. Only the small night-light and the last embers from the evening's fire lit the room.

The front door opened, then shut. It was him. Relief flooded her as she sat up. "Any luck?"

He stopped and peered into the darkness. Shrugging off his slicker, he hung it on the hook in the foyer, then came toward her. "What are you doing down here?"

"I wanted to see you," she said tentatively; then, becoming bolder, she added, "I've missed you."

He sat beside her, his arms tight around her as he leaned back on the sofa. She could feel the weariness in him, the frustration. She lay her head against his chest, listening to the steady pounding of his heart, her arms about his waist. "This isn't exactly the kind of week you were expecting," he whispered.

"Do what you must, Paavo." She lifted her head. In the darkness, the shadows were deep under his eyes. She touched his face, finding it rough and scratchy, in need of a shave. "If you didn't, you wouldn't be the man I love."

He kissed her once, twice—soft, gentle kisses. He stopped, but his hands continued to drift up and down her back while intense blue eyes searched hers. "I came in to warm up a bit. I've got to go back. We've got to find her."

"It's too late to do more tonight. Come to bed, Paavo."

"Jeffers, Bayman, and Vane are still out there some-where."

She held his shoulders. "Actually," she began, "Martin came in and passed out, so Bethel and I got him up to bed. It seems the whiskey he was using to keep warm had another effect on him. Reginald Vane came in about an hour ago, half dead from cold and weariness. And earlier, Running Spirit came in and went to Moira's room. I haven't seen him since."

"Great!" Paavo said. "The dutiful husband."

"You need some sleep."

"I'm used to long nights at work. This is no different. It'd be a lot easier if I had some real coffee, but—"

"Ah!" she cried, here a big smile brightening the darkness. "Ask and ye shall receive."

"What?"

She ran a few steps in front of him, then crooked her finger. "Come with me to the kitchen, said the spider to the fly."

He chuckled and followed.

Angie had borrowed some French roast and a handful of Hershey's Kisses from Chelsea, planning on an after-dinner surprise for Paavo. But he'd been out.

The inn didn't have a cappuccino machine, so the caffè mòca she was making wouldn't have any nice frothy milk on top. But it'd be delicious nonetheless. Being his first cup of real coffee since he'd arrived at Hill Haven Inn—was it only three days ago?—would make it particularly special.

She stood over the stove in the kitchen, stirring the chocolate so it wouldn't burn.

She found it pleasant being here in the warmth and coziness of the quiet room. When she was young, she'd loved to sit in their old-fashioned kitchen and watch her mother cook. Serefina would take boneless rump roast and cut it into long, thin strips. She'd spread the strips with chopped parsley and garlic, roll them up, and hold them together with toothpicks. Cooking them all day in a red spaghetti sauce would make the sauce thick and tasty and the meat so tender it could be cut with a fork. Whenever Angie smelled that certain blend of spices, particularly the hint of anise and basil Serefina used in her sauce, she felt right at home again.

Paavo leaned against the sink, lost in thought, one foot crossed over the other, his hands in his pockets. Seeing him in the kitchen caused her to notice anew how tall and broad-shouldered he was, how sharp and analytical his gaze could be, how stern his features. But then his gaze caught hers, and his features softened. She smiled.

"What's the smile for?" he asked.

"You." The chocolate was melting fast now. "Even though I'd hoped you'd be able to rest this week, and that we'd get to spend a lot of time together, a nice woman is out there somewhere, lost or hurt." She held the spoon still a moment. "I can't tell you how proud I am of all you're doing to try to find her."

Paavo stepped up behind her, his large hands spanning her waist; that simple touch brought a quickening in her, an awareness that prickled her skin. He had to go back outside, she reminded herself, fighting the feeling. Back to search for Patsy.

"So you've forgiven me for spending so much time away from you?" He breathed the words against her hair.

"Don't I always forgive you everything?" She stirred faster.

"Do you?" He moved closer, drinking in her scent, the soft curls of her hair tickling his nose, caressing his cheek. He shut his eyes, wanting more than anything to lose himself with her, in her. He fought the feeling.

She bent her head forward, and without thought he kissed her neck. He heard her breath catch as he slid his hands over her hipbones, then forward to her belly, holding her against him.

"I can't concentrate," she said.

"I'll concentrate," he murmured. His hands slipped under her sweater, one splaying against her stomach, sliding under the waistband of her slacks, the other finding the upper edge of her bra and inching under it. His fingers were strong, hard, hot.

She melted a lot faster than the chocolate. Where he touched, she wanted more, and wanted to touch him in turn.

To hell with caffè mòca. Still holding the spoon, she spun around to face him, her hands upraised to circle his neck. The chocolate-coated spoon smacked against the side of his nose.

He stepped back in surprise. Laughing, she dropped the spoon, gripped his shoulders, and licked the spot of chocolate.

"So that's the way it is," he said.

"Well, I didn't want it to burn you," she said. "I guess that's what's known as a hot lick."

"Not exactly."

She shrieked as he lifted her, in one quick movement, so that she was sitting on the stainless steel countertop. She started to scoot back, away from him, but he grasped her hips and slid her forward, right to the edge of the counter, one knee on each side of him. Her laughter died.

His hands cupped her face. All sense of time and place flew from her mind. Her arms circled his shoulders, his neck. He leaned over her, slowly lowering her onto the counter, her pulse pounding until finally, their lips met in an open-mouthed, groin-throbbing, sight-blinding kiss.

The chocolate sizzled against the bottom of the pan. A burning smell filled the kitchen. But none of that mattered. Nothing mattered but Paavo and the way he made her feel.

He lifted her sweater, reaching for the clasp at the front of her bra, his gaze and touch so searing she thought the clasp would melt.

"What's burning?" Chelsea's voice rang out as the kitchen door opened. Paavo yanked Angie's sweater down, straightened, and stepped away, his back to Chelsea.

"Are you cooking, Angie?" Chelsea asked.

Angie struggled to sit up and look nonchalant. Paavo's eyes were shut and his jaw clenched.

Chelsea walked up to the smoking pan and lifted it off the flame and right into the sink, where she ran cold water in it. "I thought it might be the chocolate. There I was, sleeping, and this wonderful scent woke me up. But when it began to burn, I just had to investigate."

"It's ruined," Angie said. "Oh, well, we'll try again tomorrow. Good night, Chelsea."

Chelsea reached into the pocket of her smock and pulled out a handful of Hershey's Kisses. "I don't leave home without it . . . I mean, them."

Angie bit back a groan of frustration.

"If it's stopped raining tomorrow," Chelsea said, "I'll go down to the village and buy more."

"Nifty," Angie said. To think she used to like Chelsea.

"Whenever weathermen predict a big storm, like now, it's often no more than a light sprinkle," Chelsea chattered on. "Nothing to worry about. This'll be another drought year, for sure."

Angie glanced at Paavo. He'd bent over, his elbows on the counter, and was staring at a blank wall.

"I'll melt the chocolate," Chelsea said, "and make sure it doesn't burn. Then we can all have some caffè mòca together."

"I'll just have my coffee plain, thanks," Paavo said,

turning abruptly to get a coffee mug and pour a cup of the fresh brew. The look worn by all frustrated males weighed heavy on his brow. "But go ahead, Angie. I know you love it. I need to get back outside."

"I've lost the taste for it myself," Angie said, wondering if the longing she felt sounded in her voice.

"Nonsense," Chelsea said. "I can melt some in a jiff. I even brought more coffee."

Chelsea took a clean pot from the cabinet beside the range, dropped the chocolates in, and put it on a burner. "I didn't get to be this size not knowing how to make good things to eat and drink. Anyway, I figure ghosts don't mind a little extra flesh on a woman. Heck, they're probably happy for any flesh at all!" She laughed, then sat on a stool.

There's no getting rid of the woman, Angie thought. She could see Paavo fidget, wanting his coffee to hurry up and cool so he could drink it and get out of here. Giving up, she set out cups for herself and Chelsea.

"All melted," Chelsea said.

"I was," Angie said forlornly.

Angie put some chocolate in the bottom of the mugs, poured in the coffee, then stirred them together before adding any milk. She wadded up the little foil candy wrappers and opened the big double doors under the sink to throw them in the trash. A pair of big blue eyes looked up at her.

14

Angie slammed the door again. It was all she could do to stop herself from screaming. Thankfully, she did. She hated screaming women. Unfortunately, this place was turning her into one.

Paavo hurried toward her, but she held up her hand, stopping him.

Swinging open the door, she said, "Come out of there."

A boy, about eleven or twelve years old, crawled out. He glared at her from deep blue eyes under a black Chicago Bulls baseball cap.

"Who are you?" she asked.

He looked from her to Paavo, then turned and ran to the back door. Paavo grabbed his T-shirt by the shoulder, stopping him. "Wait a minute," he said. "Tell us your name and what you're doing here this time of night."

The boy was thin and dirty. His lips were clamped shut and he shook his head.

"Where do you live?"

No answer.

"Do you know the people who live here?"

Same lack of response.

"At least tell me what you were doing in the kitchen," Angie said. "Are you hungry?"

"No!"

Angie knew a hungry child when she saw one, especially when one protested so vehemently against hunger. "I'm sure I can find something to cook up fast." She opened the refrigerator. "There're eggs, butter, jack cheese, bacon." She turned toward the boy. "How would you like a bacon and cheese omelet? I can make toast and maybe find some good jam or jelly to put on it."

"Bacon? I never—" His eyes lighted for the briefest moment, then shuttered once more.

"I can leave out the bacon," she said.

"No. That sounds good. Just the way you said it," he replied.

"All right." Angie and Paavo nodded in silent agreement not to question the boy any more until he'd eaten his fill. Paavo placed a stool beside Chelsea for the boy.

"You know, Angie," Chelsea said, "if there's enough of everything, I'm kind of hungry myself."

"You eat meat?"

Chelsea shrugged. "I'm hungry. What can I say?"

Angie smiled. "There's plenty. Paavo, I know you've hardly eaten today, and I haven't either. Four omelets, coming up."

Chelsea looked at the boy. "What's your name?"

"What's it to you?"

"Well-mannered, isn't he?" Chelsea said to Angie, then got off her stool to take charge of cooking the bacon while Angie beat the eggs and grated the cheese. Paavo made toast. Before long, the omelets were on the table.

The boy took a tentative bite of his food, then scarfed

the rest down. Angie was heaped with praises for how good the meal was.

"Well, I don't think the boy belongs around here," Chelsea said as soon as she finished eating. "Guess we'll have to hold him here until the sheriff arrives. Whenever *that* will be."

"I live out there," he offered.

"You're Quint's boy?"

"No. I'm nobody's boy." The boy ate the last of his food, then got off the stool, looking ready to make a run for the back door.

"Hold it." Paavo took hold of the child's arm and turned him around. "Where are you going to sleep tonight?"

The boy lifted his chin. "I don't have to tell you."

"No, you don't." Paavo let go of him. "But we can find someplace here for you."

"I got someplace to stay already." Distrust and caution lined his young face.

"Come by tomorrow," Paavo said.

"Why should I?"

As Paavo looked at the hard stare and the ragged clothes, he was reminded of a boy many years ago who used to approach adults with the same defiant attitude. "No special reason," he said, hooking his thumbs in the pockets of his jeans.

"Maybe I got something else to do," the boy said, adopting the same pose.

Paavo nodded. "Could be. But I saw a basketball hoop nailed to the side of an old shed. Thought I'd shoot some hoops if the rain lets up a bit."

The boy frowned. "You like to do that?"

"Sure. Do you know Horse?"

A half smile filled the boy's face. "Of course!" he said, then turned and ran from the kitchen.

They watched as he stopped at the end of the patio, reached behind a rosebush, and lifted out a long object.

"Oh, God!" Angie cried. "He's got a rifle."

"It's all right," Paavo said. "It's a shotgun."

"All right? He's just a child. Stop him!"

"There are mountain lions around here. Wild boars. Snakes. I'm sure Quint showed him how to use it for self-protection."

Angie felt as if all her blood had turned to ice. "You mean I've been walking around out there . . ."

Paavo chuckled. "Stay near the house or with others and you'll be okay. Especially during the day."

Angie wasn't so sure about that. "I wonder if we should have let him go?" she asked.

"He said he has somewhere to stay—probably Quint's. I want to know what drew him here in the middle of the night, though."

"Maybe it's just that Quint's in town and the boy doesn't like being alone," Angie suggested.

"I'd say it's more. He doesn't seem the type who's afraid to be alone."

Angie began putting things away in the kitchen. "I wish he'd talk to us," she said.

"He will." Paavo put the dirty dishes in the dishwasher. "If we get his trust, the rest will follow."

"That's a beautiful thought," Chelsea said, sitting on the stool again. "It explains exactly how I feel."

"Oh?" Angie said.

"About Jack."

Angie didn't want to hear more of Chelsea's ravings. She went outdoors with Paavo to see if the boy was anywhere nearby. If he showed any indication of changing his mind, they wanted to assure him he was welcome to come in with them.

Chelsea waited at the door while they searched. Coming back into the kitchen, they made one last inspection to be sure they had cleaned everything and put it all away, then turned off the light and crept back down the hall.

"Walk me upstairs, Paavo?" Angie asked.

He looked at his still wet slicker hanging on a hook, at Angie, and nodded.

"I wonder if Jack Sempler might come by tonight," Chelsea said, then giggled as they climbed the stairs and crossed the gallery.

Suddenly, the soft sound of crying filled the house. "It's Elise," Chelsea whispered. "She's probably upset because Jack is interested in me now and not her. This must mean Jack will be here sometime soon!"

Angie just stared after her as Chelsea hurried into her room and shut the door.

"Great friend you found there, Angie," Paavo said. "She thinks she shares a room with a ghost."

"That's an improvement for her," Angie said as she went into their octagonal room and turned to face him.

"Oh?" He put his arms around her.

"She used to think she saw Elvis."

He lifted her sweater off her and tossed it aside. "Did she tell you Elvis is an anagram for lives?"

"Not to mention evils, veils, and even Levi's."

He unbuttoned her slacks, lowered the zipper, and let them drop. She stepped out of them and into his arms. "I'm almost afraid to kiss you," he said. "The way things have gone around here, the roof might fall in."

She ran her fingers up his arms, across his chest, and down to his belt buckle. "What's the matter—do you think Miz Susannah would take displeasure at any goings-on in her room?"

He ran his hands over her shoulders, her breasts, while he eased her closer to the bed. "I could pretend to be a ghost myself, then she might not even notice."

"I don't know, Inspector," she said as she stepped into his arms, feeling his arousal pressing against her. "I don't think ectoplasm can do this."

15

"*I don't want to even think* about selling the inn, Mr. Bayman," Moira said.

Angie stopped at the kitchen door, so irritated she didn't know if she should go in or just turn around and leave. When she awoke that morning—long after she was supposed to have awakened—she discovered that Paavo had left.

Last night he'd made her feel like everything was all right; then before the sheets had even cooled, he was gone.

She knew she was being unreasonable. She knew he was right in going off to search for Patsy. Nevertheless, she would have enjoyed it, even liked it, if once, just once, during their so-called wonderful week together, she could wake up with him beside her *in* the bed. Not on top of the covers. Not telling her to get up to help Moira in the kitchen. But in it. Next to her. Ready to make love to her. Was that too much to ask?

Now she'd come down to help Moira, and instead of a

quiet Norman Rockwell country-kitchen breakfast scene, she found Moira and Martin Bayman in a face-off.

"Why not sell?" Martin asked. "It's the most natural thing in the world. You tell me Finley died intestate. As his only relative, you're the one who'll get all his property. Keep in mind that you'll have to go through probate, so there'll be court and attorney fees—no inheritance taxes if we can keep the value of this property low enough—but even so, there'll be lots of other bills to pay. You'll need cash—"

"I just lost my brother. This isn't the time—"

"You have to face it, Moira. Now. I'll help you."

Moira shook her head. "There are complications."

"Nothing that can't be worked out." Martin was beginning to sound like a used car salesman. "Trust me."

"How do you know all this?"

"I used to be a lawyer. I've still got a few connections, and—"

"A lawyer? And you gave it up?"

He looked sheepish. "Well, a few years back . . . more than a few . . . Bethel was doing quite well. Her fame was spreading. We figured she was a shoo-in to become the next Jeane Dixon." He shrugged. "Somehow, it all went to hell."

"But you still have connections who tell you private things about people?"

"They don't tell me a thing. Let's say I know where to look. Anyway, it doesn't matter. What matters is that it's true, and that you're a young, beautiful woman. Vulnerable. Helpless. You don't want to stay in such a remote area alone. It's too dangerous. For all you know, the next person who walks through the front door to take a room could be the moral equivalent of Jack the Ripper. The world's a crazy place."

"People attracted to an inn like this are not Jack-the-Ripper types, and I'm far from helpless."

"Oh? Well, I hope you're right. Anyway, I'm offering a solution so that you'll never have to worry about it one way or the other. You can live where you want, with whomever you want. However you want."

"That's true," Moira said thoughtfully as she turned away from Martin. "Perhaps for the first time I—oh!" She stared at Angie. "You startled me."

"I'm sorry," Angie said. "I see I missed helping you with breakfast. I wanted to apologize."

"No problem. It was a simple meal of fruit, oat bran muffins, and granola."

"What, no wheat germ?" Angie couldn't help asking.

"I helped her," Martin said.

"I didn't know you cooked, Martin."

"I've had to learn to do a lot of things, living with a channeler. When something needed to be done around the house and Allakazam was with me instead of Bethel, I'd do it myself. Four-hundred-year-old Eskimos are useless for doing anything that doesn't involve blubber. So I learned to be a whiz with a steam iron, I can sew on a button faster than a ghost can materialize, and I know how to cook breakfast. I'd make someone a damn good wife."

Angie looked from one to the other. She knew when she wasn't needed or wanted. Not by them. Not by Paavo.

She was ready to make herself a pair of water skis and glide right off this damn mountain all by herself.

"See you later," she said, and walked out of the kitchen. As she left, she heard Martin say, "I can offer you a good price besides . . ."

❂   ❂   ❂

About ten that morning, Paavo and Running Spirit came back to the house looking defeated. Running Spirit sat in a chair in the living room without saying a word. Aware that they'd returned, Angie, Chelsea, Moira, Bethel, Martin, and Reginald Vane, their faces pale, their eyes wide and fearful, huddled in the entry to the drawing room.

"Jeffers found some cloth that he said was from a blouse of hers," Paavo said to the group. "It was snagged on a bush a little way down on a cliff. If a person had jumped, some clothing might have become caught that way. The only thing that surprises me is that we didn't spot it there before."

"How horrible," Angie said with a glance at Running Spirit. "She might have fallen. There's no way she could have jumped—is there?"

Paavo recognized her hesitancy. "Jeffers and I talked about it already. When women do kill themselves, it's usually neat—like sleeping pills. Rarely a gun, and almost never by hurling themselves onto sharp rocks."

"Maybe she used Elise Sempler as her model?" Chelsea suggested. "Patsy talked about her a lot. And we all know that the night before she disappeared she was all upset about . . . you know." Realizing both Moira and Running Spirit were there, she didn't say more, but everyone knew exactly what she'd left unspoken.

The rain continued to fall in uncompromising sheets, and the wind blew strongly.

"The phone still isn't working," Moira said.

"And we can't get through to town to ask for help," Chelsea added.

Bethel rarely bothered to straighten her turban anymore, as the strain of these last few days wore on her. "If someone here was as good with OBEs as he says he is, he'd have been flitting about already, getting into places where no normal body could go, and would have found her by now."

"What's that supposed to mean?" Running Spirit jumped to his feet.

"God," Bethel played with her star-burst rhinestone earring. "He's even dumber than he looks!"

"Listen, you dirt-mouthed hag, I just lost my wife. You can have a little respect."

"I have respect—for her. It's the living I'm contemptuous of."

"Anyway," Running Spirit said, circling around her, "if you're such a know-it-all, why don't you ask Allakaket where she is? I think I now understand why your own husband speaks of your channeling with such contempt!"

"See here, R.S.," Martin cut in, "she's my wife, and if I want to joke about her little frozen buddy, that's my business, not yours."

"If you're all through bickering," Paavo said, his voice icy, "let's get into some dry clothes and get back out there."

Angie went upstairs with Paavo. She didn't mind watching as he changed clothes. One thing about his being a cop—he kept up a strict regimen of exercise. Where other men she knew grew soft and flabby in their office jobs, Paavo was solid muscle. Beautiful, solid muscle.

"So, what do you think?" she asked. "Is the material from Patsy's blouse?"

He quickly shucked his wet slacks, shoes, and socks. His shirt had stayed dry except for the collar and cuffs, but he took it off as well. "He says it is. But I don't know how we could have missed it yesterday."

"You think it was a plant?"

He reached for a heavy gray pullover and put it on. "Could be."

"By whom?"

He picked up a fresh pair of socks. "That's the question, Angie. Who wants us to think Patsy killed herself? It's got to be one of these people."

"Unless it's Patsy herself," Angie suggested. "What if she's not dead, but hiding? What if she killed Finley and is now hiding so that she can make her escape once the rains let up?"

Jeans went on next. "True, but we can't even be sure about Quint. What if he didn't go to get the sheriff at all, but is hiding out there?"

She moved closer to him. "It could be any one of them. And the murderer's planning to kill us off, one by one, in the most gruesome sorts of ways."

He gave her a steady stare. "I think I saw that movie, Angie. *Ten Little Indians*, was it?"

"Which version? There've been at least three. The original, *And Then There Were None*, was my favorite."

Last, dry shoes. "If you're talking movies, remember all the ones where the butler did it," Paavo said as he brushed his hair.

"The butler! Of course, Reginald Vane. Who could look more guilty than a man who wears a bow tie all the time?"

Dressed and ready to be on his way once more, Paavo stepped in front of her and smoothed her hair back off her face. "You can joke about it, Angie, but the fact is, there's a very dangerous person on this hill with us. Two people are dead, and one missing—"

"But Patsy could still be alive," Angie insisted.

"That's why we're going back out to look for her. But you've got to be careful and not trust any of these people. The only ones I'm fairly sure you're safe with are Chelsea and Moira. And even with them I'm not positive."

"Moira! Why? She's my prime suspect!"

He kissed her, then grinned. "I don't think that has anything to do with murder, Miss Amalfi."

She frowned. "Of course it does. First, when Finley was missing, she waited nearly twenty-four hours before telling anyone but her gardener there might be a problem. What could be more suspicious than that? Then, his death scarcely bothered her, and now the inn is hers. Opportunity and motive, Inspector. What else is there?"

"Inheriting a mortgage as large as this one is hardly a motive, Miss Amalfi."

"What about insurance?"

"Tay didn't carry any. He was relatively young, healthy, and couldn't afford it."

"I still say she's guilty as sin. You're being duped."

He placed his hands on her shoulders. "Forget Moira. I want you to stay with one of the women at all times when I'm not here. If I could, I'd get you off this hill right now, but we're all stuck in this together. Am I clear?"

"Quite."

"I don't want anything to happen to you," he commanded, his tone harsh, his eyes like flint.

"Yes, sir!" she said.

He looked at her proud little chin, her upturned mouth, the sparkle in her eyes, and something inside him melted. "And don't be so goddamn sassy." He gave her a kiss, hard and possessive, before he turned and walked out of the room.

Angie jiggled the phone's receiver in the kitchen. It didn't do any good. She hadn't expected it would, but then Moira had said the phone company would fix the phones soon. Why didn't they? She could have screamed in frustration . . . but she really did hate screaming women, despite what this place was doing to her.

If there was a killer here at Hill Haven, and the thought seemed more plausible with each passing hour, who would be in danger from him or her? Wouldn't the killer be anxious to get rid of a homicide inspector, someone trained to spot mistakes, to apprehend criminals? Hadn't she, then, in thinking she was bringing Paavo to an idyllic spot, actually brought him somewhere that his life was more in danger than ever?

Whoever this was had already killed two people, and if Patsy was dead, that made three. Facing capture, the killer might do anything at all to get away. What was another dead body to a fiend like that?

But who? *Who?* Much as she didn't want to admit it, not even Moira seemed capable of such action. No one seemed evil enough.

It had to be someone from the town. Someone who snuck up onto this promontory, killed, and then snuck back down off it again. Living here all their lives, people from town surely knew a way here and back despite the rain and the roads being washed out.

That was the only logical answer.

She tried the phone again. The rain was steady, and she knew that there was still no way to leave the hilltop.

People were searching all over. All over . . .

Except, perhaps, for one spot.

But there was no way she'd go alone.

She ran up to Chelsea's room.

"No. I'm not going down there," Chelsea said, folding her arms after Angie had explained.

"Everyone is out looking around for her except you, me, and Bethel, and Bethel has the excuse of being arthritic. We don't." Angie stepped into Chelsea's closet, found a jacket, and handed it to her. "We can't let the men do all the searching."

"I can."

"Where's your feminist spirit?"

"Gone."

"This house probably does have too many spirits already, but we can't let that stop us."

"I only care about one spirit. And he's got to be the most shy ghost who ever walked the Earth. Or didn't walk it."

"Maybe he'll protect you. Now let's go." She guided Chelsea through the doorway.

Following Moira's instructions from yesterday morning, Angie and Chelsea trudged across the garden in the back of the house and kept going until they reached a small knoll. The wind was howling, the rain pelting them. Angie didn't understand how Paavo could spend so much time out in such horrible weather searching for Patsy. He hardly knew the woman. She guessed that was what dedication was all about.

"Help me," Angie said as she lifted the bar that held shut the small door fitted into the slanting hillside.

"Is it safe?" Chelsea asked.

"I don't know."

"I don't think this is such a good idea, Angie."

Angie grabbed the door handle and pulled. "But it's the only place they haven't looked. Or at least they haven't said so if they did look here. But what if Patsy came down for something and fell? She could be hurt. It's worth a try. I'm not sure the others even know this house has a root cellar back here." The wind began to roar, and the rain fell more heavily. The two struggled to open the door against the galelike winds.

"In my pocket," Angie said, "I've got a candle and some matches. Take them."

"No, you go ahead. Any door that size was *not* made for

a person my size to go through. It's fate," Chelsea said. "I'll hold the door open or it'll blow shut in this wind."

"Don't be silly. Let's open the door as far as it'll go. It's heavy. It'll stay," Angie said. They pushed the door all the way open and peered through the munchkin-size doorway to steps that led down into the root cellar.

"Okay, Chelsea," Angie shouted to be heard over the sudden loud wind. "You go first."

"Me? Shoot!" Chelsea took a candle and some matches and started down the stairs. "Patsy?" No answer. "It's too creepy. I've gone far enough."

"You've only gone down three steps! Go on, Chelsea. I'm right behind you."

"That gives me lots of confidence," came the ungrateful grumble.

"Anyway, I thought you liked creepy things. Like ghosts," Angie said.

"Funny, Angie. Real funny." Chelsea kept going.

"How big is the cellar?" Angie asked.

"Uh . . . bigger than a bread box. But not exactly Grand Central."

Angie started down the steps after Chelsea. "Ah, finally I'm out of that wind. Now I can light my candle and see what's going on here." She lit it and looked around. The root cellar was surprisingly large, with shelves lined with jars of preserves, stone crocks, and bunches of drying and dried vegetables.

"Patsy," Angie called. "Patsy, are you in here?"

She went down a few more steps, then held the candle out so that she could see as much of the cellar as possible.

"I'm getting out of here," Chelsea said and turned around. Her eyed widened in horror. "No!"

Angie turned to see the door swinging closed, just as a gust of wind extinguished her candle.

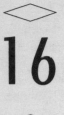

16

Running Spirit, Martin Bayman, and Paavo discovered an old bridge that spanned a deep gorge, one that almost cut the promontory off from the mainland and made an island out of it.

The bridge's dry rot was so bad it was visible with the naked eye. Paavo was surprised a strong gale hadn't blown it down long before.

"Maybe that's why we can't find Mrs. Jeffers," Bayman said. "She crossed over the bridge."

"Would she chance it, Jeffers?" Paavo asked. "The bridge looks dangerous."

"As I've said from the start, I can't believe she'd have left the house," Running Spirit replied. "She's hiding . . . or she's dead."

"Nonetheless, one of us should try to get across it," Bayman said. "We've got these ropes. We can tie one end of the rope to a tree, the other to one of us, then that person can try to cross. If the bridge falls, the others can pull the man up."

Paavo was dubious. "She can't weigh much over a hundred and ten or twenty pounds, but I still wonder if it could have held her."

"She wouldn't chance it," Running Spirit said.

"Who'll be the guinea pig?" Martin asked, ignoring Jeffers.

"She's my wife," Running Spirit said. "I guess that means I'm elected."

"The bridge would come down for sure under your weight," Paavo said. "The only one of us with any hope of crossing it is Martin. If the bridge starts to go, the two of us could pull him up easily."

Although agreeing with Paavo's contention, Martin muttered about the unfairness of it the entire time he was tying one end of the rope around his waist and Running Spirit was tying the other end to a nearby tree.

Slowly, being careful to cause the least disturbance, Martin stepped onto the narrow wooden bridge.

"Chelsea, are you all right?" Angie whispered into the darkness. Something grabbed her foot and she cried out.

"Sorry. It's just me," Chelsea said. "I'm trying to come up the stairs. It's too scary down here."

"Careful! You nearly knocked me off the steps. I'm going up to open the door." She went up two steps and felt the door in front of her. She pushed, but it wouldn't open.

"Is the wind holding it shut?" Chelsea asked.

Angie didn't think so. "I hope that's all it is. Help me." Angie pulled Chelsea up the stairs to her side.

"Put your hands on the door," Angie ordered, trying to keep her balance. "Okay, now, one, two, three, push!" They strained. The door didn't budge.

"I don't think it's wind," Chelsea cried and let go. "I had no idea the door would be so heavy."

"It's not. The bar that holds it shut must have dropped into place when the door closed."

"Don't say that, Angie! That means we're locked in."

A soft thump was heard.

"Oh, God!" Chelsea clutched Angie so hard she nearly smothered her. "What was that?"

"Nothing. Just your imagination."

"Then how come you heard it, too?"

Angie pushed at the door again, to no avail. How long would it take for someone to find them down here? And worse, what creatures were down here with them?

Angie had dropped the candle, but she still had the matches in her pocket. Should she go down the stairs to find it? How far down was the ground? And what else would she be touching in this total darkness as she tried to find the spot where the candle had fallen?

Tha-thump.

The soft sound reverberated through the cellar.

All her fears of the dark, of things that go bump in the night, burst loose, and she and Chelsea held each other and screamed for help.

The bridge swayed precariously. Its creaks grew louder and more ominous with each step.

Martin made it almost to the opposite bank when there was a sharp crack, almost like a rifle shot, and the bridge crumbled under his feet.

"Martin!" Paavo shouted as he watched the man plunge into the deep chasm.

The rope slid from Martin's waist upward to his underarms before it caught, stopping his free fall with a sharp jolt. He winced with pain as the rope tightened, cutting into his shoulders and back.

He took hold of the rope with his hands, trying to pull up, trying to lift some of the weight off his shoulders. But his feet weren't able to touch the ground, and he was left dangling in midair like a fish caught by a line tossed off the end of a pier.

"You'll be all right," Paavo called down. He grabbed the rope and started to pull on it, trying to haul Martin back to the bank. The rope, like everything else at this inn, was old and rotten in parts. He could see it starting to fray. They'd have to work fast. "Pull, Jeffers," he ordered. "Help me."

Running Spirit folded his arms.

Paavo looked back at him. "Jeffers!"

No answer.

Paavo felt Martin drop lower as the rope began to thin in one part. He tugged on it, trying to get Martin up to what was left of the bridge as soon as possible. He made progress, but it was slow. The rope tore at his hands and his arm sockets burned from the strain of Martin's dead-weight. "Jeffers, damn it, there's not much time."

Running Spirit backed up. "He doesn't belong here. Everything was fine until he got involved. It's his fault all this is happening."

"You don't know that. Take hold of the rope. You can't let him fall."

Another part of the rope started to unravel, the fibers standing straight upright where they tore in two. "Jeffers, nothing will be solved by this. He was trying to find your wife, man!"

"I'm doing for him what he'd do for me. Nothing."

Loose and muddy from the constant rain, the ground gave way under Paavo's feet and he slid forward, toward the bank. Martin dropped about three feet. His terror-filled shriek reverberated through the gorge.

Paavo's hands had gotten burned and bloodied from the rope, but he didn't let go. Wordlessly, he looked over his shoulder at Running Spirit.

"Goddammit! All right." Running Spirit picked up the rope and started to pull. Working together, he and Paavo were able to quickly drag Bayman up to what was left of the bridge. Martin was able to grab hold of it and hoist himself onto it, then scramble quickly to the bank.

Lying facedown, Martin shut his eyes for a moment and breathed deeply. Paavo said nothing. He knew there was bad blood between the two, but he hadn't realized it ran this deep.

Running Spirit stood over Bayman. "Don't thank me," he said.

Martin tried to stand, but his legs shook too badly, and he sat down again on the ground. "Thanks was the last thing on my mind," he said bitterly. "A lawsuit was first."

Their screams stopped abruptly. The cellar door rattled. Angie and Chelsea lunged against it, pushing with all their might, when all of a sudden it sprang open. A rain-soaked Reginald Vane held his arm down to them. "My goodness! What are you doing there?"

"Acting out my worst nightmare," Angie said.

"Really?" Vane asked.

Angie clutched his arm in a death grip until she was outside in the wind and rain. "Help Chelsea," she murmured as she dropped to the ground, not caring that it was wet and muddy. Her heart needed time to settle down, and her knees to stop knocking, before she could walk back to the inn.

"Miss Worthington," Vane said softly, taking both Chelsea's hands. "Are you all right?"

She nodded.

"I'm so sorry," he said.

Hearing his heartfelt kindness must have been Chelsea's undoing, because all of a sudden she burst into tears. "I was so afraid," she said.

"There, there, my dear," he said, moving so that she stood within the circle of his arms as he patted her shoulder. "I didn't know you were there, miss," he said very softly.

But Angie had heard. "What do you mean? What difference would that have made?"

Chelsea, too, stepped back, a confused look on her face as Vane's words penetrated.

Vane looked at them both, flustered. "I only meant, literally, I didn't know she was in there. I only saw Miss Amalfi at first. And while you, Miss Amalfi, have Inspector Smith to see to your emotional state after such a trauma, Miss Worthington has no one. I'm glad I could be here to help."

"What brought you out here?" Angie asked.

"I heard the thumping sound of the ghosts," Vane said. "I tried to ignore it, but somehow I couldn't. I fled the house to walk about outdoors, despite the rain. Mercifully, I heard your cries."

Angie stood up. She didn't believe Vane's story, but what was the truth? And why would he lie?

"Let's go in," Reginald said. He took Chelsea's arm and held it as they walked back to the inn.

17

"*My dear girl, what a horrible* fright you've had." Reginald Vane patted the back of Chelsea's hand, then quickly wrapped his hands around his mug of the hot chocolate he'd made for himself, Chelsea, and Angie. The three of them sat at the kitchen counter, Reginald and Chelsea side by side, while Angie felt shunted off into the corner.

"It was awful," Chelsea said.

"I don't know how you stood it. You're wondrously brave." Reginald's ears reddened with his last statement and he straightened his bow tie.

What was I, Angie thought, chopped liver down there?

Finally she got sick of the reprise of poor, brave Chelsea in the root cellar and left the kitchen, feeling decidedly sorry for herself. Not only did no one care what happened to her, no matter how frightening, but she had to listen to concern over everyone else.

She put on Moira's wide-brimmed rain hat and slicker and went outdoors, planning to walk over to the cliffs to try to find Paavo and the others. She'd like to help search for Patsy, even though she knew she'd have to struggle not to slow the men down. Staying indoors felt too claustrophobic after having been stuck in that horrible root cellar. She needed to watch, and think, and figure out what was going on here.

She stuck her hands in her pockets and walked with her head down. The rain was steady, but the wind had stopped, so walking in it wasn't unpleasant.

Speaking of unpleasant . . . her thoughts drifted to Moira Tay. She had to be the guilty one. Getting rid of Finley would make her owner of the inn. Getting rid of Patsy meant there were no obstacles to her and Running Jerk being lovers once more. And with Miss Greer gone, then what? Moira could do the cooking? No, that was no reason to kill someone. What clue was she missing?

She looked around, so lost in thought she'd paid little attention to where she'd gone. At the top of a knoll the young boy with the Chicago Bulls cap stood watching her. "Hello, there," Angie called and headed toward him. The knoll was steep and she soon found herself struggling to climb it. "Can you give me a hand?"

The boy's eyes widened and his face flushed. "Sure." He scampered down the hill.

She held out her hand. He stared at it. "Wow. You've got long fingernails. Purple, too. Just like on TV."

"Rose mauve, actually. But thanks."

The boy rubbed the palm of his hand against his jeans, then took hers. To her surprise, he was strong enough to give a hard yank on her arm as he began to run back up the knoll. Angie could scarcely move her feet fast enough as she found herself going uphill almost as quickly as she usually went down.

Angie had to bend over, her hands on her knees, trying

to catch her breath, when they reached the top. The boy laughed.

"I didn't know you'd get so tired," he said.

"Who's . . . tired?" she wheezed, then straightened, her hand on her still heaving chest. The boy's eyes traveled to the curve of her breasts, then locked for a long moment. When he stepped back, his ears had turned flaming red.

"My name's Angelina Amalfi. I never did learn yours."

The boy bit his bottom lip before replying, "Danny."

"Danny what?"

"Just Danny."

"Ah."

"Where were you going?" Danny asked.

"Toward the cliffs. I'm looking for a lady from the inn who's missing."

Danny's face paled, his eyes wide. "Mom?" he whispered.

"Who?"

"Is Moira Tay missing?" Danny's voice was small, scared.

Moira . . . Danny's mother. Angie began to slowly walk along the knoll, Danny beside her. "No, not Moira. It's another woman. Her name is Patsy. She's thin, with light brown hair. Have you seen her around anywhere?"

Danny shook his head. "How come she's missing? Did she go out alone or something?"

"It seems that way."

"You got to be careful out here. You got to know what you're doing, like I do. There's some places, if you step on them, they can give way and you'll slide all the way down the hill and end up in the ocean. It's pretty danger-ous, if you don't know it."

"So I've learned," Angie said. Danny's description brought back the memory of her own quick trip sliding down the rocks yesterday, just before finding Finley's body.

They walked in silence. Angie surreptitiously studied Danny and mentally kicked herself for not having noticed how much he resembled Moira.

"I'm twelve," Danny said after a while. "How old are you?"

Angie smiled. "Considerably older than twelve." Double it, in fact. She felt old.

"Really? I'm almost as tall as you are," he said.

"Yes. You'll be a tall young man, I think."

"Do . . . uh, do you like tall men?"

"Oh, of course."

"Good," he said with a sigh.

She did a double take.

Suddenly, he ran off.

She stood watching him disappear. Well, Angie, she thought, you certainly have a way with men. Even young, completely inexperienced ones hightail it away from you as fast as they can go.

She continued onward. The rain, which had stopped for a while, began to fall once more. A bolt of lightning flashed and thunder rolled across the landscape.

She reached the cliffs, but there was no sign of anyone. It figured. Given her luck lately, they'd probably gone in the opposite direction to search. Being out here alone was probably foolish, anyway. Time to go back to the main house. She turned around and started walking, following her footprints in the soft, damp earth. The rain fell harder with each passing minute. As she retraced her steps, the footprints grew smoother, less visible, until they disappeared altogether in the rainstorm.

Foolishly, she hadn't paid a lot of attention as she walked with Danny, more intrigued by his relationship to

Moira than where she was walking to. But at that point she was headed west toward the cliffs. It wasn't as if she could miss them.

Going back and trying to find the inn was a different story. She'd have to find footprints or a trail. They must be somewhere. Thunder clapped. She wouldn't let herself think about the mountain lions and snakes and wild boars Paavo had mentioned. It was daylight. They wouldn't come out now. Would they?

Up ahead she saw an indenture in the ground. She ran to it. A footprint. Looking at the size and shape of the shoe, she realized it was hers. Lewis and Clark, move over! She'd blaze this trail right back to the inn. Maybe tracking wasn't as hard as it was cracked up to be.

Carefully, she followed her footprints in the opposite direction from which they headed, not letting herself miss a single one. When she passed an especially gnarled tree for the second time, though, she realized something was wrong. She looked up, looked around, and realized she'd been following the footprints she'd made while walking around in circles looking for her footprints!

God, now what? No wonder she never left the city. Where was a taxi when you needed one?

Thoughts of Patsy and what might have happened to her filled Angie's mind. What if Patsy had only meant to go for a walk in the woods and then met up with . . . what? Or who? And what did that person or animal do to her?

No! It was the city where those horrible things happened. Not the country. But Angie would have known better than to go wandering into strange neighborhoods in the city. Why hadn't she used the same caution here?

"Danny!" she called. "Danny! Come back, please!"

Silence.

She made her best guess and started walking in one direction.

Up ahead, she saw a small cottage with lush plants and ground coverings, unusual since it was winter. She knew Quint had a cottage on the property somewhere. That had to be his.

As she walked up to it, the front door opened. She froze, holding her breath.

"I didn't know you wanted to come here," Danny said, his head bobbing out at her. "I thought you were going to the cliffs."

She released her breath in a whoosh. "Nope. Changed my mind."

Quint's cottage was small but clean and comfortable. It had a large sitting room with an eating area in front of the windows, looking out on what would be a lovely rose garden once spring arrived. A kitchen nook took up one side of the sitting room. Beyond the main room was a large bedroom with a single bed and, on the far wall, a roll-away all made up as if a guest were expected this evening.

"This is nice," Angie said. "So you're staying with Quint?"

"What makes you say that?" Danny struggled to keep all expression from his face as he followed her glance. "Oh, my bed."

"Don't you want anyone to know you're staying here, Danny?" she asked.

"It's nobody's business."

"That's true enough." Angie went to the window. The rain continued to fall in heavy sheets. "Aren't you afraid out here alone?"

"In here? Afraid of what?"

Angie looked around the snug, secure little cottage. Good question, she thought. "Afraid of being alone, I guess," she said.

"No. But Moira would let me sleep at the big house if I was scared or got lonely."

"Good." Angie peeled off her wet jacket and spread it over the back of a chair. "Have you always lived here?"

"No," Danny answered.

"Just with Moira, then?"

"Moira?" the boy said, trying to sound surprised. "No, I don't live with her."

"You're quite the loner," Angie said.

"That's right." Danny clamped his mouth shut defiantly.

"If you'd like something hot to drink, hot milk, or chocolate, or anything like that, just show me where it is and I'll make it for you," she offered.

"Cow's milk isn't good for you, and chocolate has caffeine and other bad stuff, so I can't have any," he answered.

Now I know for sure this is Moira's son, Angie thought. "Do you have soy milk?"

"I hate hot soy milk! The only thing Mom gives me is herb tea, but I don't much like it. I'm fine. But Gran—I mean Quint, keeps coffee for himself, so if you'd like some, I'm sure he won't care."

Gran? Quint was the boy's grandfather? That meant Quint was Moira and Finley's father? Impossible. He and Finley, in particular, weren't at all alike. For that matter, neither were Finley and Moira. What was she missing here?

"I'd love a cup of coffee. Bless Quint for having it— and you for telling me about it."

As Angie went into the kitchen area, Danny sat at the table, watching the rain. "What do you think happened to the woman who's missing?" Danny asked after a while.

"Some people think she ran away."

"What if she's dead? Like Finley."

Angie's hand stilled as she counted measuring spoons of ground coffee and put them in the filter. "You heard about Finley?"

"Yeah." Danny didn't elaborate.

"I see." Angie finished setting up the coffee, then turned to figure out something to make for Danny.

"Maybe that woman jumped off a cliff like Elise Sempler," Danny said.

"I can't imagine she'd do that."

"But didn't they find something of hers by the cliffs?"

"You do learn a lot out here," Angie said, impressed and curious about what else this boy might know. She found some apple cider and heated a cupful of it. "Do you think Patsy is much like Elise?"

"I guess not. Like nobody took her baby away or nothing."

"Her what?" Angie stepped into the living room. "Whose baby?"

"Elise's. Elise jumped because she was so sad after Susannah took her baby away."

"Who told you that?"

"I've seen Susannah's diaries, and some letters," Danny said.

Angie's heart leaped. The thought of getting her hands on the letters and diaries of the strange Semplers . . .

"They're kind of hard to read," Danny continued, "but I also heard Quint and some other people talking about what they said, so then I was able to understand."

Angie tried to keep the excitement out of her voice. "Do you know where these diaries and letters are?"

"They're here in a box. Finley wanted to throw them away, but my . . . Moira put them in a box and brought them here. She said it was evil to throw away their things. Moira believes in stuff like ghosts."

"I've noticed." And I just might start, Angie thought.

"Would you like to see the letters? I don't think she'd care. She said it's okay if I read them, but I have to be real careful not to tear them because they're so old."

"I'd like to see them. Very much."

A little while later, they sat on the sofa. Angie had a cup of hot coffee, and for Danny she made a cup of hot buttered apple tea, a mixture of hot tea and hot apple cider. For flavor, she mixed together dark brown sugar, cinnamon, clove, the zest of a lemon, and a little butter, then dropped the mixture by the teaspoonful into the hot drink until the taste was just right.

Danny gave her a hatbox filled with Susannah's memories, Susannah's life—a single dance card, a theater program from Eureka, some ribbons, a lock of fine blond hair in a small envelope, a diary, and tied in a pink ribbon, a packet of letters.

As she went through the contents of the box, Danny sat down beside her with his cider. He proclaimed it the best thing he'd ever tasted.

Once Angie became used to the flowery script Susannah used with her wide-nibbed ink pen, she was able to read through the diary fairly rapidly. The early entries were dull, talking about needlework, gardening, an occasional book read, or her dog.

She turned a page and found a sprig of dried violets pressed between them, and soon, as she read, the world of the snug little cottage disappeared.

18

May 4, 1893

    Cousin Elise arrived today. She's prettier than I expected, given the lack of fashion or quality of her dress and the shocking inferiority of her upbringing. Her manners are so vulgar I suppose it will fall to me to show her how a lady comports herself.

    Her hair is black, a most unrefined color, and she persists in wearing it in a braid down her back as though she was still a child. Her face is dreadfully browned by the sun, and her cheeks positively glow red as hot coals.

    I fear I shall have quite the task to make a silk purse out of that ear.

    I was quite surprised that Jack paid her so much attention. He gave us each a posy of violets.

The diary was filled from that point with one slam after the other at Cousin Elise. As Jack and Elise grew closer, Susannah's venom increased.

August 19, 1893

My heart is broken. Father sent Jack away, all because of that hateful creature. Something happened yesterday. No one will tell me precisely what it was, but do they think me so naïve that I don't know?

Father was in a rage all evening. This morning, he took Jack to Eureka to put him on a merchant ship where he must work off the humors of the blood that have caused his unnatural interest in his own cousin. "There'll be no Sempler by-blows in this house," Father said, not knowing I was near enough to overhear. I'm unable to cast the ugly, shocking words from my mind.

Already, I miss Jack's smile, the soft hazel color of his eyes. I'll never forgive Elise for taking him from Father and me. I'll hate her forever. Beyond forever. If possible, even beyond the grave.

Angie shuddered; but, compelled, she continued reading and found out that Jack took a position on the Titan, a cargo ship out of San Francisco that traveled throughout the Far East and South Pacific.

November 2, 1893

The worst has happened. Every day Elise grows more sickly. She's thin, pale, and constantly has trouble holding down her food. We thought she feigned love sickness for Jack. But then Father called Dr. Hayden, who informed him that Elise is with child.

How can we bear the humiliation this will cause, especially if people suspect who the father might be? Any prospects Jack had for a good marriage are now crushed. And what of my own?

Will I spend my days here, watching that woman and her child, knowing they've disgraced this family's honor and our proud name?

It must be hateful to say, but it would be a mercy if she were dead.

Quickly Angie turned the pages, skimming over the mundane, day-to-day things Susannah wrote about to find further mention of Elise or Jack. A word in passing of Jack's travels was all that she wrote. It was as if she wanted to ignore the fact that Elise was living with her and her father, until—

April 30, 1894

Last night Elise was delivered of a boy child. Father named him Benjamin. I would not look at him. Not even when I gave him over to the stable-man's wife to care for. She has such a passel of brats, what's one more child to nurse to the likes of her? Anyway, it's only until the babe is old enough to travel with the barren couple Father has arranged to give it to.

God grant that we are doing the right thing.

The next entry in the diary wasn't until two weeks later.

May 13, 1894

I don't know if I should try to capture on these pages the suffering I have endured these past weeks. If I should ignore these dreadful events, will I, in time, forget they ever occurred? No, I think not, for some events are so monumental they shape and destroy all that comes thereafter.

I think I will always remember, always hear, Elise's

*pleas for her child. We told her the boy had died, but
then she overheard two of the stableman's children
talking about their new baby, of his black hair and
hazel eyes, so different from the rest. She knew.*

*She begged to see the child, to hold him. Wasn't
it bad enough that Jack had forsaken her? she
pleaded. That he had gone away and had never
written or tried to reach her again?*

*We could not let her have any happiness, Father
and I, when she'd taken ours so completely. Her
tears did not move us.*

*I last saw her standing atop the cliffs at sunset,
staring out at the sea. Sometime last night, she
jumped, or fell. We found her this morning on the
rocks below.*

May God forgive her. And us.

The diary was blank after this.

Angie slowly put it down, back in the box where it had
lain for so many years.

She looked at the packet of letters. They were from
Jack.

Letter after letter begged for news of Elise. Why
hadn't she written to him? Was she all right? Had she
found someone else? Had she never loved him at all?

Then the letters came less frequently. Jack told
Susannah that he'd learned to face the truth—that Elise
had never loved him. He never wanted to return to
Sempler House, the site of his great folly.

Angie watched the parade of postmarks from around
the world as the years went by. But she also watched the
dissolution of Jack's spirit. Where the first letters were
warm, passionate, and full of hope, the last ones were of a
man who'd seen too much of the underside of life.

The last letter from Jack was dated February 1, 1905, and postmarked Pago Pago. His penmanship was thin and shaky.

> *Dear Susannah,*
> *The doctors here say I must return home for an extended rest or the fever will take me. Part of me longs for such a consummation, yet another part, more rational perhaps, wishes to see you, and home, at least one last time. I should be strong enough to travel in about two weeks.*
> *I look forward to seeing you, sister dear, the only good and faithful woman I have ever known. Your loving brother,*
>
> *Jack*

How could Susannah have borne it all those years, Angie wondered, knowing that her interference had caused the destruction of the lives of two people who had done nothing worse than fall in love with each other?

"Are you through? Did you like the letters?"

Angie looked up to see Danny standing in front of her. He'd been sketching while she read and now held the sketch out to her. He had drawn a good likeness.

"Why, thank you. It's lovely. And yes, I liked reading the letters very much."

"It's not raining hard anymore," Danny said.

Angie quickly glanced through the other papers and letters, but there was nothing that told her what had happened to Jack, although it was clear that the dissipation of his body as well as his soul had killed him.

Nothing told her, either, what had happened to the baby.

Her heart ached as she put everything away and went back to the inn with Danny. If unhappy souls walked the earth after death, those three surely did.

◦   ◦   ◦

"Good Christ, I thought you'd disappeared, too!" Paavo stood in the doorway, his jacket on, a fierce scowl on his face.

"I won't disappear, I promise." Angie went up to him, wanting to give him a hug, but he was in no mood for forgiveness. She hurried past him into the house, taking off Moira's hat and slicker as she went. "I was just waiting out the rainstorm at Quint's cottage and—"

"Quint's!" He paced back and forth in front of her. "Don't you know the dangers out there? Two people dead, a woman's missing, and you decide to go waltzing off to Quint's cottage!"

She walked into the drawing room to stand by the blazing fire in the fireplace. "I didn't mean to—"

"You never mean to, Angie." Paavo took off his hat, jacket, and gloves, leaving them in the foyer as he followed her. "Did you even stop to think that I might be worried about you? Did you even care?"

"Your hands!" She stared in shock at the pads of gauze and tape on his palms. Taking hold of the backs of his hands, she closely inspected his bandages and torn skin. "What happened to you?" She still held his hands, not wanting to let them go.

"It's just a rope burn. Martin was on an old bridge that broke. Jeffers and I had to pull him up."

"My God! Is he all right?"

"Just a little sore."

"But you . . . Oh, Paavo, this is all my fault. I never should have asked you to this hateful place."

He pulled his hands from her. "It's nothing. You're the one I'm worried about. First I hear you and Chelsea were locked in a root cellar, and next you disappear altogether."

"I'm sorry. I lost track of time. I was reading—"

"Reading! That's just great, Angie! Great!" He walked around as he spoke, his hard gaze never leaving her. "Here I was being stupid enough to worry—"

"There's a good reason," she cried, interrupting him.

His eyes narrowed. "I don't see how there can be any good reason for being thoughtless, not to mention careless." His voice was low, his words challenging, as if he didn't believe her.

He had to be the most obstinate man who ever lived! "I said I'm sorry! What more do you want from me?"

"That you stay put!" He turned on his heel and left the room.

Rationally, she knew he talked to her as if she were an inconsiderate child and refused to listen to her explanation because he had been worried about her, and because he was tired after spending so many hours trudging around in the mud and the rain looking for Patsy. But that didn't make it any easier to take.

Her eyes welled with tears, also caused, she realized, by her own weariness, worry, and frustration over all this. "It'll be all right, Paavo," she said aloud to herself, to these walls that seemed to have ears. "Once we get away from here, things will be right again between us."

She thought back on her afternoon as she looked around the drawing room, her gaze resting on Susannah's portrait. Elise . . . Jack . . . Susannah. Lonely, loveless, jealous Susannah.

"I'm so sorry," she whispered. "For all of you."

Then, realizing that she was standing there talking to dead people, she hurried down the quiet hall to the kitchen—the domain she knew, the world she was comfortable with. There was no sign that anyone had done anything about dinner. That she could handle.

19

Angie peered into the refrigerator. What could she cook for all these people, who didn't even appreciate the work she went through for them? Peering at a tub of soy cottage cheese, she got an idea.

In a drawer was a set of file cards that Finley had written a number of his special recipes on. She took them out and went through them, one by one, until she hit upon the perfect meal:

salad: alfalfa sprouts, celery, carrots, and onion
soup: cream of lettuce, made with soy milk
entrée: gluten, brown rice, and soybean casserole
vegetable: wheat-germ–covered spinach
dessert: soy cream custard

Finley hadn't been joking when he said he knew seventy-three ways to prepare soybeans.

This menu, for sure, would make them wake up to the interesting meals she'd been trying to cook for them.

She went into the pantry for the soybeans and rice. She'd have to find the gluten. It should be out there somewhere as well. She'd been through all the regular cabinets to see what canned and dry goods, spices, and condiments were available and hadn't seen any. She hadn't yet taken the trouble to look through the bottom cabinets and shelves, though.

Inside a bottom cabinet, a ten-pound sack of dried lentils stood beside a twenty-five-pound sack of brown rice. Next to them was a large canister. She lugged out the cannister and pried the lid off. Gluten flour. Success.

Checking the recipe, she saw she needed four cups of the stuff. She got a bowl and metal scoop and brought them into the pantry. She put one, two, three scoops into the bowl; but on the fourth scoop, an odd ropelike thing turned up. She poked at it with the scoop. It looked fleshy, but not human. She poked a little deeper into the flour. Coarse brownish-gray hairs appeared, then the base of the tail. . . .

She dropped the scoop, ran from the pantry, down the hall, and up to her room.

Paavo was stretched out atop the bed, his shoes off, asleep.

"Get up!" she yelled. "Quick!"

He was instantly awake. "What is it?"

"The rat! The rat I saw the first night after Finley disappeared. It just mooned me!"

Everyone showed up for dinner, probably because they were hungry after having run out on lunch; but they didn't look particularly happy to be there. Especially when they saw the food.

"We should all join hands and pray to the Supreme

Oneness to keep all of us safe," Running Spirit announced. "And to bring Patsy home."

"The only thing I'd pray to the Supreme Oneness for is that you shut up," Martin said.

Running Spirit looked down his nose at Bayman, then turned to Moira. "Do you feel all right this evening?"

Moira nodded.

Martin said in a stage whisper to his wife, "I wonder how Patsy feels tonight. I wonder if she feels anything at all."

"Isn't it a shame?" Bethel said. "What do you think, Chelsea? Or are you still waiting for your ghost? You know, I've asked Allakaket about that, and he doesn't think there are any ghosts here. None at all. He thinks your Jack Sempler is a myth."

"Finley wouldn't have lied about such a thing," Chelsea said.

"But what proof did he have? Probably none," Bethel said.

"It's not facts that Chelsea needs," Running Spirit said suggestively. "And it's not a ghost, either."

Chelsea's face flamed. She put down her fork, the expression in her green eyes hurt and vulnerable. Her thin lips seemed to sink and disappear altogether. "I don't understand."

"Sure you do, Chelsea." His tone mocked as his gaze slid over her.

She drank some water, trying to ignore him.

"Time to be with the living," he taunted.

"Stop it."

"There are better cures for loneliness than ghosts. You should find one. If you can."

Angie couldn't stand it any longer. "Did you hear her say to stop? Or are your ears as deficient as your manners?"

"Oh, ho!" he said, giving her a haughty look. "Feeling left out?"

"Don't even think about it, Jeffers," Paavo said quietly.

Running Spirit jerked back in his chair. It was Angie's turn to smirk.

Bethel leaned forward. Her turban slipped slightly. "I hate to admit it, Chelsea, dear, but Greg's right. I've been worried about you myself."

Chelsea turned to Moira. "What have you been saying to them?"

"Nothing, I assure you."

"Don't let it bother you, Chelsea," Martin Bayman said, frowning furiously at his water as if by will alone he could make it turn into the sort of beverage he obviously wanted to drink. "I've seen lots of spirits myself."

Everyone chose to ignore Bayman, their attention on Chelsea.

Running Spirit eyed Chelsea as he shifted sideways and hooked his muscle-bound arm over the top of his chair. His smile showed perfect white teeth. "Why don't you come with me tomorrow morning. We'll have an OBE."

"I don't think so."

"What's the matter, Chelsea? Are you afraid?"

"I have no idea what you're talking about."

"Sure you do. I think you're afraid to find out you can't have an OBE. Or maybe you're afraid if you're with me you might want to find out what a live man is all about."

Chelsea jumped to her feet, her whole body quivering and her eyes tear-filled. "You scum!"

Running Spirit opened his mouth to speak.

"Jeffers," Paavo said, his voice calm but firm. "That's enough."

Running Spirit gaped at him, then shut his mouth.

Moira leaned toward Chelsea. "Don't listen to Running Spirit. He doesn't understand."

A glimmer of a smirk touched Running Spirit's lips before he cast a cautious eye toward Paavo, then seemed to decide it was safer to shovel more food in his mouth.

Reginald Vane hurried into the room. "I'm sorry I'm late." He looked from Chelsea's stricken expression to the others. "Is anything wrong?"

Chelsea backed away from the table.

"Miss Worthington," Vane said as he reached out to take her arm.

"Leave me alone!" She brushed him aside and ran from the room.

Paavo walked into the kitchen to help Angie clean up after dinner, only to find that Martin and Bethel had beaten him to it. He left and went into the library. Jack Sempler's picture was the first thing to catch Paavo's eye. As he studied Jack looking off toward the horizon, Paavo couldn't help but wonder what the man would think if he heard about the havoc he was wreaking on lives some ninety years after his death. Paavo went to the bookshelves to see if he could find a book to take his mind off the people in this inn for a few minutes.

He found a book on the history of the northern California and Oregon coasts during the time the Russians traveled there, built forts, and established communities. It was an interesting period that he knew little about.

He walked toward the fireplace, which had been lit, to sit in an easy chair.

"Hello." Peeking out from a wing chair facing the fireplace was Moira. She'd obviously been crying.

"I didn't see you there," Paavo said. He didn't like seeing a woman cry, especially not one who reminded him so strongly of his past. Too many tears had been shed back then. "I'm sorry. I didn't mean to disturb you."

"That's all right. Come and sit. I'm glad for the company. I've been here with my own thoughts too long."

"I know what you mean."

She smiled. "What thoughts have you been with too long?"

"Thoughts of Patsy Jeffers. Knowing she might have a chance if we could just find her, or get some help in our search. Wondering . . ." No, he wouldn't say anything about Finley. As much as she didn't seem to actually grieve for her brother, it wouldn't be right to speculate on the means of his death. He ended with a noncommittal, "I don't know."

Running Spirit burst into the room. "Moira?" He saw her with Paavo. "Ah, there you are. I'd like to talk to you. Would you come with me?"

"No, Greg. I really don't care to."

He walked over and took her hand. "Come on."

She pulled it back. "No."

He leaned over her chair, his hands on the armrests, his face mere inches from hers. "Moira. I know how you feel. I can help." He touched her face. "Let's go to your room."

She turned her head. "Please go."

"Damn it—"

"Leave her alone," Paavo said.

"This isn't your business, Smith." He turned back to Moira.

"It is now."

Running Spirit straightened and faced Paavo with a murderous look. "Watch out for your glass house before you throw stones, Smith. I think you're the one who needs to leave her alone."

"I don't know what the hell you're talking about, Jeffers. And I don't care to. Just get out of here."

"Your girlfriend being a cook fooled me at first, but no mere cook wears Donna Karan and Ferragamo. Patsy buys all that stuff, too, only on her it doesn't look so hot. Now you're nosing around Moira. You tired of your woman's money? Maybe you're just tired of being bought and paid for. Big-time cop. What a joke!"

Paavo grabbed Running Spirit's vest and jerked him forward as easily as if he were a child. Paavo kept his voice low, his eyes cold and hard. "You ever say anything like that again to me, to Moira, or to Angie, and you'll pay."

Moira stood, placing one hand on each man's chest. "Please," she said.

Running Spirit put his hands up as if to surrender. "All right. She's upset. We'll finish this some other time, Smith."

Paavo let go of him. "Anytime, Jeffers."

Running Spirit backed away. When near the doorway, he glanced at Moira. "Don't waste your time falling for him, babe. Looks like little Patsy took a dive, and I'll be free soon as her body shows up."

Moira shook her head. "Get out of here, Greg. Go cause trouble somewhere else."

"I'm going back out at dawn to look for her," Running Spirit said as he turned.

"I'll be there," Paavo said.

Running Spirit cocked an eyebrow. "Whatever's right." With that, he left.

Moira studied the door long after he'd disappeared, her expression one of quiet desperation. "I wonder if the investors are right. They say I should sell this place, that it'd be a lot easier that way."

"You're thinking of selling to the Baymans?" he asked.

"Possibly to Martin and Bethel, but then Greg—I'll never get used to 'Running Spirit'—also wants to buy it. He thinks it could be the start of his ashram. I, on the other hand, would have been perfectly content to simply live here and take in a few guests now and then to help meet expenses."

"Why are they both so interested in this place?" Paavo asked.

"It's all because of zoning," she answered.

"Explain."

"This whole area is either U.S. Forest Service land or is owned by private logging companies. Between the two of them, and the old-time residents who are opposed to any change or any building along the coast, it's impossible to build a new inn or bed-and-breakfast. There's no way on Earth a resort or a complex like Running Spirit wants could be added. The only way to get one is to buy a place that's already established."

"In other words, if someone has big plans, this is the way to have them fulfilled."

"That's right," Moira said, her voice low and soft as she caught Paavo's eyes and held them. "This is the kind of place dreams are made of."

Moira soon excused herself, and Paavo, lost in thought, stepped onto the back porch to watch the rain.

This inn must be haunted, he decided, but not necessarily the way people here assumed. It was haunted with lost dreams and lost goals. The investors came here with their dreams, their hopes, on the line. Even Angie, with her dream of a special assignment, special training, that would lead to the wonderful, elusive job she sought.

What was Moira's dream? he wondered. Finley's had seemed to be this inn. He had sought a dream but found death.

Since Jeffers was going to allow himself a few hours of rest before going back out again, Paavo thought he'd do the same. The longer he was out there, the more hopeless the search became. Wherever Patsy was, he didn't think she was simply out wandering around lost. She was hurt, or dead, or purposely hiding.

The possibility that she was Finley's murderer and was hiding so that she could eventually escape also couldn't be ignored.

He was tired, though, of these people, these murders, coming between him and Angie. He had to figure out who was behind it all so that they would all be safe, but he also needed time with her. Time to remind her how much he cared. He hurried to their room.

There were too many lost dreams in this house. Angie wasn't a dream, though. She was vivid, more alive than any ten women he'd ever known. Despite all his most logical, rational pronouncements, he loved her.

Bursting through the door, he stopped short, trying to appear nonchalant. She was there, looking all warm and cozy wrapped in a thick, snowy robe, seated in front of the fireplace. A low fire was burning, and she was reading a book. She put it down when he entered and gave him a cautious smile.

"What's happening?" she asked.

"Nothing. Jeffers and I will rest for a while, then go search some more at dawn."

"Do you think there's much chance of finding her?"

"I don't know."

Angie nodded and crossed her ankles on the footstool, her fluffy pink bedroom slippers pointed toward the fireplace. By her side was a glass of white wine, a bottle, and a clean glass. "Would you care to join me?" she asked. "Bethel gave me the wine. She said the ancients originally used alcohol for its medicinal effect as a relaxant, so it was quite acceptable for us to have a sip now and then. I think she just may be right."

He grinned. Despite himself, Angie could get him to smile at the most mundane of things. "Are you saying Bethel's gone on a politically correct toot?"

Warm, brown eyes caught his, crinkling up into infectious laughter. "Very good, Inspector."

He sat in the rose-colored chair beside her, wanting to get closer, but still leery. It was too easy to say the wrong thing to her lately. As if his every word, every nuance, was under a microscope here in this small, phony world.

She poured him a glass of wine and then told him about her afternoon with Danny—her belief that he was Moira's son and that Quint was his grandfather.

Paavo had expected something like that and was glad Angie could confirm it.

She went on to tell him about Susannah's diaries and Jack Sempler's letters.

"So," Angie said as she finished the tale, "we now need to consider a missing heir lurking around somewhere—a grandchild or even great-grandchild of Jack and Elise. What if the missing heir is here, with us? What if he, or she, is one of the guests? Then wouldn't it make sense that he or she would kill off Finley and Moira, then reclaim the property?"

"There are a few problems with that," Paavo said. "First of all, Benjamin was illegitimate. It'd have to be proven that Jack Sempler was in fact his father. Remember, Jack had been away for a while. No one knows what Elise was doing to ease her heartbreak. Also, Susannah inherited

Jack's share of the property upon his death. That part of the inheritance would have to be overturned. Then, depending on what Susannah's will stipulated—"

"All right, all right. Still, it seemed plausible to me." She rubbed her eyes, feeling herself growing weary. "Maybe the heir is just really pissed off that Moira and Finley are living here instead of him or her, and for that reason decided to kill them."

"Then why is Patsy missing?"

"Maybe she saw who bumped off Finley?"

"That's all too possible. Much as I hate to think it, it seems one of these people must have killed him, the cook, and maybe even Patsy."

"What a group," Angie said. "Right before our very eyes—greed, hypocrisy, con artistry, lust, naïveté, self-delusion, arrogance. Just about every frailty except gluttony." Then she remembered Chelsea's stash of candy and the way she and Chelsea devoured it. All right—gluttony, too."

"Given all that," Paavo said, "what was the one thing that drove someone to murder?"

"I don't know." Angie took another sip of her wine, then lay her head against the back of the chair and shut her eyes. "Maybe no one killed anyone. Finley cracked his head on a rock as he fell, Patsy jumped and was carried out to sea, and Miss Greer's heart gave out. All we have to worry about is Running Spirit starving to death because he won't shut up long enough to eat."

Between not having a decent night's sleep since she arrived and drinking a glass of wine now, she knew she wasn't making much sense. Who cared, anyway? She was weary, but sleeping was one thing she wasn't going to do. She planned to stay awake and find out exactly what it was that kept Paavo occupied every night.

Besides that, going to sleep in this place seemed just a little too dangerous. You might not ever wake up again.

She yawned. My eyes are open, she told herself. My eyes are open. My eyes . . .

Suddenly, she felt herself being lifted. She put her arms around Paavo's neck as he carried her to the bed, then set her down on it and pulled the covers over her. "You've had a busy day, little one," he said, then kissed her.

She shut her eyes, a warm, lethargic feeling coming over her. "I'm not going to sleep," she whispered as her eyes fluttered shut.

20

Angie awoke with a start. In the darkness of the room, it took her a moment to orient herself, to remember the inn and the ongoing nightmare her vacation had become.

The chilling sound of Elise Sempler's cries broke the silence.

She turned, flinging her arm across an empty bed. Paavo wasn't beside her, but then he hadn't been throughout their few days together.

"Paavo?" It was foolish to call, perhaps, but she was always a fool where he was concerned.

The room, the inn, seemed absolutely still.

She checked the dressing room and bathroom. As she'd expected, Paavo wasn't there. She opened the door to the hallway and peered down it. Only a small nightlight lit the long corridor.

The memory of the diary and letters she'd read came back to her, and she could imagine Susannah, alone in this house, looking down this very hall, thinking she heard a strange noise in the night.

She shut the door and jumped into bed, pulling the covers up to her neck.

Paavo must be downstairs with the others. Maybe, hearing the sounds of Elise, he went off to investigate. Decided to check on Moira. Went to her bedroom . . .

Impossible! She was letting her imagination run wild.

Slowly, as she came more and more awake, the quiet of the night struck her. The rain had stopped, and so had Elise's cries. For the moment, at least. Angie sat up. That's no ghost, she told herself. And with startling clarity, she knew her thought was the absolute truth. Who or what was making that noise? And why? Why was anyone going to such lengths to scare her and the others at the inn into believing the place was haunted?

She threw back the covers and went to the window. The soft mist created a halo around the moon. Beyond the lawn, the trees appeared as no more than black shadows. Just as she was ready to turn away, a beam of light appeared back by the trees. It seemed to be moving. A flashlight?

She could just make out a shape—Paavo! She'd know that man anywhere.

Quickly putting on her shoes and a robe, she stuck her head into the corridor and listened. No sobs from Elise, no strange thumps, not even humanlike footsteps. Scurrying down the hall, she paused by Chelsea's door. No sounds of Jack Sempler, either.

She flew down the stairs and out the front door.

As she ran across the lawn, her pale robe billowing, the mist swirling, and the moonlight streaming down upon her, she gave a quick glance back to the dark mansion. She felt like the heroine on the cover of a gothic novel.

But no supernatural mystery was involved here. The troubles at the inn were being caused by a very human, very dangerous person. That realization was a lot more frightening than the possibility of it being one, or even three, unhappy spirits.

The flashlight she'd seen from her window had either been turned off or Paavo had gone in another direction, because ahead of her all was dark. Reaching the trees and shrubbery where she'd seen the light from her bedroom, she stayed on the edge of the lawn area and strained to see into the thicket. "Paavo?" she called in a loud whisper. "Paavo? Are you here?"

Suddenly someone grabbed her arm. She began to scream when a hand clamped down over her mouth.

"Ouch! Angie, stop kicking and don't yell. You'll wake up the whole house." He lifted his hand from her mouth. "What are you doing out here?"

"What were you trying to do? Scare me to death?"

A voice from behind Paavo slurred, "Don't be annoyed, fair damsel. He was trying to save me." Martin Bayman leaned against a tree, swinging a bottle of bourbon as he spoke. "Trying to save me from the creatures of the night, from the powers of the occult, and most of all, from myself." With that, he attempted to bow with a flourish, and nearly toppled over.

"I heard some noise," Paavo explained. He grabbed hold of the shoulder of Martin's jacket and helped Martin stay upright. "I looked out the window and there was Martin sitting on the lawn. I came out to see what was wrong."

"I'd slipped on the wet grass," Martin said, still swaying. "That's all. No need for worry. Never need for worry. Eat, drink, and be merry. As long as it's not soybeans or soy milk."

"Are you all right?" Angie asked.

"Just fine, lovely lady."

She glanced at Paavo. "Should we get him inside and up to bed?"

"The problem is, Angelina," Martin waved her closer, then changed his voice to a stage whisper, "I don't want to go inside. And I want to go to bed even less. How easy do you think it is to live with someone who channels?"

Angie felt a sinking in the pit of her stomach as she saw how the clever, poetic man under the moonlight was now reduced to this slurring mess. "I don't know. I never have," she said.

"Well, don't, if you can avoid it." Martin hiccuped. He grabbed hold of a low-lying branch, then tottered as the branch swung from side to side. "Bethel's been at it for years and years. She's got quite a following. Or at least she used to have. Once lots of people wondered what Allakazam had to say. Lots and lots of people. In the sixties, he used to talk—should I say yak?—about planetary cooling and the coming of the next ice age. These days he worries about just the opposite—the polar ice cap melting and drowning us all."

"Maybe we should help you inside," Angie said, trying to take hold of his arm.

He kept moving it out of reach, and the branch he held swayed further, making him totter more, like a drunken Tarzan, until Angie stepped away, afraid she was doing more harm than good.

"Did you know that Bethel still has people who throw good money at her to get this joker's advice on how to deal with global warming? Who would know better than a dead Eskimo, right?"

Martin planted his feet, let go of the branch, then started to unscrew the cap on his bourbon bottle. Paavo reached out and stopped him. "Time to go in now, Martin," he said firmly. He took Martin's arm with no trouble and began walking toward the house.

"Go in, goin', gone!" Martin shouted, waving his arm,

then turned around to go in the opposite direction. "Beautiful dawn," he cried to the sky. "No, poor dawn. It's time for Running Mouth to come out and destroy you."

"Destroy dawn?" Angie asked, walking around in circles beside Martin as Paavo tried to get him headed toward the inn.

"If he's not astrally projecting himself," Martin said, "he's out here beating on his drum trying to commune with his brotherhood or sisterhood or whatever damn thing he last heard he was supposed to commune with. Why the hell doesn't he project himself into another dimension?"

"Maybe he should have been called Drumming Spirit," Angie suggested.

Martin stopped moving around. He laughed bitterly, then said, "I wish to God and the devil he'd turn into Disappearing Spirit."

Angie grabbed his other arm and she and Paavo were finally able to steer Martin toward the house.

"Have you and Bethel known Running Spirit long?" Angie asked.

Martin tried to think. "Five days? Six? It seems like an eternity. No, actually we met Greg Jeffers the first day. Then he had a session with Moira and found out that he was Running Spirit in another life. Or something like that. Who the hell knows anymore? Who cares? It's all over, anyway."

"What's over?" Paavo asked.

"It was supposed to be empty. That was the whole idea."

Angie asked, "What was supposed to be empty?"

"Let me ask you," Martin began. "Does this look like a well-run establishment?"

Paavo frowned as he and Angie took hold of Martin's

arms again. "It doesn't look like anything in the middle of the night. Come on, Bayman."

"Nanook of the North told her to worry, but Nanook never explains anything. I'm the one who has to do that. It's all up to me." Martin looked at Paavo. "She's thinking of opening an institute. To study psychic phenomena. Can you believe it? She thinks she'll attract government grants. She'll probably attract the IRS. Then what?"

"Come on, Martin," Angie said soothingly. "Let's get you inside."

"There's no money in it. I know how to get money. Disneyland. That's the way."

"Let's go, Martin," Angie coaxed.

"No, listen." He stopped walking. "A Disneyland for the ages—the New Ages—get it? I've got it all worked out."

"I'm sure you do," Angie said as she and Paavo finally got him walking toward the house again.

"All those books, all those talk shows, and where are we now? Too much competition. Channelers are coming out of the woodwork. Like cockroaches."

"Aren't you a believer, Martin?" Angie asked.

"What does it matter?" He sighed wearily as Paavo walked up to the front door and held it open for him. "One way or the other, 'The ghosts are gonna get you if you don't watch out.'"

21

Angie sat on the bed, Paavo in a chair.

"Is everyone acting stranger than ever, Paavo, or is it just my imagination?" Angie asked.

"It's not your imagination at all." Paavo's expression was as grim as his words.

"It's as if this inn is part of a spring that's being wound tighter with each passing day we're stuck here," Angie said. "Whoever killed Finley for sure never imagined we'd be marooned here. They probably thought the investors and townspeople would travel back and forth, arguing and hurling threats about opening the inn. If, in the midst of all that, Finley was discovered murdered, there'd have been all kinds of suspects."

"Instead of just one houseful," Paavo added.

"I wonder if Miss Greer might not have died, or if Patsy might not have disappeared. Now, though, how much more will whoever is behind this try to get away with?"

Paavo shook his head. "Whoever's behind it all is smart. Smart enough to know the noose is tightening with every passing day, with every statement made. There's a possibility that someone will slip, that something will be said or done that will turn suspicion around to the right person."

"Besides the murderer worrying about getting caught, the others see people dying or disappearing—and are getting more and more nervous that the same will happen to them. No wonder it's as if we're sitting on a powder keg ready to ignite."

"It'll blow soon, Angie."

"Will it?"

She never heard his answer. They jumped up. The sound of a crash from the next room had jarred them. Was it danger, or just an accident? Then a voice, a woman's, was crying out for help.

"Oh, God!" Angie cried. "Chelsea!"

Paavo grabbed his .38 revolver from the bureau. Angie hurried down the hall behind him. He tried Chelsea's door. It was locked. Ramming it hard with his shoulder, the door and frame sprang apart. Chelsea screamed again.

Paavo flicked on the lights.

"In there," she cried, pointing at the dressing room.

Paavo stepped to the side of the dressing room door. Holding his gun barrel up, he pushed the door open. Once, twice, he darted his head to look into the room, and when no one shot at him, he entered. The dressing room and the bathroom beyond were empty.

The walls in the dressing room were paneled—the kind that opened up in old movies to reveal secret passages. But that was only in the movies, wasn't it? God, Paavo thought, he was starting to think like Angie.

Chelsea sat on her bed in Angie's arms, sobbing quietly. Swathed in a loosely billowing pink ruffled cotton nightgown, she looked three times bigger than Angie, rather than the usual two.

"What happened?" Paavo asked her as he slid the gun under the waistband at his back.

"I'm not sure." Chelsea's sobs grew louder. Her body shook like warm custard. "I was asleep, and suddenly I felt someone in the room with me. I reached for the lamp but knocked it over. I saw him step forward, almost as if he were going to help. I screamed, hoping you'd hear. Thank God you did."

"Then he ran into the dressing room?"

"Yes."

"You're sure?"

"Yes!"

"Describe him to me, Chelsea, as best you can."

"I don't know!" she wailed. "It was so dark."

"It's all right, Chelsea. Take your time." Paavo sat on the edge of the bed. His voice nearly purred. Angie gawked—she'd never heard him sound that way outside of the bedroom. "All I'm wondering is if he was big or little, short or tall."

"He didn't move." Chelsea pulled at her thick red hair. "He was just a blob. A scary blob."

"What was your impression?"

"Big. Huge, actually."

"Do you mean muscular or just heavy?" Paavo asked. "Was he big like Running Spirit?"

"Running . . ." Chelsea stopped speaking as she thought a long, long moment. "I couldn't say. To me, he seemed a lot bigger than even Running Spirit. More like the ghost of John Wayne."

"Running Spirit, of course!" Angie jumped up. "That loud-mouthed blowhard, that disgusting creep. After the nasty things he was saying at dinner, who else—"

"No!" Chelsea covered her ears.

"I think we should find him." Angie waved her fists in the air, more convinced with every word she spoke. "Confront him and see what he has to say for himself!"

"Don't!" Chelsea screeched. "Please, don't do that."

"Leave it for now, Angie," Paavo said. "We have no proof. Anyway, whenever someone breaks into a person's room or house, the intruder seems to be at least ten feet tall."

"Who else could it be?" she asked.

He looked back at Chelsea. "Are you certain it was a man?"

"Well . . ."

"Could it have been a woman?" he asked.

"I thought . . . maybe . . . it was . . . Jack."

Paavo and Angie glanced at each other, then back to Chelsea.

Her face fell. "You're right. It couldn't have been Jack. He wouldn't have scared me. He wouldn't have run off." She covered her face in her hands. "Good God, am I a fool to have believed Finley Tay? I just don't know. I don't know. Maybe I just imagined the whole thing."

"Can you think of anything said to you or that you overheard," Paavo asked, "that made you feel uneasy in any way?"

She rubbed her forehead. "Don't we all feel uneasy with these deaths?" Her eyes began to tear again.

"What if whatever happened to Patsy," Angie said slowly, "happened the same way? Someone might have been watching her, then grabbed her. She was awfully frazzled that last day before she disappeared. We all thought it was because of Running Spirit and Moira. But what if it was a lot more than that? What if the killer is after us, all of us, for another reason, a reason we haven't figured out yet? He or she went after Finley, Miss Greer, Patsy, now Chelsea—"

"Angie, enough!" Paavo ordered.

Chelsea was close to hysterics. Angie patted her hand. "I'm sorry," Angie said. "I just wanted to consider all sides of this, since the sheriff obviously doesn't think it's important to come here to protect us."

"You saw the road, Angie," Paavo said. "Even after it stops raining, he'll have to dig his way in."

"They could send a helicopter."

"In this storm? And he has no reason to think there's any emergency."

"That's just ducky. Before Butz bothers to think anything, how many more of us will have been killed?"

"Oh, God!" Chelsea wailed. "I want to go home."

"We *all* want to go home." Angie helped Chelsea put on her robe, then took her hand and pulled her from her bed. "You're not staying here alone tonight. Come to our room."

A flicker of relief lit Chelsea's eyes, but she pulled her hand free. "No, I couldn't intrude that way."

"It's no intrusion," Paavo said. "Angie's right. You shouldn't be alone after this."

"Thank you." Chelsea picked up her pillow and hugged it against herself as she walked with Angie and Paavo down the hall.

Once back in their room, Paavo took his pillow from the bed and tossed it onto a chair by the fireplace. "You ladies get into bed. I've got a few things I want to check out."

"I couldn't take your bed," Chelsea said.

"It's all right. I wasn't planning to use it tonight anyway." He glanced at Angie and remembered his fleeting thought of making up with her when he first came up to the room tonight. It seemed like centuries ago. "Not much, at least." He took his gun from the back of his waistband and put it on the nightstand next to Angie. "Keep this near, in case you hear anything strange."

"A gun?" Chelsea cried. "Oh, my God."

Angie couldn't believe Paavo would leave them. "Where are you going?"

"I'm going to check out her room. There's got to be another way out of it. Men don't disappear."

Angie stood up. "I'm going with you."

"Don't leave Chelsea alone."

Angie saw that Chelsea was still fixated on the gun. "I guess you're right. But be careful." She ran across the room, threw her arms around him, and kissed him.

Paavo held her close, then gave a single nod and left the room.

Paavo eased open the door to Chelsea's room. Before entering, he checked to see if anyone was there or if anything had been disturbed. It appeared the same as when they left it.

Shutting the door so softly he could scarcely hear it latch, he tiptoed across the room to the dressing room. Carefully eyeing the way the clothes hung in the closet to see which might have been disturbed, the nap on the carpet to see where someone might have stepped, and the way the panels fit into the walls, he found the spot where a secret panel would be—if one in fact existed.

He racked his brain trying to remember the things he'd learned in robbery detail about the various kinds of doors and latches and ways to break into them. He remembered that a lot of them used a spring latch mechanism that simply required two spots to be pressed at once. Remembering that most people didn't have the height or long arms that he did, he shortened his reach. All of a sudden, when he wasn't even too sure which magic duo he'd touched, the panel sprang open.

He pushed the panel open as far as it would go—it was hinged on one side like a door—and went into the passage. No lights or light switches. In Chelsea's room there'd been a gaggle of candles of varying sizes and thicknesses, arranged in a circle on her dresser. He went into the bedroom, picked up the largest, and lit it.

Back in the passageway, he saw that the walls hadn't been finished but showed the beams that held the building's structure.

As he descended the stairs, he felt more and more like a character in a Vincent Price film. At the bottom stood a panel much like the one he'd entered from. He placed his fingers along the edges near the spots where the spring locks had been placed upstairs and pushed. The panel sprang ajar and began to turn.

"What's that?" Chelsea asked as she sat up on the bed, clutching the blanket to her breast.

Angie stopped stoking the fire. Her fingers tightened on the poker. The rain had stopped, and now soft keening sounds could be heard. "Someone's crying."

"Elise Sempler," Chelsea whispered.

"Or someone in the inn trying to make people believe in ghosts for their own crude purposes—like what happened to you tonight."

"No, it's real."

As abruptly as it started, the sound stopped. "I guess she's gone back to sleep," Angie said. "We should, too."

"I think the sound came from outside," Chelsea whispered.

"Let's take a look." Angie shut the off lights in the bedroom to better see and the two crept to the windows. As they neared, the cries began again. She found Chelsea's hand and held on tight.

A misty, whitish glow appeared at the edge of the cliffs, then disappeared almost as quickly. A few seconds later it appeared again, but only for an instant. This happened three more times before it disappeared altogether. The cries were heard twice more. Angie watched, fascinated, unsure what she was seeing.

"It's Elise!" Chelsea exclaimed. "And seeing her proves that Jack is here. Maybe it was Jack in my room."

Angie frowned. "If it was Jack, he sure isn't the man you thought he was."

Paavo stepped into the library. He'd always thought tales about secret passageways in old houses were a myth. He learned now that he'd been wrong. Someone, who was it? had said old Ezra Sempler was a survivalist. Was that why he had secret passages and panels put in the house? What else had he built here?

He opened the door to the hall and looked up and down. No one was there. Creeping down the hall toward Finley and Moira's quarters, he heard voices.

"I don't care what you say!" It was Moira.

"You can't blame me for this, Moira. It's your fault. All of it is," Running Spirit said.

"I hate you!"

"Do you, now? How can I believe that when you asked that I come here and head my own ashram?"

"I never did any such thing!" Moira's voice was indignant.

Running Spirit gave a low, crude snort. "Finley told

me all about it. How you've wanted me all these years. How we have to get Patsy out of the way."

"Anything between us was a lifetime ago. You made your decision then. It's taken a lot of years, but now I can thank you for it. You did me a big favor."

"Bitch!"

"How articulate of you."

"I'm warning you, Moira. This inn is the answer to a lifetime of dreams. I won't give it up. Do you understand me?"

"This inn will be mine soon, and I'll throw you out of it."

"Yours? The bank's, you mean. Without Patsy's and my backing, you'll lose it even faster than Finley would have. With Patsy's money, I'll get it—and anything else I want. Including you."

"How do you know Patsy's dead?"

"She's got to be. There's no way she wouldn't be with me if she was still alive."

"You're so damned arrogant. Same as ever."

Paavo heard Running Spirit's loud laughter. "Good night, Moira, love. Pleasant dreams."

Paavo ducked back into the shadows. Moira's "Go to hell," reverberated in the hallway as Jeffers left her room, chuckling to himself.

Paavo quietly entered his bedroom. The glow from the fireplace was the only light. He tiptoed over to the bed.

Angie and Chelsea lay back to back, fast asleep. He stood and watched them for a moment. The thought struck him that that might have been what Jack Sempler was doing, just standing there watching her sleep, when Chelsea woke up and saw him. God, he thought, he was likening his actions to those of a ghost. This place had to be getting to him.

Turning away, he crossed the room to the little rose-colored chairs and sat. After removing his shoes, he tried to curl his six foot two inch body onto one chair, his feet up on the other, in some way comfortable enough to be able to sleep. No matter how he twisted or turned, some part of him didn't want to fit.

He finally put a spare blanket on the floor, his pillow on top of it, then lay down.

As he listened to the sound of Angie's and Chelsea's deep, sleep-filled breathing, he imagined the reaction of the guys in Homicide if he told them he'd spent a night in a secluded inn with two women in his bed. His old partner, Matt Kowalski, would have bombarded him with jokes and innuendos, not paying any attention to Paavo's explanation of what actually had happened. But Matt was dead now, gunned down just a few months before. Paavo had been off-duty that night, and Matt had died on the street, all alone.

If ghosts were as real as Chelsea and everyone else in this place seemed to think, he'd have liked to see Matt's ghost. If nothing else, he'd have liked the chance to tell Matt how much he missed him, to tell him he was the best friend Paavo ever had. He'd have liked the time to say good-bye.

Hell. His eyes shut as he tried to push the thought away. There was no such thing as ghosts.

22

No one but Chelsea cared about eating breakfast, Angie realized. The others seemed to stay up most of
the night and sleep away the morning—except Moira,
who never seemed to sleep at all. Wasn't that a trait of
zombies? With this crew, anything was possible.

Force of habit and misplaced duty caused her to join
Moira, once again, in the kitchen to assemble the same
boring breakfast of soy coffee, oat bran muffins, granola,
and orange juice.

Paavo and Running Spirit gulped down hot coffee, cold
orange juice, and then left to continue their search for
Patsy. Martin, Bethel, and Reginald didn't show up at all,
while Chelsea ate two muffins and a bowl of granola. Her
fright last night had increased her appetite.

Since Martin and Reginald were still asleep, Angie
wondered if one of them might have been Chelsea's
nightwalker. On the other hand, she didn't know when
Running Spirit had left Moira. It wouldn't have surprised
her to learn that Moira threw him out of her room, leaving

him more frustrated than ever, and as a result, he went looking for Chelsea, thinking she'd welcome the attentions of a live man. But she couldn't imagine Chelsea being an object of lust for Robinson Crusoe while still on his desert island, let alone for Running Spirit.

Angie decided she'd reserve judgment on what the nightwalker meant to do with Chelsea, if anything, until she learned who he was. None of these men could be potential rapists. But then she couldn't see any of them, or the women either, as potential murderers. Which just went to show how poor a judge of character she must be.

After the kitchen was straightened up, it was time for Moira to change the bed linens and do what had become her usual routine of cleaning for her small battery of guests.

Meanwhile, Angie went to visit Chelsea, who had gone back to her own room. There Angie discovered that not only had Paavo found a secret passageway in Chelsea's room last night, but he had been in there while breakfast was being served and had put slide bolts on it so that no one else could use it to break in.

"He's so clever," Angie said proudly. "Cute, too. At least to those of us who like our men tall, dark, and handsome with baby-blue melt-your-heart-away eyes, rather than pining for ghostly apparitions."

Chelsea agreed. "For a man, he is nice. He also showed me how to spring the secret lock."

"Really?" Angie was impressed. "He's a regular Houdini. Show me."

Chelsea slid back the bolts—one high and one low on the panel—then, as Angie watched, she hit the sensitive points and the panel sprang open. They pushed it open further, then, holding up candles, peered into the spider-infested passageway.

"How disgusting," Angie said. "Paavo actually went in there? It's all full of spiderwebs."

"I know," Chelsea said. "I was going to try using it, but I think I won't. Paavo said it just went down to the library, where there's a door like this one."

"If that's all, I'll take the regular route," Angie said.

She soon left Chelsea to do just that, deciding she ought to figure out what to serve for lunch before she got involved in anything else.

The first floor of the inn, as far as Angie knew, was empty except for Moira, who was dusting the drawing room.

But as she neared the kitchen, she heard some noise coming from it and froze. Utensils in a drawer rattled as it was being shut, then the refrigerator door was opened, then closed. It could be any number of people, she told herself. Someone from the outside could have come in, or from upstairs could have come down. She shouldn't feel so skittish.

Still, she stepped up to the kitchen door very carefully, ready to run if anything looked the least bit untoward. She held onto the door frame and slowly bent her head forward, just enough to see inside.

Danny stood at the counter. He had a small paper bag, and she watched as he cut a thick slice of cheese from a brick, put plastic wrap around it, and put it in the bag, following it with an orange. When he glanced up and saw Angie in the doorway, he snatched the bag of food and stepped back.

"What are you doing?" Angie walked toward him. "You can eat with us if you're hungry."

"Oh." He bit his bottom lip. "I was going to go looking for that lady myself. And when I got here I felt a little hungry. . . ."

"You don't have to hide. No one would care if you wanted to take any food."

"I'm not supposed to be here."

"That's hard to believe." She was going to have to confront Moira about the boy and why she didn't want him to be known to these people.

"See you. Bye." He grabbed the sack and ran off.

Angie didn't bother about lunch, but went back to Chelsea to convince her that the two of them ought to go out and look for Patsy. Everyone else, it seemed, was already doing so.

Paavo sat alone in the kitchen, eating toast, three eggs that he'd fried for himself, and having a cup of reheated soy coffee. One thing he could say about soy coffee—reheating didn't make it any worse.

It was long after breakfast. He'd just come in for a break from the Patsy search, felt hungry, and wasn't about to trouble anyone for food. Particularly not Angie.

Moira stepped into the room. "Oh, I didn't think anyone was here."

"I helped myself," he said. "Hope you don't mind."

"Not at all."

He saw that she hesitated near the doorway. "Join me?" he asked. There was a lot he wanted to ask her about, but yesterday the pain of her loss had been too fresh. Today she looked a bit better.

"All right." She filled a teakettle with water and put it on the stove to heat. After placing her favorite herb tea mix on the counter, she began rummaging through the back of a cupboard. "Ah. Success." She held up a tea bag. "Lipton's."

He grinned. "Lady, you've made my day."

She got out the cups, then sat beside Paavo at the counter, silently watching him eat and waiting for the water to boil. He knew she didn't mind the silence—would probably relish it, in fact.

Why did he know that about her? Was it just because she looked and acted so much like Sybil, or was there something more to this woman, another dimension that he was open to? Good God, but he hated how he was thinking that way more and more these days. He'd probably go back to Homicide as a goddamned Edgar Cayce or something. Might help with a few tough cases, though.

The tea was ready just as he finished eating. She placed his cup in front of him. "I've wanted to ask you about your brother," he said, "and if you have any idea why this happened to him."

She folded her hands. "I'm not terribly surprised."

Her words surprised him. "You're not surprised he was killed?"

"Not really. To Finley, people were like mice, and he was a very big, very clever cat."

He heard both bitterness and sadness in her voice.

"You're saying he treated people here that way? You?"

"All of us." She dropped her hands, drawing deep breaths as she tried to find her composure, then she stood to leave. "Excuse me."

He took her arm. "Tell me about it. If someone here killed your brother, or harmed Patsy . . ." He didn't have to list the dangers any of the rest of them might be in. "Is there anyone that you suspect? Is there anyone who particularly hated him?"

"Hated him? I guess the one who hated him the most was me."

"You?" Was she saying she killed him?

"I didn't do it. Despite some very unpacifistic ideas I

may have had from time to time about doing just that. But I'm sure others have felt the same way. All the investors wanted to kill him."

"Why?"

"He duped them. Every one of them. He found out what their dreams were, and he played with them, holding their dreams and hopes out like bait. The people you see here are the ones who reached for that bait. He hooked them and reeled them in. Now they're stuck, bleeding, dying. And they hated him for it."

He wanted the facts that she held so closely. "I need to know about it, Moira. All of it. Before anyone else is killed."

She shook her head, her hands covering her eyes.

He pressed on. "Tell me about Jeffers. His wife is missing and might be dead. What brought them here? Do you know?"

"I'm not sure." He could tell she was lying, hesitant. Was she afraid to tell him? Or was the story she would tell too painful? He waited and finally the hesitancy passed.

"Finley met Greg several years ago at an ADOBE convention. That's Atlantis, Dolphins, and Out of Body Experiences. Greg had, even then, some idea of becoming a guru, or whatever it is he calls it. Anyway, it all boils down to the same thing—a charlatan. He planned to get rich by feasting off the disaffected, the unhappy. Finley cultivated a friendship with him. A blood brother, so to speak."

Her chuckle was directed inward, and he could see that there was much more to this story than her words revealed. "I understand you and Jeffers knew each other long ago. Was it before this ADOBE meeting?"

"Yes. Years earlier. Finley didn't meet Greg back then, though."

"I see. Go on," he urged.

With a sigh, she came back to the present and her story. "Finley met a wealthy heiress named Patricia Mannington. She was plain, lonely, and had been taught all her life that men wanted only one thing from her— her money. She was a nervous woman, fragile, and very wary of Finley. He saw that if he tried to date her himself, he'd simply scare her off. He had a better idea."

"Involving Greg Jeffers, I take it?"

She nodded. "Finley looked up his old ADOBE friend, told him about the inn he hoped to buy someday, and went on to tell Greg that Finley believed he would be perfect as a homegrown Maharishi Yogi—all he needed was the financing to get his face, body, and ideas before the public, and someplace to call his ashram."

She began to play with her braid, twisting it, her hands shaking and her manner agitated as she continued talking. "Next, Finley began to tell Greg all about the very straight-laced, innocent woman he knew, and how no man had ever been able to penetrate her self-control and wariness of being married for her money. At the same time, Finley worked on Patricia, telling her of the aesthetic young man who had no interest in anything material in this life. A man who thought only of spiritual things. He talked about them to each other for over three months, telling Greg that Patricia refused to meet him because he was a man and she was afraid of his 'baser instincts,' and telling Patricia that Greg refused to meet her because she was a woman who might divert his mind from pure, lofty, and spiritual thoughts."

"Very clever," Paavo said, watching Moira's closed, guarded expression as she told this story.

"Yes, wasn't it?" She took a moment before she continued. "When they met, I learned from Finley that Greg held himself back, scarcely looking at her, so all Patricia saw was a wonderfully handsome, virile man, afraid of her as a woman. No one had ever paid her such a compliment before. She fell head over heels in love. Greg played his role so well that in the end Patricia, or "Patsy" as he lovingly called her—the height of irony—proposed to him. She convinced him that through the sanctity of marriage their relationship would continue to be pure and spiritual, even though their flesh would be as one. He fell on his knees and thanked her."

"I wouldn't think he could be that good an actor."

"There you're wrong. He's an excellent actor." Her words were bitter.

"So Patsy bought Greg his ashram," Paavo said. He could see the pale, desperate woman giving Running Spirit Jeffers whatever he wanted.

"What actually happened was that Greg tried to leave her out of it. He cut a deal with Finley, giving Finley money to put into this inn in exchange for Finley's written promise that the inn could be used and advertised as Greg's ashram. Greg believed he was being terribly clever, duping Finley into giving away control of the whole inn for only a small portion of what it would cost if he owned it."

"Sounds good," Paavo admitted.

"Too good. Apparently Greg was madder than hell when Patsy pointed out that all he had for his money was a piece of paper that was worth about two cents. It was a contract a first-year law student could break, and Finley was a lot cleverer than many bar exam graduates. Patsy called Finley on it, only to learn that Greg wasn't the only investor, and that the Baymans planned to use Bethel as the inn's main attraction."

Paavo had to laugh.

"Don't laugh yet," Moira said. "You don't know the half of it. After talking to Finley, Patsy got on the phone and called the Baymans, demanding that they pull out of the inn. That was the first they'd heard of the Jefferses. When the two couples approached Finley, he let two more bombshells drop—namely, Reginald Vane and Chelsea Worthington."

"But Martin Bayman's no Greg Jeffers," Paavo said. "He wouldn't just hand over thousands of dollars to Finley for promises on a piece of paper."

"Apparently Martin had been in charge of Bethel's finances all these years, but when the economy began to turn sour, along with her career, he took bigger and bigger chances, until he lost everything. The only way to get money was to begin again, to try to make Bethel the star she never quite became the first time around. For whatever reason, he turned to the inn. No bank would lend him money, so he couldn't be a mortgagee. Instead, he got money somewhere to buy a share of the inn directly from Finley, believing he could maneuver Finley into running it the way he said. But he couldn't."

"And Vane?"

"Apparently, as a single man with a job as an electrical engineer, he was able to save a lot of money. Investing in the inn was the way he wanted to finally enjoy some of the money he'd worked for all these years."

"Chelsea?"

"Her parents apparently believe getting her out of their lives is worth any amount of money."

"It sounds like Finley did his homework well. What brought everyone here?"

"Patsy did. She got on the phone and called them all and asked that they meet here. Greg and Bethel were the two most obviously in conflict, as far as which would be the inn's main attraction. But Reginald, it turns out, doesn't want anyone here disturbing the spirits. Only Chelsea seemed to want the place to be an inn, just as Finley proposed."

Paavo frowned. "That's suspicious in itself."

For the first time, Moira smiled. "I agree."

"And you," Paavo said. "Knowing all this was going on, how did you cope? Why did you stay here?"

Her face drained of what little color it had. "Sometimes we don't have choices, Inspector."

"What do you mean?"

She shook her head.

"Did he do something to you? Hurt you?"

"No one cares about that."

"I suspect more care than you imagine."

She reached out as if to touch his hand, but one glance at him and her hand stilled, then rested on the table near his. "Thank you. It's been a long time since I've heard anyone say anything like that to me."

"Oh!" Angie stood in the doorway, her gaze jumping from one to the other. "Excuse me. I didn't mean to interrupt . . . I was just . . . lunch . . ."

Paavo stood. "We were talking about Finley."

Angie's eyes were wide. "Yes. Of course." She turned and ran down the hall.

"Pardon me," Paavo said to Moira, hurrying after Angie.

She was already at the stairs when he reached the hallway. "Wait a minute!"

She didn't.

He took the stairs two at a time, grabbing her elbow as she reached their room; but she pulled herself free.

Just before she could shut the door, he put his foot in the doorway. "Angelina, will you listen?" He pushed the door open and entered.

"I'd like to be alone," she announced. He could feel how hurt she was.

"Is that so?" He pushed the door shut and circled around her.

"Please, Paavo, just go." She held her ground. "You don't seem to have much to say to me, anyway. Not nearly as much as you have to say to Miss Tay."

"And just what have I said to Miss Tay that has caused this outburst?"

She turned her back to him; her voice was low. "I'm sure that's between the two of you."

He stepped in front of her. "We were talking about her and her brother."

One eyebrow rose and she folded her arms. "Oh? And that caused you two to hold hands?"

"No need for sarcasm, Angie. Besides, we weren't holding hands. Hers was next to mine."

Angie's look was long, low, and seething. "Same difference."

"No, it's not."

"You weren't exactly pulling away."

He took hold of her arms. "You walked in on the middle of something, made assumptions about it, and now you're getting upset for no reason."

"Who's upset?" She pushed him away.

"You are." He stepped closer.

She put her hands against his chest, stopping him. "I've seen the way you've looked at her ever since we arrived. What is it with you? I know you have some kind of special feelings for her, but I don't know what and I don't know why. Do you deny it?"

"Special *what*?" He just stared at her. How could she suggest such a thing?

"Don't tell me you knew her in a past life. I don't

believe in reincarnation, either, despite what everyone else here says!"

"You don't get it, do you, Angie?" Here he'd been acting like a lovesick schoolboy around her, leaving his job, home, everything familiar, to be with her. Now he just wanted to get to the bottom of what was going on around here, but all she saw was him talking to another woman.

"This isn't about me, Paavo. There's more here than you're telling me. I know you. I can feel it."

"Intuition, Angie? Next time—if there is one—trust me." With that, he left.

23

Angie lined up mushrooms, celery, cucumber, spinach, leeks, and onions on the kitchen counter. This inn menu was supposed to be vegetarian. Fine. That's what she'd cook. Nothing else she cooked was appreciated. She wasn't appreciated. Not by anyone.

But she wasn't about to cook another Finley concoction. That was too much a case of cutting off your nose to spite your face—or in this case, eating soybeans to spite your stomach. Instead, she'd cook the vegetables à la Grecque, simmering them in a court bouillon of water, olive oil, lemon juice, parsley, thyme, fennel, and peppercorns, letting the bouillon boil down, then pouring it over the vegetables. She'd then serve them cold as part of a buffet with some risotto and onion soup.

She started slicing the onions. As she sliced and diced the vegetables, her thoughts strayed to the people here. Paavo the onion head. Moira the mushroom. Bethel was like a celery stalk; Chelsea most definitely a cucumber; Reginald, spinach; and Martin, leeks. But Running

Spirit? What was he? A fat yellow squash came to mind for some reason.

Darn, she didn't have any.

She didn't have much of anything, in fact. Her supply of food was dwindling fast. If they didn't get off this damned hill soon, she'd be reduced to cooking the way the peasants did in *The Good Earth*, where they counted how many grains of rice each person was given to eat.

She continued to slice the onions, her eyes watering more with each stroke of the knife. She let the tears flow. No one here even considered the fact that it was hard work to cook for all these people. Granted, the dishes she came up with were fairly easy, but the quantity was enormous, and that alone made cooking time-consuming. Did anyone care? No. She'd tried to make light of this mess, but she couldn't any longer. Everything she'd tried, or planned, had gone inside out and backwards.

All she wanted to do was show Paavo that they could be together day in and day out in harmony and happiness. So what happens? She brings him to a hill with a bunch of homicidal lunatics. He's off investigating, and for all she knows, he could be next on someone's hit list. Or she could be. And on top of that, they weren't getting along well, either.

She had to be the most unlucky person who ever lived.

Having finished with the onions, she wiped her eyes and took a deep, cleansing sigh. Chopping onions always made her feel so much better.

She picked up the mushrooms and began slicing them into thin pieces. Moira the mushroom. What was this fascination Moira held for so many men at this inn? Moira seemed spooky, as far as Angie was concerned. She'd never understand men. Particularly homicide inspectors.

"It's nice that you're here, Angelina," Bethel said, her hands flicking the sides of her caftan so they poofed out around her as she walked into the kitchen. She peered into the pot as Angie stirred the bouillon.

Nice for whom? she wanted to ask. "Thanks."

"I mean it, dear girl. Whatever would we do if you weren't here?" Bethel stole a stalk of celery from the counter. "Why, even I might have to cook."

So it wasn't her company Bethel enjoyed, it was having a live-in cook. Heck, if she were Julia Child, Bethel would probably be doing cartwheels.

"Is that soup?" Bethel asked, pointing with her celery. "It seemed a trifle thin, don't you think?"

"It's called *Soupe du Jardin Mort.*" Even dead garden soup sounded classy in French.

"Of course," Bethel chuckled. "I should have recognized it. One of my favorites. *C'est magnifique!*"

"Right," Angie replied.

"And if I might be so bold . . ." Bethel began.

Was there no getting rid of her?

"Bringing a homicide inspector here with you was a simply marvelous idea. I feel much safer knowing he's here. He doesn't have a gun, though, does he?"

"A gun?"

"I'm opposed to guns."

"Don't worry. He'd only use it to stop a criminal from killing an innocent person, such as yourself," Angie said.

"Oh, well, in that situation, guns are all right."

Angie wondered if Bethel's turban had been worn too tight for too many years.

"Have you seen the inspector lately?" Bethel asked.

Angie tried to push aside the memory of Paavo and Moira holding hands, or nearly holding them, but it wasn't easy. "I saw him a while ago."

"I wonder if he's got any idea who killed Finley and the others."

Angie looked at her closely. "I don't know."

"It scares me to think it might be someone from the town." Bethel finished her celery. "But it scares me even more to think it's someone in this house. I think about it day and night."

"We all do," Angie said. "Do you think it might be someone here with us?"

"Impossible. Unless it's that Running Spirit, of course." Bethel watched as Angie placed the vegetables, tender after having been simmered, onto serving dishes. "I never trusted him from the minute he declared his new name. He's just a charlatan, you know."

Angie's gaze drifted over Bethel's lime-green caftan and matching turban. "Oh, really?"

"It's terrible. Once people would come to see me, and they'd simply believe me. Those were good, honest times. But these days, there are so many who've been ripped off that they want me to prove what I'm doing and saying. Now, I ask you, how can anyone prove that a four-hundred-year-old Inuit is channeling?"

"I have no idea." Angie stirred the bouillon.

"Me, neither. Then, for some reason I don't understand at all, many of the people who know about spirituality are also into computers. Do you understand that?"

"No."

"They seem to think I can relate spiritual space to cyber-space, spiritual reality to virtual reality. I don't even understand the concept of virtual reality. It sounds like a contradiction in terms. But they say that spiritual reality sounds the same way. They seem to think that if Allakaket isn't up on this cyber-punk stuff he isn't real. I don't know what to do. I don't understand any of it anymore."

"I guess you could try to learn what your audience is interested in."

"I asked Reginald to teach me, since he knows so much about electronics. He said I'd hate it, and he won't even try."

"That's terrible. Can Martin help any?"

"He's worse than I am about such things."

"Why don't you just ask Allakaket? Since he knows about twentieth-century things, even though he's from the sixteenth century, it seems he should understand virtual reality as well." The bouillon had boiled down sufficiently to form a tasty sauce. Angie spooned it over the vegetables.

"Now you sound like my ever-dwindling audience. No one understands properly. That was why Martin and I were so happy when Finley approached us about being part owners of this inn."

Finley approached the Baymans? Had he approached others as well? This was a surprise. "What do you mean?" Angie asked.

"He was going to let me run an institute here. I would explain to the public what I was doing and offer classes and a quiet place for contemplation and retreat. Martin liked to call it a Disneyland for New Age types, but he was wrong. It was going to be a college—like one of Oxford's, for example. And I'd be dean. We thought we couldn't afford to get in on this opportunity, but then Martin found a way to arrange it. He's so clever and brilliant."

Angie couldn't imagine being so desperate as to have to rely on Finley Tay. "I had no idea. How terrible it must have been for you and Martin."

"Ah, Angie, to be young again. To have dreams for the future. Now I have none, except to hope that somehow I can come away from this with the business I'd hoped for. If that fails, I have no idea what I'll do."

Angie carried the dishes of vegetables to the refrigerator. "I'm sure something will come up for you or Martin."

"Not Martin." Bethel snatched a cucumber slice and popped it into her mouth. "Mmm. Delicious. Martin's totally dependent on me. Actually, there's one person I've been talking to who had an idea."

"Who was that?"

Bethel loudly licked the sauce off her fingers. "Chelsea. She said she had the inside track with someone and suggested I try to channel with him. He's modern, with a built-in audience that would bring me lots of publicity, and therefore money, immediately."

"My goodness, who could that be?"

"Elvis."

"It's impossible to find anything in that storm. It's kicked up again." Reginald Vane opened the front door but stayed on the stoop as he shook some of the water off and scraped the mud off his shoes; then he walked into the house. Paavo did the same and came in behind him.

Angie and Chelsea sat in the drawing room listening to Bethel talk about the first time she'd channeled Allakaket and how frightening it had been. Bethel stopped talking and all faced the door as soon as they heard Reginald's voice.

Paavo's gaze caught Angie's, but she turned away.

"Is Running Spirit still searching?" she asked Reginald.

"He was right behind us," Reginald replied, "but he said he wanted to go over to the cliffs first."

Martin was next to enter the house, but he headed toward the library, where the liquor was kept.

Reginald greeted Chelsea. "Are you all right, Miss Worthington? I heard you had some trouble last night."

"Trouble?" Bethel chimed in. "What trouble?"

"It was nothing," Chelsea answered quickly. "I'm quite fine, Mr. Vane. Thank you. My only concern now is for Patsy and Mr. Jeffers."

"I wouldn't waste my sympathy on him," Bethel said, "if you know what I mean."

"You wouldn't?"

"If anything, he's the one who should be missing in action, not poor Patsy. Who did she ever hurt?"

"I hadn't thought about it that way, but you're certainly right," Chelsea agreed. "Do you agree, Mr. Vane?"

"Absolutely," Reginald said, looking at her in a way that made Angie sure he'd agree if she said that Running Spirit was San Francisco's uncaptured Zodiac killer. "He made her terribly unhappy, I believe."

"He should pay," Bethel said.

Suddenly a massive blast, followed by a second, then a third in quick succession, rocked the house, rattled the windows, and caused the investors to put their hands to their ears, ready to duck.

Moira ran into the drawing room. "What was that? Is everyone all right?"

They waited a moment, wondering if another blast would hit. Paavo headed for the French doors. "It came from out there."

The rain was falling hard, but despite that, they could see a huge cloud of black smoke. On the ground, a few fires burned, then quickly fizzled out. Still, they had to get close before they could clearly see that where a small toolshed once stood, there was now nothing but a few smoldering boards and a smoking pit blown into the earth. Angie reached Paavo with effort. Her shoes stuck in the mud, and her clothing and hair were quickly drenched. Paavo put his arm out. "Don't come closer."

"What happened?" Angie asked.

He pointed. Not far in front of him lay one of Running Spirit's tooled-leather boots, and just beyond, near some shattered boards, she saw the other one. But no Running Spirit.

"Oh, my God," she whispered, staring, unable to turn her head. She felt woozy. Paavo put his arm around her, letting her bury her face against his chest. Her body shook from the horror before her, her stomach recoiled, and she wasn't sure her lunch would stay down.

"Well, well," Martin Bayman said, suddenly at her side, shielding from the rain a glass of what appeared to be straight whiskey. "It looks like our friend just had the ultimate out-of-body experience."

24

Paavo and Reginald Vane found Running Spirit's body several yards from the toolshed site. He was dead.

"What could have caused this?" Angie asked as the frightened, horrified group huddled close together, watching Paavo and Vane.

"It was dynamite." Moira had to shout to be heard over the storm. "Finley put it in that shed. He'd planned to use it to widen a stream that flowed near the garden."

"Why would the man be hiding in a toolshed?" Bethel asked. "He was supposed to be looking for his wife!"

"He smoked, but didn't want anyone to know it," Moira said. "So he came out here to hide."

"But you knew he smoked," Angie said.

"Yes. I suppose Patsy and I were the only ones he'd told."

"Well, they always say smoking's a killer," Martin said.

No one was in the mood for his quips, though, and all fell silent.

Paavo asked for tarps or other waterproof materials to be put over the whole scene without disturbing anything more than absolutely necessary. He watched as the others followed his orders, then he took Angie's arm and led her up to their room, wishing he could lead her much farther away from the morgue that Hill Haven Inn had become.

"I find it hard to believe he was a smoker," Angie said quietly. Paavo sat on the bed, his back against the headboard. Angie lay down at his side, her head resting on his chest. He gently stroked her hair, every so often letting a strand of it twist around his fingers. She sat up. "I can't believe he's gone, Paavo. It's like a horrible dream. A trick of some sort. Why is all this happening? God, but I wish we could leave here."

He drew her close again. "We will. Soon. It won't rain forever, and we'll be off this damn hill and able to turn all this over to the sheriff."

She lay her head on his chest once more, listening to his strong, steady heartbeat. "Not forever. Just for forty days and forty nights. We'd better start loading the animals two by two."

"It's been a long four days," Paavo said. "Five days for you."

Ironically, she'd invited him to what she thought was her world, and they'd ended up in his. These murders only served to remind him of how different their worlds were.

"This might have been an accident. Don't you think, Paavo?"

"It might have been." He couldn't hide his skepticism.

"How could anyone have lit the dynamite without Running Spirit seeing them? And everyone was with us inside the inn."

"There are a number of ways. A simple kind of timing device to use, since Running Spirit was in there smoking and wouldn't have noticed the smell, would be to light a cigarette and wrap the fuse around the bottom of it. When it burns down, the fuse will light, and whoever put the cigarette there in the first place could be long gone."

Angie wrapped her arms tighter around Paavo. "I don't want to believe anyone here would do anything so cruel."

Brushing her hair back from her face, he felt the silky strands slide through his fingers. "Believe it. We're staying with a murderer."

Paavo wandered away from the investors and Angie as they huddled in the drawing room, trying to make sense out of Running Spirit's death and trying to convince themselves that it had nothing to do with Finley's murder, Patsy's disappearance, or Miss Greer's supposedly natural death. Paavo didn't want to hear their speculations or excuses. What they were saying was meaningless. One of them had just killed another person, and that fact wasn't being even remotely acknowledged. Not out loud, at least.

Moira wasn't with them, and she was the one Paavo was most interested in talking to right now.

He found her alone in the library, her eyes red from crying. He crossed to a wing chair at her side and sat. "Do you feel like talking?" he asked.

She blinked, then wiped her eyes with a Kleenex. "I suppose you want to ask all kinds of police procedural questions now. Right, Inspector?"

"No. Those questions seem to be going on in the other room. But the answers there are completely false."

She smiled. "Yes. I couldn't take any more of it myself."

"You knew Greg Jeffers better than any of them, I suppose."

She shut her eyes a moment. "Better than you or any

of them have ever imagined." With her dark-eyed gaze on him, in her slow, otherworldly way of speaking, she said, "He was Danny's father."

Paavo stared at her, thinking back on her story of how Finley had introduced Jeffers to the rich woman he married. Finley, she once had said, liked to play with people the way a cat did a mouse. Did he play so cruelly with his own sister?

"So Danny is your son?" Paavo asked.

"Danny told me that you had met. I'm sure you figured out that he was mine long before tonight."

"Did Jeffers know about the boy?"

"No. And I didn't want him to know. That was why Danny stayed with Quint."

"Finley didn't know who the father was either?"

"Oh, he knew. He hated Greg for it."

"Yet he invited him here."

She folded her hands. "That was only because he hated me more."

"I can't believe that." Paavo once had a sister. He couldn't imagine ever hating her.

Moira took a deep breath. "It goes back a long time. Finley, you see, isn't my real brother. He's a stepbrother. My mother married his father when I was ten years old. Finley was twenty-one at the time, and already out of the house, on his own. I was a very shy little girl, and he was nice to me—the only one who had ever paid any attention to me since my mother left my father. But that's another story."

Paavo nodded, encouraging her to go on.

Moira continued. "My mother's second marriage was even shorter than her first. After four years, she divorced Kendall. A year later, her own drunk driving killed her. No one knew where to find my father, and I would have been made a ward of the court except that Finley heard about it. When my one-time stepfather didn't want Veronica's brat, as he called me, Finley brought me to live with him."

"He was then about twenty-five or twenty-six?"

"Yes. That was the problem, you see. I was a fifteen-year-old kid, and I developed a king-size adolescent crush on him. He was a *man*, after all, not just a boy like I saw in school, and he had protected me from foster homes and juvenile care centers. He, though, fell in love."

Paavo drew in his breath. He could imagine that Moira had been a strange child, not the type that's popular in high school. He could see her turning to Finley in her awkward loneliness.

"But you didn't actually love him in return," he said.

"No. As I grew older, I began to meet people I could relate to. People who didn't find me weird, but interesting. Not ugly, but mystical. I found friends."

Paavo understood. The growing-up process that teens go through, the maturity that causes them to want to leave home and go off on their own, caused Moira to want to leave Finley.

She hung her head. "We fought all the time. He said he wanted to marry me, and I called him a lecherous old man who took advantage of a young, innocent girl. In time, I even convinced myself it was true. I ran away."

"Where did you go?"

"San Francisco. I'd learned a lot about food and nutrition and its effect on the spirit from Finley. He'd been interested in that sort of thing as long as I'd known him. Even before it became fashionable. So I moved to the Haight-Ashbury, where I could disappear among all the other runaways and lost souls."

Something about her tone made Paavo say, "That was where you met Greg Jeffers."

She nodded. "He was like no one I'd ever known before. Charming, fun, and the handsomest man I'd ever seen. He was living with an older, well-known lawyer, a woman. He'd take me to her place while she went to work."

"Nice guy," Paavo said. It seemed Jeffers had made a career of living off rich women.

"I know." Moira rubbed her forehead. "I should have known better. I guess I did, deep down. But I ignored everything except Greg, and how much I loved him. Then one day the woman walked in and found the two of us together. He refused to see me after that. Later, I found out I was pregnant. I never told him."

"How did you support yourself?"

She gave him a grim smile. "I read tarot, rune stones, crystals, I-Ching. I'd have read tea leaves if it meant a buck. I took all the beautiful, spiritual things that Finley had taught me and used them in the cheapest way. I felt like hell for it."

"Why didn't you leave?" Paavo asked.

"Where would I go? It was a horrible life, though. Horrible. I learned that there is much to fear in this world. When Finley found us—Danny and me—he said as long as there was no other man in my life, I was free to go with him. If I hadn't, I would have been lost. Do you know what I mean, Paavo?"

He knew, and understood even better why she reminded him so much of Sybil. "Yes."

"I knew it," she whispered.

She didn't have to say that she never came to love Finley. In fact, Paavo suspected that if anything she resented him for the hold he had over her. "Did you keep your promise to him?"

"I had to. I'm a weak woman, Paavo. I knew what it was like to live on the streets, and I was afraid to go back to them. As Danny grew older, though, I thought more and more about leaving Finley. I'm sure he realized it, because one day Finley found my father working as a gardener in a small town in Sonoma County. Quint is my father."

"Quint." Angie had been right. "Go on."

"Finley had a dream for our future," Moira said, "one that also became my father's and Danny's, that we would run an inn together."

"And so you stayed?"

"Yes. I couldn't disappoint my father or my son. Then one day I looked in the mirror and saw that the strong young girl I once was had disappeared long ago, and in her place was a weak, frightened, loveless old woman. An apt partner for Finley. I learned to resent him as much as he did me."

"There's no reason to continue feeling that way," Paavo said.

"No, not now that Finley's gone. I guess this makes me your prime suspect. Doesn't it, Inspector?"

25

Angie watched Paavo, Martin, and Reginald Vane as they set out to check, once again, on the mud slide that blocked the road. The storm had eased a little as the afternoon wore on, and they hoped they could soon begin the long, tedious process of digging themselves out. Since Jeffers's death, everyone was more frightened than ever and even more anxious to get off this promontory.

Angie, Chelsea, and Bethel made a pact to stay together. Bethel had what she called a "touch of arthritis" in her hips and knees and couldn't walk very far. Chelsea was too heavy to move fast, and Angie, although she could walk far and fairly fast, remembered her difficulty climbing over the headland rocks on the beach with Paavo and didn't want to do anything to slow down the others.

Moira didn't want to be with anyone, preferring instead to lie down in her room. As much as Angie and the others thought it was foolish for her to be alone, it was clear that no one was willing to argue with her.

Seated in the drawing room, Bethel asked Chelsea to tell her about Elvis. Angie did her best to ignore them by trying to figure out, if it were up to her, how she'd redecorate the inn to make it more inviting. She loved redecorating. At the moment, the inn reminded her of something out of *Wuthering Heights*.

To begin with, the library was much too dark. A gloomy library wouldn't attract anyone. She'd love to play around with the window coverings and furniture.

"Why don't we go into the library?" she asked.

Engrossed in their discussion of Elvis, neither woman bothered to answer.

"We need to find a new angle," Bethel said. "Something that hasn't been done before."

"But what?" Chelsea asked, then sighed wearily.

Angie couldn't believe them. "You can always play 'Love Me Tender' backward. Call it a way to conjure spirits. Or at least to cause a primal scream or two from the audience."

"That's an idea," Chelsea said.

Bethel didn't move or say a word. She was either giving it serious thought or she'd been struck catatonic by how ludicrous it was.

"I'm going to the library," Angie said. "Anyone care to join me?"

"'RedneT eM evoL'," Bethel said thoughtfully. "I believe it can lead to a higher spiritual consciousness. Don't you, Chelsea?"

Rolling her eyes, Angie left.

In the library, she pulled back the heavy drapes. They needed to be tied or hooked back off the windows. Even better would be to take the drapes down and replace them with light, lacy curtains or simple wooden blinds in white or cream.

She slid small wooden chairs beside the windows, then lifted the drapes over the back of each so she could get a sense of the room with more light in it. If it ever stopped raining, she'd open the windows and let the place air out. She hated the constant damp, decaying, musty smell in the air.

On each side of the fireplace stood a high-backed, peacock-blue armchair, and beside the chairs stood bookcases, so that the chairs were wedged between a hot fireplace and dusty books. Not a comfortable spot to sit. As a result, no one ever used them.

She pulled one of the chairs out from its wall and decided to place it in front of the fireplace, first facing the mantel. No, it would look better, friendlier, if the chairs faced each other. She went to the other chair and tried to pull it out into the middle of the room as well, but it wouldn't move. Tugging harder, she watched an electric cord fly loose as the chair suddenly pulled free of the wall.

The wire ran upward from beneath the chair to the top of the wainscoting midway up the wall, then disappeared behind the bookshelves, probably into an electrical outlet.

She got down on her hands and knees and peered under the chair to see what the cord had been connected to. A little black box was taped to the bottom of the seat. She yanked it off.

It looked like a miniature projector, with a tiny lens. She plugged the cord into it, but couldn't figure out how to turn it on. The entire device must have been operated from some remote location. But what was it? And why was it there?

Only one person in this inn seemed to have any idea about electronics. Reginald Vane.

So much had already happened around here that had made her suspicious of everything and everyone. The thought that it had all been orchestrated by a mad scientist made a lot of sense.

Who else could it be but Reginald? On the other hand, she had been warmed by his obvious interest in Chelsea. The two seemed somehow peculiarly right for each other. Or would be, if only Chelsea forgot her macabre love for a dead man. Could Reginald be a murderer? And if so, could his interest in Chelsea put her life in danger?

Angie had to find out. She needed to show this to Paavo, to tell him all about her finding.

She put the projector back under the chair and slid the peacock-blue chairs back against the wall. No sense alerting whoever had put it there that they'd been found out. What could the projector possibly be for, though? Could it be used to make ghostly holograms on demand? Just like at Disneyland's haunted house? Chelsea said she saw a ghost the night of their séance, and Reginald Vane said he believed her.

Angie went into the hall to check on Bethel and Chelsea in the drawing room, since they'd agreed to keep an eye on each other. They were there, still planning Bethel's return. They were fine since, after all, the house was empty.

Empty.

The perfect time for checking out Reginald Vane's room—the sole room up on the third floor. Angie had never even been up there yet. If Vane was behind this, if he used electronic devices in some strange way, his room would be the perfect hiding place for them.

She really ought not go searching, though. She ought to wait for Paavo. To tell him about it.

Of course once he returned Vane would return, too. They couldn't very well search Vane's room with him looking over their shoulders.

She'd have to do it on her own. Paavo wouldn't like it, but then he wasn't here, was he? If she didn't find anything, she wouldn't have to tell him she'd even looked. And if she did, he wouldn't mind that she'd looked. Case closed.

She went into the kitchen to get the set of spare keys, then snuck up the stairs to Vane's room. As she'd suspected, the door was locked. Angie unlocked it and walked in. The room was immaculate. If Vane wasn't an electrical engineer, he should go into the housecleaning business. Angie would hire him in a minute.

This had been Elise's room, the pathetic, lonely, ever crying Elise. It was small, with a peaked ceiling and two dormer windows. But the view of the ocean was breathtaking. The room looked directly out upon the cliffs from which Elise had jumped.

Suppressing a shudder, Angie began to look around the room.

No electronics were lying about, but that didn't surprise her. The man could hardly keep such things out in the open. She searched his closet. Nothing.

Judging from the outside of the house, the roofline was quite a bit wider than the room, which meant there could be eaves on either side of it creating attics. Now all she had to do was figure out how to get into them.

In the back of a closet, she found a small, half-size door. She opened it. Two VCRs, a reel-to-reel tape recorder, a timer, a small framed mirror, batteries of all sizes, and several flashlights filled the space. No televisions, so just what Vane did with the VCRs was anybody's guess.

Incredible. How did he get so much paraphernalia in here? she wondered. Were Finley and Moira so oblivious that the man practically set up his own Radio Shack and they hadn't even noticed? But as she thought of Finley and Moira, she realized, maybe so.

What did he do with all this stuff? It had to somehow be connected to the mysterious ghost sightings around Hill Haven. He was the one who kept running around warning people of the ghosts, telling them that they ought to leave. Was all this equipment to back up his pronouncements? Obviously he had planned all this before ever coming to the inn, but why? And just what did he do with everything?

She'd get Paavo up here and he'd be able to figure it out. He wasn't exactly Mr. Fix-it, but men seemed to understand this sort of thing. As if it came with their Y chromosome or something.

She backed out of the attic and quietly shut the door. She had to get out of here; no telling when they'd be back. Wouldn't Paavo be surprised when she told him!

She was crossing Vane's room when she glanced at his bureau. What if, just as he brought the equipment before he ever arrived at the inn, he also brought something that explained his actions?

It might be right there, in one of those drawers. How long could it take her to find out? Not long. They wouldn't be back quite yet. At least she hoped not.

She dashed over to the drawers and began to open them. Socks. T-shirts. Purple bikini shorts. (For Reginald Vane? Unbelievable.) Waffle-textured thermal underwear. (That was more like it.)

She shut the drawer and went on to the next. It was empty. So was the one after that.

But in the bottom drawer of his dresser she found a large padded envelope and inside it some papers and a Bible. Could this be what she was looking for?

She could feel her nerves tense as she carried the envelope to the bed and slid the contents out. Would she find something here that could cause a man to commit murder?

She picked up the Bible. It was old—old like the diary and letters that belonged to Susannah. The dried leather cover felt as if it might crumble to dust under her fingers.

The pages, almost tissue-thin, had gold leaf on the edges. Carefully turning them, she saw nothing unusual until she reached the back cover. There she found a hand-written paragraph in an ink so faded, and a hand so stylized, she wasn't sure she'd be able to read it. Following it was a list of names, written in different inks and by different hands. Her glance traveled down the page to the bottom where, in bold, black letters, she saw the words, "Reginald Vane, born 1950." The Vane family Bible.

But why bring it here?

She wove back through the list of names, reading about Vane after Vane, until she reached the topmost entry. The room was growing dark as evening fell and she turned on the lamp on the nightstand to better see the faint ink. Under the bright light, reading slowly and carefully, she was able to read the words:

I give this book to my adopted son, Benjamin Arthur Vane, to record for all time that, although he came to us as a poor orphan, the son of Jack and Elise Sempler, he is now and evermore shall be known as a Vane. Let him and all his heirs record the Vane family on these pages, and may they prosper on this earth. Your loving father, Lucas Allen Vane.

Jack and Elise. The Vanes, then, were the childless family that Ezra and Susannah Sempler gave Jack's son to. Ezra must have told them that the child was an orphan, and they took him and clearly opened their hearts to him. And now Reginald was here. The last survivor of Jack's line. Was he coming to proclaim his heritage?

She unfolded the sheets of paper. An article entitled "Ghosts of the Pacific Northwest" from a 1967 copy of *Look* magazine lay before her. In it she found photos of the Sempler house, Jack's and Susannah's portraits, and a brief retelling of the love story of Jack and Elise.

As Angie looked at the papers in her hands, she was struck by the sadness of it, the senselessness, and the loss.

Could Elise's great-grandson be murdering people because of her story? That seemed too horrible to contemplate. But what other explanation could there be for the happenings at Hill Haven?

Quickly she put the material back in the envelope and placed the envelope in the drawer. As soon as Paavo returned, she'd tell him everything. She turned around.

Reginald Vane, his bow tie bobbing in agitation, stood in the doorway watching her.

26

"*It's still a mess out there,*" Paavo said to Moira as he walked into the drawing room. "We couldn't even get close to the area near the mud slide. As it was, we nearly lost Vane in a slide of his own making." He went to the fireplace, trying to thaw his nearly frozen hands and feet. Bethel and Chelsea sat at a table scribbling on a large notepad, oblivious to the outside world. "Where's Angie?" he asked.

Moira sat facing the fireplace. "Does it look at all promising?"

"The water's going down, but still running too fast to try to cross. There's a chance it'll be crossable tomorrow, as long as we don't get any more heavy rains. Why isn't Angie here with you? Have you seen her?"

Moira looked around. "I'm sure she's nearby. What about the search for Patsy?"

"We've scoured the hill, over and over. She had to have been swept out to sea, got off this hill somehow, or is deliberately hiding."

"Are you giving up?" Moira asked.

"No."

Moira nodded.

"I told Angie to stay with you," Paavo said. "Didn't she?"

"I was lying down. I just got here."

"Bethel, Chelsea." Paavo walked toward them. "Where has Angie gone?"

"Angie?" Chelsea looked around. "She was right here."

"She gave me a wonderful idea for my channeling," Bethel added. "She's so clever."

"Damn!" He ran up the stairs two at a time to their room, and in scant seconds he was back. "She's not up there. What about the kitchen?"

"I don't know," Moira said. "She might be there."

"I don't believe this," he muttered as he hurried down the hall, looking in the dining room and the kitchen, his heart beginning to beat a little too fast, a little too fearfully, in spite of himself. She wasn't there.

She was nearby, he told himself. She was fine. She was just poking around where she shouldn't be, but that didn't mean she'd come to any harm. She never listened, that was all. Someday maybe he'd get her to listen. If he didn't wring her neck first for worrying him.

He ran to the library. If he knew her, she was probably sitting in there reading a book.

Small chairs had been moved near the windows and draperies lay over them. "Moira," he shouted. "Come here. Fast." He had no patience for her slow, sleepwalking ways now.

In no time, he heard her gasp. "What happened?"

"I'd hoped you would know."

"It's much too bright in here," she said, walking into the room.

He ignored her and ran to the foyer. Which way? Where could Angie have gone?

The banging of a door, followed by shouts and the sound of running footsteps, stopped him cold.

"Good God," Moira cried, looking toward the ceiling where the cry had come from. "The ghosts are sounding more human all the time."

"That's no ghost," Paavo said, running up the stairs. "That's Angie."

He put his arms out and Angie ran into them full steam, clutching his neck in a stranglehold. He held her tight, relief filling him.

Reginald Vane was right behind her, bellowing almost as loud as Angie was shrieking. "You caught her! Thank God!" he cried. "She's a thief! I wouldn't be surprised if she is a murderer as well."

"Arrest that man!" Angie yelled. "He's a murderer. I have proof!"

"You idiot woman!" Vane yelled. "You won't get away with this. I caught you red-handed. The jig's up."

"You won't get away this time, you, you . . . Sempler!"

"Quiet," Paavo ordered. "Both of you. Let's go talk this over."

"Where's your gun, Paavo?" Angie asked as Paavo held her arm and led her toward the library, where Moira waited. "You can't trust him."

"Don't worry about it, Angie."

"She doesn't have to worry," Vane said, "but I do. You came here with her. How do I know the two of you aren't in cahoots?"

Angie glared at Vane as Paavo took her to the center of the library and stopped. "Will you can't stop using that Wild West jargon, Reginald? It won't go any easier on you just because you sound like Wyatt Earp."

"This is the Wild West," Vane intoned. "And I just caught Belle Starr."

Angie flushed. "You—"

"Both of you sit down," Paavo ordered. "Now."

They sat without argument.

Paavo gave each a long, cold stare. Angie could imagine what it must feel like to be on the hot seat in Homicide. "Let's start at the beginning. Angie?" he said.

She sat primly on the edge of her chair and cleared her throat. "Well," she said. "It's good we came to this room, because it all started here."

Paavo glanced at the room with the draperies and chairs all out of place. "I suspected that."

"I decided to make the room better looking. Sorry, Moira. I moved the drapes and chairs, but when I did, I found a cord and a little electronic device attached to one of them. It's under the seat on that one."

Paavo walked over to the peacock-blue chair Angie pointed to and tilted it, finding the mini-projector. He looked the thing over, then gave it to Moira.

"That projector," Angie continued, "made me think of who, of the people here, knew the most about electronic devices. I came up with Reginald." She cast a pointed stare his way. "I decided to look in his room, and sure enough there were tape recorders, VCRs and other things in the attic off his bedroom. I know it was wrong of me to look—but we're dealing with murder here."

"We're dealing with breaking and entering!" Reginald roared. "So what if I have electronic equipment. Most people do, Miss Amalfi! Finley wasn't electrocuted. His head was smashed in. Forgive me, Miss Tay." He looked at Paavo helplessly. "I fail to see any connection."

"You haven't heard the most important part." Angie glanced from one to the other.

"Go ahead," Paavo said.

"I found his family Bible."

"Did you both hear that? There! She admitted it. I demand she be arrested," Vane yelled.

"I put it back exactly where I found it. But the thing is, the Bible showed that Reginald Vane is the great-grandchild of Jack and Elise Sempler. It proves he's the killer."

"My good woman," Vane said, jumping to his feet. "It proves no more than that my family has passed a Bible from one generation to the next. Years ago I came across a magazine article with the names of some ghosts here in the States. The same names as in my family Bible. That was when I learned about the American side of my family, when I learned that there was more to me than being the last of a rather unimportant line in Canada. I discovered a home, a heritage. A birthright."

"But it's not your home," Moira said. "Finley bought it."

"That's the problem," Vane admitted. "With this much land and this view, even a vacant house was priced much higher than I could afford. The owner was a distant relative who lived in Connecticut, never even saw the place, and cared nothing about it."

"So why are you here now?" Angie asked.

"Six months ago, I learned someone was interested in buying the place. I also found out that Tay was having trouble getting together enough cash for the sale. I volunteered to pick up a piece of the house on the condition that if Finley couldn't make a go of the inn, I could assume his bank loan, and he would lose his down payment. He agreed, in writing, to those terms."

"That was a terrific deal for you," Angie said. "A good reason for you not to want to see this inn succeed."

"Yes." He folded his hands. "It was. Unfortunately, I wasn't the only one Finley duped into making a partner. One day I received a call from Patsy Jeffers, saying she and her husband were part owners, and that there were others. I knew then that I had to find a way to scare them off, to have them pull out of the deal with Finley or we'd all end up in court. I could no more afford a lawyer than I could this house." Vane lowered his head and sighed.

Worry and weariness lined Vane's high forehead; his mouth had taken on a grayish cast, his lips turned down in a frown. Even his straight, thinning hair seemed somehow to have shrunk.

"In other words," Paavo suggested, "if you got the others to pull out, Finley would be that much less solvent, and you could get the inn that much sooner."

"That was my thinking. So I brought my equipment and pretended to be a spiritualist. I thought I'd scare them away. I never expected that the group Finley brought together would think that the place being haunted only made it that much more attractive!"

"Killing Patsy and Running Spirit," Angie said, her certainty that Reginald Vane was behind all this beginning to slip away, "also lessened the competition for the place."

Reginald shook his head. "So what? Once Finley was gone, I learned he'd made agreements, written and verbal, with everyone here. The legal fees alone to sort them out would be far more than I could afford. My dreams of owning this house are gone. Everything is."

"Why did you continue with the noises after we learned Finley was dead?"

"It seemed right. There are those in this house who want to believe in the Sempler ghosts. I let them."

Paavo leaned back in the chair and looked at Moira. "Questions?"

She studied Vane for a moment. "How did you make the thumping noises?"

"The magazine article said that my great-great-grandfather Ezra was very paranoid about his wealth.

He moved to this hill for that reason. These days, one would call him a survivalist, I believe. Anyway, he was rumored to have built this house with secret passages so that he could hide if it ever was attacked. From an engineering standpoint, it's a simple matter to determine where any such passages might be located. Equally simple was to rig up speakers. Using the VCR timers, I set up prerecorded tapes with the kinds of sounds I wanted."

"But Chelsea and I saw Elise's ghost one night," Angie said, then glanced at Paavo. "I should say, we saw what we thought was Elise's ghost."

Reginald laughed. "I heard the commotion that night and knew you and Miss Worthington were awake and that no one was outdoors. I used a mirror and flashlight from the attic and reflected them on the rocks near the cliffs. I thought it might help Chelsea, I mean, Miss Worthington, get over being upset."

"Because you knew what had upset her," Paavo said.

Reginald stared at him. "No!"

Paavo paced. "Since you knew about the secret passage, you also knew it led to Chelsea's room."

Angie sat upright in her chair.

"I didn't," Vane said.

"You had to have known, between your engineering background and going up and down the passageway— and your obvious interest in Miss Worthington."

Vane stood. "Don't tell her. I beg you."

Angie stared at him, appalled. "You went into her room!"

Vane spun toward her. "Don't look at me that way. I meant no harm. I'd never harm her. This world is hard on her and she's retreated to the spiritual. I understand that. She loves someone else. She'd never care for me. Good God, I'm twice her age! But that night she'd been so upset at dinner I was worried. I just wanted to see that she was all right."

Angie was furious. "Considering the deaths that had happened here, how could you frighten her like that?"

"I don't know." He hung his head.

Angie looked at the lonely man before her, hanging his head at his adolescent stunt, when all he wanted was to be close to Chelsea and to see if she could care for him. "Tell her what you told us," Angie said, her voice low and gentle. "Tell her it was just you."

He blushed, but his eyes were bleak. "You're right. It was *just* me. She should know that. She shouldn't be worried that it was someone who meant her harm. Or some ghost. It was just a very foolish person."

"I'm sorry, Reginald," Angie said quietly.

He drew himself up and smoothed his bow tie, the epitome of the British stiff upper lip. "She has every right to hate me for this."

Angie mentally crossed her fingers for Chelsea's sake. "She might surprise you."

"One more question, Vane," Paavo said. "What was the projector for?"

"I planned to liven up one of Moira's séances," he said. "Using a remote, I could turn on the projector to where I have a tape of the Sempler photos. Unfortunately, when she finally held a séance, you were nearby, Inspector, and I was afraid you might walk in on us. I couldn't chance it—except for about one second—the other night."

"Moira," Paavo turned to the woman, who'd been sitting in quiet surprise listening to all this. "What do you think of Vane's story?"

She hesitated only a moment. "I believe him."

Paavo stood and slowly paced back and forth in front of Angie. "That leaves the most troublesome part of this afternoon's episode, Angelina—the fact that you broke into and entered his room, without permission."

Mr. Inspector, not Paavo, stood before her, carrying the full weight of the law in his hands. She felt as if all the blood had drained from her body. "I did not! I used the key. I'm an employee here. I had every right."

"Mr. Vane might want you to argue that to the sheriff. Mr. Vane has rights, too."

"The sheriff?" Angie shuddered at the thought of being in the hands of Sheriff Clark G. Butz, even if it did give her the chance to find out if his middle name was Gable. "But I was just trying to help!"

Paavo leaned over her chair, his blue eyes piercing. "That's why there are police, Angie. If you suspect something, you call an officer of the law, you don't take the law into your own hands. Is that clear?"

"Yes." Her voice was tiny, her eyes wide. She glanced at Reginald, wondering what he'd decide to do.

"I hate the idea of anyone going into my room uninvited," Vane said evenly. "I hate the idea of anyone going through my things."

Angie's hopes sank.

"On the other hand, my actions practically invited anyone with an inquiring mind to do just that. This was all my fault. I couldn't possibly press charges against her. I can only hope Miss Worthington will be as forgiving."

Just then, Angie saw Bethel and Chelsea walk into the library, arm in arm, smiling broadly. "We thought we heard voices," Chelsea said. "Did we miss anything?"

"Nothing at all," Angie replied.

"Good," Bethel said. "We've got a surprise for all of you. We've been practicing in secret all afternoon, but we think we're ready. Chelsea?"

Chelsea nodded.

"Okay, here goes. 'Love Me Tender,' backward. *La, la, laaa*," she trilled, so that they could both start off on the same key. More or less.

27

"I feel sorry for Reginald, despite everything," Angie said as she and Paavo walked into their room.

"It's hard to believe he thought he could scare people away when money is involved. Money makes people desperate. They'll risk their lives before they walk away from it," Paavo said. The room was chilly. He knelt in front of the fireplace and began to stack kindling and logs.

"Reginald had reason, opportunity, and motive." She sat on the bed. "He confessed to rigging up the house with his electronics. Why do I find I want to believe him when he says he's innocent of doing anything more?"

"Most murderers can be quite persuasive," Paavo said. "Especially when they have no reason to confess."

"We can't overlook Chelsea, even though she's my friend." Angie kicked off her shoes and scooted back against the headboard. "Running Spirit made fun of her, Finley duped her, and who knows how she felt about Miss Greer or Patsy. I guess anyone who claims to be in love with a ghost could be capable of anything."

Paavo couldn't help but smile at Angie's forlorn words.

"Now Bethel," Angie continued, "I think would be a lot more capable of murdering someone than Chelsea. Especially after the way Finley and Running Spirit didn't take her seriously and wanted to cut her out of the inn."

"That's true." Paavo stood and watched the kindling burn, waiting to see if the logs would catch. "Martin's reasons would be the same."

"And Bethel said Martin had borrowed money to invest here. But why would they want to harm Miss Greer or Patsy? Maybe we're going about this the wrong way. Instead of thinking about the suspects, we should look at the victims."

"We don't know that Patsy is a victim," Paavo replied. "She's also a suspect. No one here knows anything about Greer, which makes it tough to figure out who'd want her dead. I don't think that's going to work."

"Hell. There's only one person who knew them well enough to want them all dead."

"Who's that?"

"Moira Tay."

Paavo came and sat beside her. "Moira once said a lot of people brought their dreams to this inn. I think that's where the key is."

"Interesting," Angie said. "Her words went along with something Bethel said to me earlier today."

"What was that?"

"That this place, this inn, was supposed to be a dream come true for her and Martin. It was supposed to give her a big comeback."

"Like Reginald's foolish dream about returning to his birthright." Paavo reached for the matches.

"Running Spirit came to find success. He'd lived a life of selling his love to women with money. Isn't it ironic that his dream could go no further than to fraudulently sell himself to a larger public? To have lots of people pay for the pleasure of loving him spiritually?"

Paavo took her hand. "Don't forget Patsy, whose only fault was to love too completely and too thoughtlessly."

"Yes," Angie said. Leave it to Paavo to recognize the foolishness of love. "Chelsea, too, seeking in a past life what has eluded her in this one. Pinning her hopes on a ghost, like a heroine in a fantasy novel, only to discover the reason they're called fantasies."

As she watched Paavo add more kindling, she realized she too had come to the inn because of a dream—not only Finley's false promise of an interesting, creative job, but of being here with Paavo and it being a place their love could grow and flourish.

"Then there was Finley," Angie said, going to his side, "conning everyone just so he could get money to show people his food philosophy. That seems so trivial for all that happened."

"He had another reason," Paavo said. "He and Moira weren't brother and sister. Their parents were briefly married, but soon divorced. Finley, though, fell in love. She thought she still loved Danny's father—Greg Jeffers—"

"Greg!" Angie exclaimed as she sat down, her initial surprise giving way to understanding as she thought of all she'd seen and heard over these few days. "That explains a lot, doesn't it? Especially the strange way Moira acted over Finley's death. I found it hard to believe anyone could be so unmoved by the death of a brother."

"She hated Finley," Paavo said, sitting on a chair beside her. "Finley introduced Greg to Patsy, got him out of the way, but it still didn't cause Moira to love him. He brought Jeffers here so that Moira could see what her dream lover had become. But he didn't want Jeffers to know he had a son. That was why he had Danny hide while Jeffers was here."

"The whole thing is sick." Angie couldn't hide her disgust.

"I think Finley's dream was Moira. To find her love."

"And what was Moira's?" Angie asked softly.

"I don't think she has one," he said.

Angie had to smile. "The most spiritual one here, and she's the realist. Wouldn't you know it?" But her smile faded as she thought of how Moira's gaze followed Paavo. She knew, then, what Moira's dream was, even if Paavo didn't.

"When you met Moira," she began, her words slow at first, hesitant; then they picked up and soon tumbled out. "I don't know why, I don't know how, but that changed you. And you were never the same with me."

She waited, but he still didn't answer. She reached for his hand.

"It wasn't her," he said finally.

She didn't speak. It was his turn to talk, to explain.

"It wasn't Moira. It was someone she reminded me of." He walked away from her then and went to the window to peer out at the blackness below. After a long while, he spoke again. "You know what first love is like, Angie. The kind that you have when you're still pretty much a kid. The sun rises and sets on that person. Even their flaws seem perfect. You think you'll die if they leave you. And if you live to be a hundred, you'll always remember the special feeling you had with them. A feeling that never comes again, maybe because you learn to never give yourself so completely again."

"I know." Her words were quiet. Sometimes it wasn't only a first love that made you feel that way. "It's heaven and hell at the same time."

"Seeing Moira made me remember." Blue eyes lifted

to her. "I remembered how I'd vowed to never open myself up that way again. Not to anyone."

Angie shut her eyes at the pain in his voice.

"I remembered how it was to be young and in love, with lots of years, lots of dreams, ahead of me," Paavo said.

She stared at the floor, unsure she wanted to hear this.

"I walked out on her, Angie."

Shock coursed through her.

"When the woman I thought I loved needed me, I wasn't there. I failed her. Moira Tay's so damn much like her that if I can help her, I will."

She stared at him.

"Yeah." He gave a wry laugh. "Here I bet you thought I was perfect." He walked to the window and looked out, his hands in his pockets again in that 'do not touch' pose that had become so familiar to her.

"You're close enough to perfect for me," she said.

"All your words about being proud of me looking for Patsy—she's a stranger. I guess you never thought about how I treat women I supposedly love."

"Maybe you couldn't have helped her, and deep down you knew it. Or maybe this time you did fail. It happens, even with people you love. That's why there's this thing called forgiveness."

"Why don't you go see how Chelsea's doing, or something."

She'd never known what it meant to be lonely or to be rejected until she met a cop who didn't know what it meant to be loved. He was teaching her; she had to do a better job teaching him.

He had turned his back to her, but she went to him and wrapped her arms around his waist, pressing her face between his shoulder blades. "I'm not going anywhere, Paavo."

"Don't." He pried her arms loose and walked toward the door. She followed.

"We talked about dreams," he said. "This inn did show me the stuff dreams are made of. Things like waking up next to you each morning." As he opened the door, he bent forward to give her what was only a quick kiss, yet it carried his longing, his loneliness. "Why do you think I never dared to?" he whispered.

"Coward!" she cried.

His features sharpened in response to the word.

"You're right about this inn," she said. "It's no more than a dream. It's not at all what our lives would be like if we were together, because then we would have to deal with families and jobs and friends and all those day-to-day things that get in the way of two people simply enjoying being with each other. But that's what life's all about."

"I'm just not sure, Angie. I need time."

"I know." She touched his face, ran her hand along the side of his hair, his ear. "My handsome, logical, analytical Paavo. I know this doesn't make sense to you. Maybe not to me either. You've got time. I can wait." She smiled. "A little while, at least."

Slowly his serious expression broke into a grin and he took her in his arms. "I love you, Angelina. If I can't be definite about much else, at least believe that."

He gave the door a light kick and it swung shut.

The next morning, the good news was that the rain had stopped. The bad news was that the fog had come in, as thick and damp as the traditional pea soup.

Angie and Paavo rode with the Baymans, Chelsea, and Vane down to the mud slide in the Bayman's old station wagon. They were going to try to find a way past it.

Paavo drove slowly and cautiously, visibility rarely more than five feet in front of him. But no one could bear to stay a moment longer than absolutely necessary at Hill Haven. Especially not with Miss Greer's, Finley's, and now Running Spirit's corpses rotting around them, along with the ever-present terror that one of them just might be next. Safety in numbers was their constant slogan. No one, ever, wanted to be alone.

When they reached the last spot in the road wide enough to turn the station wagon around, they stopped and parked. They didn't want the same thing to happen to it as had happened to Finley's van the first day it rained.

They walked toward the slide area.

"Now that the rain has let up, why don't we go down to the beach and simply walk along the coast?" Chelsea asked.

"Because the beach disappears in parts and becomes a straight drop from cliffs onto rocks that are underwater during high tide," Paavo said.

"Besides," Martin added, "I don't think there's a town or road along the coast for twenty-five miles in either direction."

"Oh," Chelsea responded. She glanced at Reginald, but he turned his head.

Angie and the others hadn't said anything to her about Reginald's behavior, hoping he'd tell her. It seemed to Angie that he hadn't—and wasn't about to.

Finally, they reached the mud slide. They took shovels, buckets, hoes, and spades and worked to fill the buckets with mud and then empty them by tossing the mud off the edge of the road to drop to the ocean. They huddled close, because any one of them who wandered too far could be lost in the fog.

It was slow, tedious work, made even more so because the mud was so soggy that as they dug, more slid down to cover the spots they cleared.

After a couple hours, they saw the fruitlessness of their task. If it didn't rain again, though, the following day the ground would be a lot drier. Perhaps then they could clear the road, find Sheriff Butz and tell him their horrible story of the madness at Hill Haven, and then, go home.

Seeing that the mud slide was impossible to clear, they used their energy pushing and otherwise coaxing the van backwards up the narrow road until it could be turned around and driven back to the house. At least they achieved something.

Wet, cold, and hungry, the group returned once more to Hill Haven. Angie decided to cook an early dinner, since everyone had missed lunch.

She looked around for Moira, then decided to make a cheese soufflé with braised vegetables, boiled potatoes, and a salad. It would be fast, but filling.

She went out to the root cellar to get a bunch of potatoes. She'd discovered, after her fright with Chelsea, a leather thong to hold the door open while she was down there. On her way back, she heard familiar voices. She couldn't see anyone through the thick fog, but they were close. She leaned against a tree, listening.

"I've never known anyone like you," Reginald Vane said. "In this day, to find a woman whose heart is so pure, so generous, as to forgive me. You're a miracle, Chelsea Worthington."

"I'm not, Reginald. I'm nothing, not even pretty. I'm plain—and fat."

"Your figure is full, like those of beautiful women throughout history. You have the hips of Venus, the waist of Godiva, the—pardon me—the bosom of Marie

Antoinette. Your hair is the color of a Titian, your eyes the pools of Rome, your lips perfect as a Rembrandt."

"You're making me blush, Reggie. You're so clever. I don't have any such words."

"You don't have to speak, Miss Worthington. To be with you is heaven. I'll just look."

"Not . . . not touch?"

Angie strained to see, but the fog was too thick.

"I wouldn't presume."

"I love noble men!"

"Oh! Miss Worthington! Are you sure you want to do this?"

Angie stepped closer, tripped over a tree root, and fell with a splat onto a mud puddle.

"What was that?" Reginald whispered. "Let's go back to the house. I won't have your reputation compromised."

"Anything you say, Reggie."

Angie sat up. She and the vegetables were covered with brown, sticky mud. And now there was nothing left to see or hear. *Damn*!

Angie changed her clothes and had completed all the dinner preparations except for putting the soufflé in the oven when she began to gather everyone together. She wanted them in the dining room and seated before she served the soufflé.

She found everyone but Moira.

The others quickly grew anxious and worried over Moira's absence. They were ready to go on a search for her when she burst into the house.

"Paavo!" she cried. "Have you seen Danny? Was he with you?"

"Who's this Danny person?" Bethel asked.

Moira ignored her and spoke only to Paavo. "I haven't

seen him all morning. I went to Quint's house, but he wasn't there. He was supposed to come for his home study. He's never late like this!"

"Who is this person? I demand to know," Bethel repeated.

"He's my son," Moira said.

Bethel's mouth dropped open.

"I've searched everywhere—the house, the grounds—calling his name, but he never answered." Her eyes filled with tears. "Help me, Paavo. Whatever this, this horror is, it can't happen to Danny, not my boy."

He gripped her shoulders. "It'll be all right."

"I tell myself that, but I'm so scared. Where can he be? I want him home. Safe."

"We'll find him. We'll search the house and the grounds."

Her eyes held a hint of hysteria. "Just like we did the night Patsy disappeared."

Paavo maneuvered Moira toward Angie, who placed a comforting arm around the woman's waist. Paavo let her go. "We'll find Danny."

Anxiety and worry showed on everyone's faces. Angie offered her hand to Moira, who gripped it so hard Angie feared her bones might snap. She walked Moira to the drawing room to sit.

Chelsea began to cry. The others spoke in low murmurs. The similarities with what had happened to Finley were at the fore of all their minds, and Patsy was still missing.

Angie refused to consider that anyone would hurt a child, no matter how deranged he or she was. Danny knew this land like the back of his hand. He was busily doing some very boyish thing and lost track of time. They all did. But even as she told herself that, she knew Danny wouldn't do anything that would cause his mother this much worry. As fear prickled her skin, she felt her own eyes well with tears. "We'll find him," she said to Moira, trying to find courage in her words.

Paavo, Martin, and Reginald decided they'd look for Danny outdoors. Bethel, Chelsea, Moira, and Angie would search the house and nearby grounds.

"I'd feel better if you came with me," Paavo said to Angie.

"I'd only slow you down, stop you from climbing around in areas that a boy might go. I'll stay with the women."

"Don't get separated. You'll be safe if you're all together."

"I'll be careful."

"Take this." Paavo handed her his .38 revolver. "Put it in your pocket." He glanced at the tight slacks she wore. "Or somewhere that you can get to it fast."

"I don't want it."

"Whoever it is has killed more than once. I won't leave here until I'm sure you can defend yourself, if necessary."

"All right." She took the gun. "But now you have to be extra careful."

"I will." He kissed her hard and then quickly turned away and went to join Martin and Reginald outside.

She went back to Chelsea and Bethel, who were waiting for her in the drawing room. Moira had joined them.

"Should we go out and check the root cellar?" Angie asked.

"Martin will," Bethel said. "He mentioned it to me as he left."

"What about the passage between the walls that Paavo found, and the space under the eaves off Reginald's room?" Angie asked.

"Chelsea can look in there," Bethel said. "See if her friend has been up to anything."

"He hasn't been."

"How do you know? He could be behind all this."

"How do you know it isn't Martin?"

"Because I've lived with him for twenty-nine years," she snapped. "I know the man. Martin wouldn't hurt a flea. But you've just met Vane. There's no reason for you to believe him."

"He's a nice man!" Chelsea said stubbornly.

"*Stop it!*" Moira clenched her fists, then raised them to her forehead. "Everyone here is either too nice, or too crazy, or too damn old to hurt anyone. But my son is missing! I don't want to hear one more word about anyone being too nice to do any of this, because it just isn't true!"

"It has to be someone from the town," Chelsea said. "Someone who doesn't want the inn to open."

"They can't get up here," Moira said. "The road is closed and the bridge is out."

"There might be a way that only townspeople know about," Bethel said. "You and Finley haven't been here long enough to tell something like that."

"But Quint and Danny have traveled all over this property, this whole promontory. They know every inch of it."

"Maybe that's it," Angie said. "Maybe Danny knew another way—a way that kids around here learn when they're little, and keep the knowledge of when they grow up. You know, playing haunted house or something, seeing who's brave enough to come up here at night, anything."

"Maybe Danny's missing because he knew something like that," Chelsea offered.

"No!" Moira's eyes welled. "Danny doesn't know anything. There's no reason anyone would hurt him."

"I'm sorry," Chelsea said. "I didn't mean it."

"I'm getting out of here," Moira said. She grabbed the raincoat she'd thrown over a chair. "I'm looking for him myself."

"I'm coming with you, then," Bethel said, reaching for her coat.

"Me, too," Chelsea said, putting on her rain slicker.

Angie looked at the rain slicker she'd worn earlier. It didn't have any pockets, and she wanted one to be able to carry Paavo's gun with her.

"I have to go upstairs and get a jacket," she said. "I'll be right back."

"I don't care what any of you do," Moira said. "Why don't you stay here and talk about how nice you all are, and how some boogeyman from the town has come up here and spirited my son away. Why don't you leave me alone? You've all been nothing but trouble ever since you arrived. All of you!"

She charged out the door, Chelsea and Bethel right behind her. "Hurry up, Angie," Chelsea called. "Catch up with us, okay?"

"Okay." Angie ran up to her room and found a jacket. She put the revolver in it and was hurrying back down the hall when she passed Chelsea's room and remembered Chelsea's remark about Reginald Vane searching the secret stairwell.

How could he search it, though? He'd gone out with Paavo.

Hell. She put the jacket on the bed, lit one of Chelsea's candles, unlocked then entered the secret passage. Inside, she lifted the candle upward, throwing light along the house's support beams and the backside of Sheetrock. She was, literally, inside the walls of the house, between the interior and exterior walls. The area was covered with dust and cobwebs. This time, though, she had no choice but to go through it. Quaking with disgust, she pushed the cobwebs aside, brushed imaginary spiders out of her hair and off her face and arms, then ran down the stairs.

The back of a paneled wall stood directly in front of her. Instead of pushing against the panels and ending up in the library, as Paavo had done, she decided to explore further and turned to the side, to an open area that looked like storage space. She knew that the library was to her left. The room to the right of the library was Finley's room. This open area had to be between the two.

"Danny?" she whispered, her voice sounding loud in the dark quiet.

She saw boxes piled high and opened one. It was full of old, dusty books. *The Castle of Otranto*—how appropriate. One of the first gothics ever, 1878 edition. Some book collector would probably love to get his hands on this.

She raised the candle. As best as she could tell, the space above her was essentially open all the way to the third floor and Reginald Vane's room.

Checking thoroughly to make sure Danny wasn't here and unconscious, or worse, she went over to the library panel. Paavo had said it was necessary to push on two spots at once. She looked it over with her candle. Putting the candle down, she placed her fingers on one corner, then carefully stretching against the wall, did the same on the other corner. She pushed.

A spring snapped loose. Angie didn't even have time to think as the wall spun around a half turn, nearly lifting her off her feet as it twisted her around.

"What the hell?" she muttered. She was in the library. She hadn't seen anything like this since some old Abbott and Costello movies.

Paavo hadn't said anything about the whole wall spinning

around. She'd had the impression he'd merely released the spring, opened the panel, and walked through. Right now the library looked awful, with this unfinished wall instead of a bookcase. She needed to turn the wall back into place. She popped the springs, but before she could jump aside, she was spun around and once again found herself out in the between-the-walls passageway.

This would never do. She blew out the candle—she wasn't planning a return trip—then pressed the spring releases and like magic was in the library once more. She felt downright dizzy.

Instead of pushing both buttons, she pushed the wall; sure enough, it began to slowly rotate for her. She kept it going until the bookcase appeared. It stopped on its own with a click as it gyrated into place and the spring lock took hold. She touched it, and found it felt like a solid wall once again.

Shaking her head, she walked out of the library. She was going to have to hurry to catch up to Moira and the others. She just hoped she could find them.

From the foyer, she looked down the east wing toward the dining room and kitchen and couldn't help but think that if there was a secret passage on one arm of the house, why not on the other?

The east arm was a little more complicated because it held the dining room, then the kitchen, pantry, and utility rooms. Angie paced off the width of the dining room, then of the kitchen. Sure enough, the length of the hall from one room to the next was longer than it would be if the two rooms met side by side. Something was between them. But how did she get in there?

Finally, she found it. A broom closet just off the kitchen, with its inside walls paneled. A dead giveaway. Nobody paneled walls inside a closet.

She pressed two corner spots on each panel, just as she'd done in Chelsea's room. On her third try, the panel sprang open. She pushed it wide enough to step through. She was in a square, unfinished room. A ladder led from it down into the darkness.

She wished she had someone here to help her check this out, but if Danny had somehow gone down there and been hurt . . . She went back into the kitchen and grabbed a powerful flashlight, then bent into the well, shining the flashlight to see what was down there. It was a cellar.

Maybe she should get Paavo before going any further? On the other hand, it was a just a cellar. Maybe the same as the one that held Miss Greer's body. It didn't look the same, though, from up here. The smell of dampness and decay was stronger than ever.

Still, cellars were nothing to be afraid of, and they were certainly the sort of place a boy would explore. He might have come down here to play gopher, or some such game, and gotten hurt.

She slowly descended the ladder, making sure the rungs were solid and would hold her as she went.

Already, claustrophobia was rearing its head. It was one thing to be crawling along secret passageways within the walls of a building and quite another, she discovered, to be beneath it. She didn't want to be down in the ground until that sorrowful day—hopefully seventy or so years off—when she wouldn't know the difference.

The thought of turning around and going right back up that ladder was tempting, and she would have done it if she hadn't noticed that some of the ground showed signs of disturbance. Parts of the area here were completely covered with dust, but at the bottom of the ladder, and going off in one direction, the dust had been packed down, as if someone had walked on it. Whether that someone walked on it yesterday or fifty years ago was anybody's guess. But it might have been Danny.

"Danny?" she called. Her voice echoed in the dark, silent chamber. "Danny, are you here?"

Nothing. Well, at least she'd tried. Time to get out of here.

She aimed the flashlight one last time on the area where it seemed there were footprints. She stopped, feeling as if someone, something, was with her.

She aimed the flashlight a bit ahead, then a little more, a little more. She gasped. Shoes . . . women's black shoes, then slacks, a jacket. Her heart was pounding with fright as she raised the light to the face.

"Hello, Angie," Patsy said.

28

"*How nice of you to come* to see me, Angie."
Patsy smiled. Her eyes were red. "It's been lonely down
here."

"Actually, I think I'll go back upstairs." Angie turned
and ran toward the ladder. She scrambled up it as fast as
she could, but Patsy grabbed her ankle. Angie was ready
to give a hard kick when she saw that Patsy held a carving
knife against her Achilles tendon.

Where had Patsy found a carving knife? If this had
been a proper vegetarian inn, Patsy wouldn't be wielding
anything more dangerous than a potato peeler. "Okay,
Patsy," she said, trying to keep her voice calm. "If you
want my company, I'm all yours."

"Come down here. And don't call me Patsy!"

Angie slowly descended the ladder. "Relax. Everything
will be fine. I didn't realize you didn't like your nickname.
Would you like me to call you Patricia?"

"That's not my name."

"No?"

"My name's Susannah."

Here we go, Angie thought. She swallowed, but her voice still squeaked. "Susannah?"

Patsy nodded. "Now go back there. Jack and Elise's child is there."

"What?" Angie turned to look at Patsy, but Patsy jabbed the knife in her direction, so Angie hurried on, out of the blade's reach.

In the back of the cellar, Angie saw a small opening. She stepped over a high threshold and found herself in another room. She could hardly breathe—this was the source of the damp, decaying smell that permeated the house. It had to be aired out and dried somehow. But such thoughts vanished when she saw, scrunched in a corner near a kerosene lamp, Danny.

"Oh, my God," Angie said, hurrying to the boy. He had a gag over his mouth and his hands and legs had been tied. "Danny, honey, are you all right?"

He gave a brave nod, but she could see that his eyes were wide and frightened.

"Let this child go," Angie said. "He's frightened."

"They thought they could hide him from me, but I found them out. I figured it all out."

Angie sat down on the ground beside Danny and put her arm around his shoulders. He snuggled against her. "Let's take this gag off his mouth. I know you don't want to hurt him."

"Don't touch it! Just leave him be."

"But why are you doing this?"

"Don't you get it? He's Jack and Elise's child. But Jack's dead now. And all I have left is his child."

"Patsy, this isn't Jack's child. Danny is Moira's son."

"Who's Moira? Her name is Elise. She had this child without even being married. She and Jack. My Jack."

Angie stared at her.

"Look at the boy's eyes. Tell me if they aren't Jack's eyes."

She looked at Danny. His eyes did have the same periwinkle shade as Running Spirit's.

"His eyes are nothing like Jack's." Angie deliberately lied, deciding that to confuse Patsy was her best course of action. "I don't think he's Jack's son."

"He is. I snuck out one night to get some food, and I overheard Elise speaking with some policeman who's staying here. This boy is all I have left now that Jack's gone." Patsy's eyes filled with tears. "I did love him so, even though he never cared much for me. I didn't want him to leave me for *her*, but I didn't want him to be dead!"

Angie found the knot that bound Danny's hands and started tugging at it, trying to untie it. "So tell me, Susannah, why are you down here? Why aren't you still upstairs?"

"I had to come here. Jack wanted to get rid of me now that he's with Elise again."

"What did he do?"

"I told him about my meeting with Ezra."

"Ezra?" Angie's head was spinning. "Your father?"

"Yes. I asked him to sell me the house so that I could throw Elise out of it—keep it for Jack and me. But he wouldn't. He tried to push me. But I ducked and he missed. He lost his footing and fell down hard, his head hitting a rock. But he wasn't dead. I swear, he wasn't dead."

"This was on the cliffs by the ocean?" Angie asked. Did Patsy think Finley was Ezra?

"Yes." Patsy sighed. "I ran back to our room. But then Ezra didn't come home. I told Jack what had happened, and Jack said . . ." A sob caught in her throat. "Jack said he must have died. That leaving Ezra there was the same as killing him outright. He said the constable would arrest me, that he'd hang me for Ezra's murder. And then Jack said he'd cover for me if I gave him money and left him here alone with Elise."

Angie's confusion grew worse. "You say Finley . . . I mean, Ezra . . . fell when you were with him, but he was still alive. But then Jack said you'd killed him?"

"Yes. When Jack scared me, when he told me he wanted my money, that was when I knew I had to get away from him."

So Finley had been alive when Patsy left him, but later Running Spirit told her Finley was dead. Running Spirit then tried to blackmail her, telling her to leave her money with him and go away. Did that mean Running Spirit had killed Finley? But if he did, who killed Running Spirit?

Having finished untying the ropes on Danny's hands, Angie scooted between him and Patsy, hiding Danny with her body. She reached behind her and found the knot that bound his ankles. "And so you hid down here?" she said, as nonchalantly as she could, considering she had her hands behind her back.

"I couldn't get away. It was raining too hard. So I tore my blouse and put a piece of material on the rocks where they'd see it, so they'd think I killed myself. The boy found me. I told him what happened and he helped me find this place, brought me food. He's a good boy, my Jack's son." Patsy was sobbing harder now.

Her words gave Angie the creeps. "You heard that Running Spirit was killed yesterday?"

She nodded. "I don't know why you call him that, but yes, my Jack was killed. Now I'm alone except for his son."

"Jack's son?" Angie said. "He's not Jack's son, Susannah. He's Elise's son, but not Jack's."

"You're wrong!"

Angie finished untying the rope around Danny's ankles. She turned around, facing him, and ran her hands over his hair, lifting his chin. "No. Look at his blond hair, just like his mother's." She whispered to him to stay still, then continued talking to Patsy. "His father is someone from San Francisco. Someone Elise met before she ever came here."

"You lie!"

"And you know what else," Angie continued, her voice calm and filled with logic, "you're not Susannah. Susannah was Jack's sister. But you're his wife. You must be Elise. You're all confused."

Patsy clutched her head. "Stop it! You're the one who's confused. I never bore Jack's child. Elise did. Jack never touches me as he would a wife. So I must be his sister, don't you see? Jack would love a wife differently than the way he loves me. So I'm his sister. Because he does love me! He really does."

Suddenly, Angie had a brainstorm. "Remember how Jack was sent away by Ezra?"

"Ezra?"

"Your father."

"Ah, yes."

"Ezra sent Jack to sea because he wanted Elise for himself!"

"No!" Patsy clutched her head as if it were beginning to ache.

Angie almost felt sorry for the pitiful, confused woman before her, but she shouldn't because Patsy was a killer. She had to be. Angie watched her closely. "Ezra loved her, and he was jealous of Jack. So he sent Jack away;

then he had no rival. He got Elise to make love to him, and they had a child. The child wasn't Jack's son, he was Jack's brother."

"No, no, no!" Patsy sat on the ground, her hands against her ears. "It doesn't make sense."

"It's true;" Angie screamed at her.

"You're confusing me!"

"No, you're the one who's confused," Angie shouted. "You don't understand any of it. You don't know who you are."

"Stop!" Patsy let out a loud wail as she curled into a ball, her eyes shut.

Angie motioned to Danny to head toward the exit while she moved toward Patsy and kept her voice low, almost like a chant, to hide the sound of Danny's footsteps. "It was always Ezra who caused all the trouble, wasn't it, Susannah? He made your mother go away first, leaving you and Jack alone out here, with no friends, no one to love you. You had only each other. Then he brought *her* here, the pretty little girl from the South. Jack and Ezra were both taken with her, weren't they? And they ignored you. For her. Because of her. No wonder you hated her. Then, as Jack and Elise grew older, the love for the little girl turned into something much more. Ezra realized that both he and Jack loved her. But Ezra was the one with the power, so he sent Jack away, and then you, poor Susannah, you were left all alone with just the two lovers. No wonder you hated them."

As Patsy moaned and rocked, Angie jumped to her feet and made a dash out of the cellar.

Where had Danny gone?

29

Paavo walked by Reginald Vane's side, traveling over all the areas where Danny liked to play between Hill Haven and Quint's cottage. So far, they had found nothing.

The fog remained as thick as it had been that morning, making it close to impossible to see—even if Danny were just a few feet away. They had to rely on sound more than anything else and called out every few seconds, then waited, hoping for a return call.

They searched the ground as they went, since any footprints that had been formed in the soft mud within the last four or five hours would still be there. But there weren't any.

The possibilities of who it could be committing the murders went round and round in Paavo's head. The deaths here seemed to follow some plan. But what? If he just concentrated on the known victims—Finley and Miss Greer and Jeffers—and ignored for the moment Patsy, whose body had not been found, who did he come up with?

For Finley and Jeffers he had a surfeit of motives. The murder of Miss Greer had to be the key. Since none of

these people seemed to have known her before their little excursion to the inn, her death had to have been
related to something she was doing or something she
saw. Something in the kitchen, perhaps.

The kitchen. Was there something about the kitchen?

Paavo shook his head. None of it made any sense.

Angie scrambled up the ladder as fast as she could, slid
through the open panel in the closet, then shut it. With
any luck, Patsy would stay down there in her mad, confused state for a long time, but Angie got a chair from the
dining room and wedged it under the closet doorknob just
in case. If Patsy tried to get out, she wouldn't be able to.

When Angie turned around, Danny stood behind her,
holding up a baseball bat as if ready to swing. "Is she
going to be able to get out?" he asked, slowly stepping
closer to her.

"I don't think so," Angie said.

"Good." He lowered his arms.

"You're pretty brave," Angie said.

He proudly puffed out his thin chest. "I didn't want
her to hurt you."

Angie touched his shoulder. "Are you all right?"

"Sure." He dropped his gaze. "It was just kind of
scary."

Something in Angie's heart did a flip-flop as she
watched this young boy trying to act so strong and self-
assured, when she was quite sure he wanted nothing
more than to be held by his mom. She'd never thought
about having a son before, but if she ever were to, she
hoped he'd be just like Danny.

"Let's go," she said. "We need to find Paavo and tell
him where Patsy is. Oh, wait." She'd left Paavo's gun up

in the bedroom with her jacket. Should she go get it? It'd take time, and Patsy was locked in the cellar. Angie couldn't imagine needing to use such a thing on crazy Patsy, anyway. Paavo could handle her.

"What's wrong?" Danny asked.

"Nothing. We're outta here." She held Danny's hand as the two of them ran toward the cottage. Luckily, he knew the way perfectly. Angie would have been hopelessly lost in the dense fog.

After a short while, though, her side began to ache. "Stop. I'm not as energetic as I used to be," she said.

"I wonder if she's trying to get out of the closet." He gave a fearful glance toward the house. "I didn't mean to do anything wrong. She was a nice lady and I felt sorry for her. But after she snuck upstairs and heard people talking about how her husband died, she went bonkers."

"You must have a room in the inn, then?"

"'Course! It's next to, uh, Moira. I been staying there most nights since Quint's been gone. She didn't want me to stay in the cottage alone because of all the weird stuff going on."

"Good for her." They moved quickly, a cross between a fast walk and a jog that allowed Angie to keep breathing as Danny all but pulled her toward the cottage. For sure, when—if—she ever got back to San Francisco, she'd do what she'd been putting off for years and join *Herobics*, a women's aerobics studio run by one of her many cousins. She wondered if she'd ever again see a cousin, or any one of the members of her large family, or if she'd be stuck wandering around this damned hilltop the rest of her life.

She stopped suddenly, yanking Danny back, near her. She'd heard a noise. She might not be good at running, but she was exceptional at paranoia, especially when it involved strange footsteps or other noises.

"Quiet. I heard something," she whispered.

Danny pointed past a group of pines. "Over there."

"Maybe it's Paavo." They crept near. Angie wasn't sure why she didn't want to yell and make herself known, but she didn't. Not until she was sure it was someone she could trust.

"Martin!" Angie called when she made out the figure of the older man through the mist. She waved and ran toward him. "Look, I found Danny."

He looked up and smiled broadly. "Danny," he clutched the boy by the shoulders. "Are you all right?"

"Yes. It was Patsy."

"Patsy?" Martin stared at Angie. "Patsy's alive?"

"She's been hiding in some strange cellars."

"My God. She's the one behind all this?"

"That's right, although the first death was an accident. She and Finley fought, and he slipped and hit his head. Then, somehow, he died."

"Poor Patsy. I suppose she killed Running Spirit out of jealousy."

"That must be." Did she, though, Angie wondered, when she still loved him so much and his death caused her to go over the edge? "Weren't you with Reginald and Paavo? Where are they?"

"We weren't having much luck, so we decided one of us should come back to see if you ladies were all right. Where are the other women?"

"I don't know. We split up."

"Where's Patsy now?"

"She's still in the cellar. Having a not-so-quiet nervous breakdown. She's terribly confused."

"The root cellar?"

"No. That's the thing. It's totally separate. You get there by a secret panel in the hall closet near the kitchen.

You have to push on both sides of the panel at once, at about the height of my shoulders, and it pops open."

Martin nodded. "Clever. Someone said old Ezra was a survivalist and built this house with lots of secrets. I wonder how Patsy learned about them?"

Angie glanced at Danny. He wasn't about to confess. "I have no idea," she said.

"Well, you hurry far away from here," Martin said. "Find someone, particularly that boyfriend of yours, and send them to the house. He and Vane were heading toward the gardener's cottage, then the beach. I'll guard Patsy and make sure she doesn't get away."

"Okay."

"Good luck," Martin said.

"You, too." Angie and Danny started toward Quint's cottage again. Angie looked back and saw Martin stop and pull a pack of cigarettes out of his shirt pocket. He shook one loose and lit it.

Paavo and Reginald searched Quint's cottage and the land around it. No sign of the boy.

"Let's head toward the road," Reginald said. "Maybe he was trying to get to town."

"All right." Paavo started walking, but with each step his legs felt heavier and heavier, and he had the strangest feeling, some intuition almost, that something was terribly wrong. He slowed down, not understanding what was happening to him. He'd never felt anything like this before.

Angie's step slowed. Something was bothering her, but she couldn't figure out what. It had begun when she saw Martin with the cigarette. She hadn't seen Martin smoke before, but it shouldn't have surprised her. These days, lots of people huddled out of doors to smoke, since no one wanted them inside. She'd heard that in large office buildings, in particular, there were whole subculture networks of smokers who had secret signals for each other to go out and have a cigarette.

But all that meant was that Martin most likely knew Running Spirit smoked when most of the others didn't. Martin, as well as Running Spirit, might have used the shed to smoke in. So what?

So nothing. But Angie was bothered nonetheless.

It couldn't mean anything. After all, Martin was going after Patsy. Martin, suddenly brave, was willing to go after the killer of two men and one woman all by himself. Of course it was because he assumed she wouldn't be dangerous.

But why would he assume that? He'd never been brave before.

He'd been the one most opposed to Finley's food. He had the most costly ideas for the inn. It was obvious that he'd hated Running Spirit's influence over Moira. It was clear that he'd feared Running Spirit would ease him out of the picture. And it was known that all his money, and then some, had been invested in the inn.

All were reasons for Martin to want to get rid of his two chief rivals for control of it.

No, she had to be wrong. She was being misled, again, by hunches and assumptions. Paavo told her to be wary of them. She couldn't let . . .

But she couldn't ignore her feelings, either—that Patsy had been telling the truth about Finley and had loved Running Spirit too much to kill him.

Whoever killed those two had to also have killed Miss Greer. Martin Bayman had no reason to kill her.

But then, neither did Patsy.

Bayman's only connection with Miss Greer was when he said he wouldn't serve the food she'd cooked—using Finley's recipe—to his cat. Next thing, there was a dead rat in the kitchen.

Could there be a connection? There was something a bit droll, she had to admit, about the dead rat on the plate with the soy-lentil cutlets. Something in keeping with Martin's weird sense of humor.

Miss Greer had complained to Angie about finding strange people in her kitchen. Angie thought the cook had been talking about her, but what if she'd meant Martin? What if she'd found him in the kitchen when he was trying to dispose of the rat, and he'd shoved it into the bin in the pantry cabinet so she wouldn't see it? But she would have seen him. . . .

No, that was purely circumstantial. Speculative. Emotional, as Paavo would say accusingly.

Yet she couldn't ignore the fact that it rang true for her.

Martin Bayman had plenty of reasons for wanting to be rid of Finley and Running Spirit. Putting the blame on Patsy would be the icing on the cake. And if she, too, was dead, who'd be the wiser? Martin would have committed the perfect crime.

"Danny, I need you to be very careful and very brave," Angie said. "Go toward your grandfather's, find Paavo, and show him how to find the cellars. Can you do that?"

"No problem."

"When you find him, tell him about Patsy, and tell him that I think Martin Bayman is the one we want. I'm going to go try to get Patsy out of there before Bayman shows up. Got it?"

"Bayman?" he said. "But you just—"

"I know. Hurry!"

He nodded and ran into the forest, disappearing almost immediately into the mist. She turned around to face back toward the inn, then said a little prayer that she could find it in the fog—a prayer for herself, and especially for Patsy.

She ran back in the direction she'd come from, circling around the section where she'd met Martin. She could only hope he was continuing at his normal, leisurely pace, and that he might be even less familiar with this area than she was.

The back way would provide quicker access to the cellars. Hurrying, she ran to the back door and let herself in, then went to the kitchen broom closet. After pulling the door shut, she jammed the chair rail as hard as she could under the inside doorknob. It would slow Martin down.

She opened the panel that led to the cellar and made her way down the ladder. Halfway down she saw Patsy standing there with the carving knife.

"So you're back," Patsy said, crying. "You tried to confuse me and you stole Jack's child."

God help me, Angie thought. Maybe she should simply let Patsy and Martin face each other. But Patsy was so far gone she wouldn't stand a chance.

"Susannah, you put that knife away. I wouldn't have come back here if I meant to harm you. I'm here to help."

She sobbed louder. "I don't believe you."

"I'm telling you the truth. There's a man who does want to hurt you, Martin Bayman. Do you remember him?"

"I don't know anyone by that name."

"No, I guess not, since he's living about ninety years in the future. Anyway, he wants to kill you. We've got to hide."

"He wants to kill me? But why?"

"Because he can pin a few other murders on you if you're dead."

"Maybe I should be dead. What do I have to live for? Nothing. Jack's gone. So is his child. I don't want to go on."

"You've got to."

"Let whoever it is come and kill me. He'd be doing me a favor. I can't bear this any longer."

"Listen to me—"

"No!" Dropping the knife, Patsy put her hands over her ears, then sat on the ground. "It'll be easier this way."

Angie heard the rattling of the door handle. Martin had reached the closet. He was trying to open the door.

She grabbed Patsy's arm. "Come on. We can't stay here. We've got to hide until Paavo comes for us."

"I want to die. Jack's gone."

"You don't want to die! It's not Jack you're grieving for. It's Greg. Running Spirit. Your husband. He's dead. The man who's coming here killed him. You've got to help me prove to the police that he did it, so he'll pay for his crime."

"I don't care. Jack never loved me."

"He did. He wants you to know that he's sorry, Patsy. He's sorry he treated you so badly. He's sorry he didn't love you the way you loved him. If he had, you two would have been happy—just the way you always wanted."

Patsy's head jerked up. "How do you know that?"

Angie was taken aback. She was just making things up—she had a propensity to do that, especially when crazy men were after her, wanting to kill her. "I just know it."

The house shook as Martin slammed something against the closet. His shoulder? An ax?

"He's coming! Please, Patsy."

Patsy stared at her. "Jack! I miss him so."

"Jack wants you to live, to tell the police everything

you know. Come on, Susannah. We've got to find a place to hide."

"Jack said that?"

"Yes."

"All right. We can go this way." Patsy stood up and ran into the storage room they'd been in earlier, where Danny had been held. She picked up a lantern, ran toward a corner, then seemed to disappear.

Angie stopped, dumbfounded.

Patsy stuck her head out—there was a narrow opening within the wall. "Come on. Jack will lead us out of here."

At those words, for the life of her Angie couldn't figure out if she would be better off following crazy Patsy or having a face-off with homicidal Martin.

The noise from the top floor made it sound as if the whole house were being ripped apart.

That decided it. She turned down the wick on the kerosene lamp in the cellar, casting the room in darkness, then ran into the opening after Patsy. The opening narrowed down till it was only about four feet tall. Angie was afraid to go into it. What if it dead-ended? They'd be trapped in there, with Martin coming after them. Why hadn't she held onto Paavo's gun? As it was, they were helpless.

"Patsy, darling?" She heard Martin cooing. "Patsy, where are you?"

A cold chill ran down Angie's back. She scrambled after Patsy, who luckily had paid no attention, since she was convinced she was Susannah.

"Come here, Patsy, sweetheart," Martin called. "No one's going to hurt you."

Crawling through the maze, following Patsy, after several twists and turns Angie found herself in a long tunnel.

"Don't get me mad at you, Patsy. Come here. I'll take

you to Greg. Don't you want to see Greg again?" Martin's voice was sounding closer. "Maybe you can go up in smoke, just like Greg—or should I say, Fricasseed Spirit?"

"Hurry, Susannah," Angie cried. She saw light up ahead. Daylight. She crawled faster, getting ahead of the slow-moving Patsy, then grabbing her arm and trying to pull her along at a quicker rate. Martin had to be getting close.

As they neared the mouth of the tunnel, it became wider, taller. The two of them were able to stand again. Now running and stumbling, they went as fast and hard as they could.

Just ahead was the end of the tunnel. They ran to it, hoping for safety, but instead came to a screeching stop.

Below them was a sheer drop to the ocean and the rock-laden cove; above them, the wall of a cliff, the top invisible in its shroud of fog. And not far behind them, working his way through the maze of cellars to the tunnel, was the clever, murderous Martin Bayman.

30

"*Paavo!*"

Paavo turned to see Danny running over the hill toward him. He and Reginald had passed Quint's house and were heading toward the beach.

"Thank God," Paavo murmured, relief flooding through him at the sight of the boy. "Where have you been?" he shouted. "You scared your mother half to death."

"I know." Breathless, Danny stopped in front of him. "Angie told me. She got me away from Patsy."

"You were with Patsy?"

"She hid in the cellar 'cause she thought she killed Finley. Running Spirit told her she did. But then he was killed, and she, like, went nuts. She thinks she's Susannah."

"She *what*?"

"You got to hurry. Angie needs help."

A dozen questions died unspoken on Paavo's lips at the boy's last words. "Where is she?"

"She's going back to the house. She said to tell you Mr. Bayman's the killer."

"Bayman? Angie said Bayman?" Paavo repeated, incredulous.

"Where are the other women?" Reginald Vane shouted. "Where's Chelsea?"

"I don't know," Danny answered. "All I know is Mr. Bayman's going to the house after Patsy, and Angie's trying to stop him."

"Good Christ!" Paavo said.

"We'll stop him," Vane declared. "I've got to warn Chelsea and the others as well. I've got to find them." He ran into the forest.

Paavo had started toward the inn when he suddenly felt a sharp pain in his ears. He stopped and took a deep breath. Nothing like that had ever happened to him. He tried to go on, but his whole head was pounding so hard he could scarcely see. Ignore it, he told himself; he had to reach Angie. He stumbled forward, but it was no good. Blindly he put his hand out, groping until he found a tree for support. Leaning against it, he fought the dizziness that overwhelmed him.

"Are you all right?" Danny asked.

"Cellar's too far," Paavo said, breathing hard. "Bayman will reach her long before we get there. Is there any other way?"

"There's the tunnel from the sea."

"What tunnel?"

"Old Ezra dug it. Where it starts, he used to have a rope ladder to the beach. But it's just a hole in the cliffs now."

The cliffs weren't very far. "This tunnel leads back to the house?"

"To the cellars. That's where Patsy's hiding."

"Show it to me."

"Okay, but we'll need a rope to get down to the opening. Grandpa's got one."

"Let's go." They ran back to Quint's shed for the rope, then to the cliffs. With each step Paavo's headache lessened.

Desperate, Angie and Patsy huddled at the mouth of the tunnel. The swirling fog lent a murky dampness to the air, a surreal quality to the setting. But this wasn't some avant-garde movie. It was life and death.

A few feet away, the cliff dropped off, ending in jagged rocks and raging surf. Above them, the cliff rose just as steeply. The top, covered with fog, wasn't visible. Angie clutched Patsy's hand tighter.

"Elise—" Patsy stepped closer to the edge.

"No!" Angie jerked her back. She searched her mind for an answer—up or down? If they went down, they could be trapped there. One slip, one tall wave, and they could be swept into the ocean. Angie could imagine Martin's sneering laughter as their bodies floated out to sea.

Going up was the only way to safety—if they could make it in one piece.

A little way from the tunnel's mouth, a deep crack in the rock face angled upward. It looked wide enough for her and Patsy to wedge their feet in, and along it were the scraggly roots of small scrub. They could hang onto them and work their way up.

"Come on!" She had to shout to be heard over the sound of the wind whipping against the cliffs and into the tunnel. "We've got to get over to that little ledge."

Between the tunnel and the crevice they needed to reach was a small expanse—only about four feet wide—of sheer, slick rock. Just wide enough that they'd have to jump to reach it.

Patsy looked at the cliff. "Over there?"

"You've got to." As best she could, Angie maneuvered

Patsy to the side wall of the tunnel. "Don't look down. Aim for that spot. You can do it."

"Jack will help us," Patsy said.

"I'm afraid we might be meeting him a lot sooner than I ever expected," Angie murmured.

Patsy was taller than Angie. Pressed against the cliff face for balance, she was able to stretch her legs enough that her foot reached the crevice without the need to jump. Loose rocks fell, bouncing to the water, but Patsy maintained her toehold and was able to pull herself onto the cliff face, her feet wedged in the protection of the crack in the rock.

"Go up," Angie said, her heart still in her throat from the sight of those loose rocks. "I need room."

"Up?"

"Up! Hurry."

Patsy pulled herself up a little way, leaving enough room for Angie.

She looked at the crevice Patsy had stepped into. It was too far for her to reach. She'd have to jump.

But then she made the mistake of looking down. Her nerve failed her. It was too far. Too frightening.

"Angie?" Martin sounded surprised.

She spun around to face him.

"Angie. What are you doing here? I was looking for Patsy."

She racked her brain for something to say to talk Martin out of harming them. She'd talked her way out of plenty before. If Patsy would climb up, while she talked, Patsy would be safe and so would she. Martin wouldn't try to harm her, would he?

If Martin thought she suspected him he would. And why else would she be running away from him? "I was looking for Patsy, too," she said finally.

"Oh? Why? You knew where she was."

"To help you. Patsy's a murderer. Killed her own husband. How could you stand a chance?"

"He knows," Patsy called.

"What?" To her dismay, Angie saw that Patsy hadn't gone very far up the cliff at all, but had stopped and was watching them.

"Well, well," Martin said, stepping out far enough onto the edge of the tunnel's mouth that he could see Patsy. "What do we have here? Our own little Lizzie Borden."

"He saw me," Patsy said slowly, "when I killed Ezra. Ezra fell and hit his forehead, and when I was running away, I remember he was there. Who is he?"

"He . . . he's Martin." Tongue-tied, Angie prayed Martin couldn't figure out what Patsy was talking about.

"Ezra?" Martin's eyes narrowed as he looked at Patsy. "And what's your name?"

"Susannah."

Martin's eyebrows rose. Angie tried to diffuse his suspicions. "Patsy doesn't know what she's saying."

Martin ignored her and called to Patsy. "What about Running Spirit?"

"His name is Jack," Patsy insisted.

"And if Moira is Elise, Finley must be Ezra," Martin said thoughtfully. His face filled with sudden anger as he realized Patsy had seen him nearby when Finley was killed.

Angie knew then that he would try to kill her and Patsy. Too easily, he could make it appear that they had an unfortunate slip on the rocks. He would literally get away with murder.

He wasn't going to. She wouldn't allow it. Using all her strength and courage, she leaped for the crevice. The foot she led with slid into the spot perfectly, and she pressed her body against the cliff, holding on for dear life. Then she brought her back foot forward. As she stepped onto the cliff with it, the rocks broke loose. Her foot jerked downward, finding only air, pulling her down with it.

She screamed, her body rocking back away from the cliff, but Patsy reached down and grabbed her sweater at the shoulder, holding on as she steadied herself and found a new place to put her foot.

"Okay?" Patsy asked.

Barely able to breathe, Angie whispered, "Okay."

"Look at you fools!" Martin shouted. He tried to stretch his foot into the crevice, but Angie kicked him. He reached his hand toward her, but she picked up a loose rock and smacked it hard against his fingertips.

"Climb, Patsy!" she screamed. "Get away from him."

"Wait, Susannah!" Martin shrieked. "Jump! You've got to jump—just like Elise."

Patsy stopped and looked down at the ocean.

"I hear voices out on the cliff," Danny said, running back to the pine where Paavo was tying the heavy rope.

"They're outside the tunnel?" Paavo asked.

"I can't see. It's too foggy."

"Hell." Paavo gave a heavy tug to tighten the knot, then ran to the cliff. Danny was right—the fog was so thick he couldn't see what was below. Wrapping the rope under one thigh and over the opposite shoulder, he hoped the training he'd had years ago in the army wouldn't fail him; then he stepped off the edge, dropping quickly into the foggy mist.

He could hear Bayman's and Angie's voices before he saw them, but nothing prepared him for the sight of Angie clinging so tenuously to the side of the cliff. He was afraid to call out, afraid to do anything that might cause her to lose her concentration.

As much as anything, he had to worry about Bayman and hope that Angie, in her usual headstrong way, hadn't challenged and accused him. Cornered, Bayman might try to take others down with him. It was the kind of cowardly, cruel thing he'd seen murderers do before.

Forcing his voice to sound calm, he called out, "I see them, Bayman. I'll help. Just hold on tight, ladies. I'll get you off there." His eyes never left Angie's hands as he quickly rappelled down to her and Patsy.

"Paavo! Oh, God, Paavo, be careful," Angie cried. "Martin's—"

"I know, Angie. He's trying to help. Now, I'll get you off the cliff, then we'll get Patsy off. Thanks, Bayman."

"Sure," Martin said.

Paavo climbed down to Angie's level; then, with her pressed flat against the rocks, he wrapped his body behind her so she couldn't fall, and holding her with one hand, the rope with the other, he helped her back into the tunnel's mouth. "Go on," he whispered. She tried to hurry out of Martin's reach, but her body trembled so badly she could scarcely move.

"Let go of me!" Patsy screamed. "I want Jack!"

Angie turned back to the mouth of the tunnel. "Susannah! Come on, we'll find Jack. Let Paavo help you."

Listening to Angie, Patsy stopped struggling and let Paavo help her off the cliff.

Angie reached out to take her hand, but Martin suddenly snatched Patsy away and pulled her to his side. He stepped to the edge of the cliff.

"Let's get her inside, Martin," Paavo said. "She might be a danger to herself."

"Patsy's a killer," Martin declared.

"Is she?" Paavo asked, trying to sound innocent.

"She killed Finley and kidnapped Danny."

"How did she do it? How could someone as slight as she is toss Finley off a cliff?" Paavo asked.

"She could have just rolled him off the edge."

"Why would she?"

Martin grimaced. "She wanted his place for her husband. Tay wouldn't sell. Everyone knows it."

"Tay wouldn't sell to you, either," Paavo said.

"Bethel and I had this dream, but no more than that. I mean, this was no big deal to us. If it didn't pan out, we'd be okay."

"I thought Bethel said it was your last hope," Angie said. "She was the one who always had to figure out everything, but this is the one time you took an interest. She was proud of you, Martin."

He stared at her a long moment before he began blinking hard. "No." The word was whispered.

"This Disneyland idea of yours was your big dream; then you found out you weren't the only one here with plans. That made you mad, didn't it, Bayman?" Paavo asked.

"No!" His grip tightened on Patsy. White, tense lines appeared around his mouth. "It didn't matter."

"Even after Finley was gone, you saw Jeffers moving in on Moira, making himself even more influential. You saw yourself as being pushed aside. To these people, Bethel was no more a crazy old lady, and you were her drunken sot of a husband."

"Shut up!" His eyes reddened.

Paavo slowly eased closer to Bayman. He dropped his voice, making it now seem friendly—a ploy often used in homicide interrogations. "What happened, Martin?"

"Nothing!"

"Finley was no good. I know it, just like you do," Paavo said. "His own sister told me as much."

"Finley laughed when I told him about my plans,"

Bayman said bitterly, taking a step nearer the edge. Paavo stopped moving toward him. "Finley had the money, he had the inn, and he had a bunch of people so busy bickering with each other over how to run the damn place, he could make all the decisions. He screwed all of us. Not just me! I'm glad he's dead. He deserved to die. I'm glad Patsy killed him."

"With Finley gone, I guess Moira would have sold you the place; but then Jeffers messed it up for you, didn't he?" Paavo asked. "He was as bad as Finley."

"I would have convinced Moira to listen to me." Bayman spat out the words. "I can be very charming, you see. I would have convinced her, if it wasn't for Jeffers. He confused her. He was scum. He deserved to die, too."

"And Patsy killed him?" Paavo asked.

"Yes!" Bayman's face was flushed; perspiration dripped from his forehead. Patsy just stood there, rag-doll limp, lost in her own world.

"What about Miss Greer?" Paavo asked. "What made Patsy kill her?"

"She just—!" Martin stopped. His gaze darted from Paavo to Angie, then seemed to deaden as the enormity of his crimes struck him and he realized that they knew. He shut his eyes for a moment before speaking. "She saw me in her kitchen the night Finley disappeared. I had just finished hiding the dead rat. I didn't think anyone had seen it, but I was wrong. Angie had. That night my shoes were caked with wet sand, my clothes and hair damp from the night mist. The next night, the cook asked why I'd been in her kitchen, why I would have moved a rat. She said that if the rat was there for Finley, how did I know he wouldn't come home to see it—unless I knew what had happened to him. They were all good questions." He chuckled mirthlessly. "And I had no answers."

The calm in Bayman's voice chilled Paavo to the bone. Angie tried to step closer, probably hoping to grab Patsy, but Paavo put out an arm to stop her. He'd seen too many Good Samaritans get hurt or killed in situations like this. He didn't know what Martin was planning; all he knew was it would be bad.

"Bring Patsy back in the tunnel, Martin. Let's go and talk about this." He reached for Patsy.

"Don't! No closer." Bayman rocked precariously on the edge, Patsy with him.

"Come on, Martin," Paavo said. "Let's go inside."

Bayman shook his head, looking down at the rocks. "God, I wish I had a nice stiff drink."

"We'll get you a drink. Step back now, you and Patsy. You both need to get away from there."

"I don't think so." Martin peered down at the rocky beach below, then at Patsy. "Ironic, isn't it? So many plans, so much care, only to be done in by someone who thinks she's a ghost."

Patsy smiled at him.

"Yes, Susannah, dear. Why not smile? It's better in your world, isn't it?" With that, he kissed the back of her hand and let her go. "Go over to that man, Susannah. I'm sure he wants to sign your dance card."

Paavo grabbed Patsy and pulled her out of Bayman's reach as soon as Bayman let go of her. Angie started to lead her away from the edge when Patsy broke free and ran into the tunnel toward the house. Angie let her go.

"Your turn, Martin," Paavo said. "Come on."

Martin shook his head.

"Give me your hand," Paavo said, inching toward him.

"No closer, Smith. This is for me to figure out." Martin arched forward, away from the rocks, straining toward the sea.

"Don't do it," Paavo said. "It's not worth it."

"Martin, please don't," Angie cried. "Think of Bethel."

Bayman studied the cold Pacific for a moment, and he laughed. "Bethel will understand. I always said I wanted to make a big splash."

Then he jumped.

31

Angie heard a distant scream, almost like an echo bouncing off the cliffs, and then only the whistling of the wind and the crashing of the waves. She stepped to Paavo's side and watched in horror as a wave washed in, picked up Martin's broken body, and carried him out to sea.

Paavo held her tight. "Are you all right?" he whispered.

She nodded, despite the roiling in her stomach, the trembling that threatened to overtake her.

"There's nothing we can do," he said gently. "Let's get away from here." He helped her walk. She felt drained of all strength, all feeling, all emotion, and every bit as limp as Patsy had been in Martin's grasp.

They found Patsy sitting in the storage cellar. "Let's go find Jack," Angie said. Patsy quietly followed them out of the cellar to the upstairs hallway.

They walked through the inn and out to the front yard. Somehow they'd have to find the others and tell them.

Bethel, Chelsea, and Moira were walking toward the house as Paavo, Angie, and Patsy were coming out.

"You found her," Bethel said.

"Look!" Chelsea cried.

Danny was running toward them. Moira screamed his name and the boy and his mother ran to each other.

"Where's Martin?" a worried Bethel asked Paavo. "I thought he was with you."

"I'm sorry." Paavo hesitated a moment. "We were at the cliffs."

"What?" Her face turned ashen. Angie stepped closer.

"It seems he was the one behind the deaths," Paavo said.

"No," Bethel cried.

"He couldn't live with what he'd done."

She said nothing but stood, stonelike, with unseeing eyes. Then they filled with tears. "Oh, Martin." She looked suddenly old and weary as she lifted a shaky hand to her face. "I was afraid of this. I didn't want to believe it could be, but . . ." She began to cry.

Angie and Chelsea closed around her, reaching out and touching her in sympathy.

The roar of an engine broke into their tight little circle. Angie looked up to see a four-wheel-drive Jeep carrying the sheriff, his deputy, and Quint barrel down the road toward them, stopping with a screech of the brakes. Quint jumped out and hurried to his daughter and grandchild.

The sheriff casually got out of the Jeep.

"Butz," Paavo said. "How did you get through?"

"After Quint told me Hilda Greer died, and I thought more about it, I decided—what with Finley Tay disappearing and then his cook conveniently dropping dead— well, I figured you people might be in danger, after all. Soon as the rain let up, I got county workers with a bull-dozer out here."

"You're a little late," Paavo said.

"Late?"

"Angie figured out that Martin Bayman was behind the murders. Knowing he'd been caught, he jumped off the cliffs. If you've got a radio in that Jeep, you ought to call the coast guard."

"Sparks!" Butz ordered.

"Yes sir," the deputy replied, "I'll do it."

"Any chance he's still alive?" Butz asked.

Paavo shook his head.

"Bayman, huh? The old boozer, right? Why would he hurt anyone?"

"He wasn't an old boozer." Tears ran down the grooves of age and weariness that lined Bethel's face. "He was brilliant. He'd had a brilliant career as a lawyer, but he gave it all up for me. All for me."

Patsy's shrill voice cut through the ensuing silence. "He didn't kill Finley."

"What?" the sheriff faced her.

"Sheriff, you've got to understand," Angie began, but he put up his hand, stopping her explanation.

"Go on," he said to Patsy.

"I killed Finley!" Patsy cried, then rubbed her forehead. "I mean . . . no . . . not Finley. Who's Finley? I killed Ezra. He slipped while we were talking after dinner. We were near the ocean. He tried to push me but fell and hit his forehead."

Paavo touched her arm. "Finley died by a blow to the back of his head, not his forehead. It wasn't your fault at all."

Patsy shook her head. "Who could it have been? There was no one here but me, Elise, Jack, and Ezra."

Angie put her arms around the woman's waist. "You'll be all right, Patsy."

"I'm Susannah."

Sheriff Butz made a long, low whistle. "I think we'll take her back to town with us," he said softly. "There's a nice hospital up the road a piece. Oh, by the way, Miss Amalfi, would you come to town with us, too?"

"Me?" Angie glanced from the sheriff to Paavo. "Why? I haven't done anything."

"No, but your mother's called me every day to make sure you were all right. Last I heard, she'd phoned the president of AT&T and demanded he come out here and personally reconnect the phone line so she could contact you directly. I'd say she's a wee bit upset."

"My poor mother! Yes, I'll come right now."

"I told her Inspector Smith was here with you, but that didn't seem to help. Not at all. She sure can speak that Italian lingo fast, can't she?"

"Oh, dear," Angie groaned. "Maybe it's good I found those cellars to hide in."

The morning sun was bright in the octagonal room as Angie put on a dab of *Quelques Fleurs* perfume, then zipped up her cosmetic case and put it in her luggage bag. "Well, Susannah," she said to the walls, "it's all yours again until the next guests arrive. I do hope you treat them better than you did me."

Paavo walked out of the dressing room with his luggage. He'd spent most of the morning out playing basketball with Danny. "Talking to ghosts now, are you?"

"Why not? Everyone else seems to. At least it was a most lovely room."

"It was," Paavo agreed. "Not exactly a vacation I'd recommend, but it had its moments. Are you ready?"

"Am I! Offer me hamburgers, fries, and a shake, and I'd follow you anywhere."

Paavo grinned as he picked up their bags to carry down to the foyer.

As Angie pulled the door shut, she looked over the room one last time. "Good-bye, Susannah. Pleasant dreams."

Chelsea and Reginald Vane were already downstairs, their bags packed and side by side.

"So you're leaving, too?" Angie said.

"Yes," Chelsea replied. "I'm taking a trip to Canada. I've always wanted to see the great Northwest." She took Reginald's hand.

"Miss Worthington has accepted my invitation for a visit," he said, his cheeks and ears tinged with pink.

"I told him he could stay in the room with me this time." Chelsea winked.

Reginald blushed furiously, then straightened his bow tie. "It was nice to meet you and the inspector," he said awkwardly, shaking Angie's and Paavo's hands. "Have a safe journey back home." Then he turned to Moira, who stood quietly in the back of the foyer, almost in the drawing room. "Good-bye, Miss Tay. And good luck."

"Thank you for continuing to support the inn," Moira said. "Thank you both."

As Reginald picked up the suitcases and headed out the door, Chelsea ran over to Angie and grabbed her hands. "Finley was right, you know. He said I'd meet and fall in love with the ghost of Jack Sempler. Well, in a sense I did—Reggie is his only living relative. Isn't he the dearest man?"

"He's perfect for you," Angie said.

"Yes, he is, isn't he?" Chelsea gave Angie a hug.

"Write to me," Angie said.

"I will," Chelsea called as she hurried after Reginald.

Moira stepped forward. "I guess this is good-bye, then." The front door banged open and Danny ran into the room, his eyes on Angie. "Grandpa says you're leaving. Can't you stay? Mom doesn't know anything about cooking. She needs help."

Paavo turned toward Moira. "You're going to try to make a go of the inn?"

"Yes. I asked Bethel if she'd stay and help until she figures out what to do. And last night, Patsy was apparently starting to remember who she was. She said she'd like to come back here when she's stronger."

"That's good," Angie said. She couldn't help but reflect on how silly she had found these people when she first came to the inn, but now she cared about them. "She needs time. They both do. Listen," her tone brightened, "I'll send you menus, like I promised Finley, and I'll put in a number of easy-to-prepare recipes."

"I'd appreciate it," Moira said.

"What about the town?" Paavo asked.

"My father talked to the people there while the road was closed," Moira said. "He thinks if I try to work with them instead of fighting them as Finley did, and if the inn brings tourists to town, they'll accept us." She took a deep breath. "It's scary, though."

"You can do it, Moira," he said. "You've got the strength. Now you'll be able to use it."

"I hope you're right." Moira's eyes filled with tears. "And thank you both for your help. I know this was terrible for you, as it was for all of us. But I'm eternally grateful that you were here."

"I'm glad we could help," Angie said.

"One thing I still don't understand, though," Moira said to Paavo. "What made you go to the cliffs to find Angie? Why didn't you go back to the house with Reginald?"

He paled slightly and tugged at his ear without speaking. "Danny told me about the cliffs," he said evasively.

"Don't you remember?" Danny asked. "Your head hurt. You couldn't walk."

"That explains it," Moira said. "It was the ghosts. They do things like that sometimes, if they like you. Nudge you in the right direction, so to speak. They're really very benign ghosts, you see."

Angie couldn't help staring at Paavo. Had she heard right? Her logical, practical, cut-to-the-quick detective was communicating with spirits?

"I'm sure that's not it," he said, trying to act as if Angie weren't looking at him as if he'd sprouted two heads.

"Of course it is," Moira insisted. "Especially Susannah—she probably wanted to make sure you helped Patsy. I'm sure Susannah was quite flattered by Patsy's attention."

Paavo looked stricken.

"There's another explanation," Angie said with growing enthusiasm. "It's that we're so close there's a psychic bond, an ESP, between us. That we're so in tune we scarcely need words to communicate."

"Sounds a little far-fetched to me," Moira offered, frowning.

Talk about the proverbial pot calling the kettle black, Angie thought. "It makes more sense than egomaniac ghosts."

"But you and Paavo? I understand him bet—"

"I think it's time to go," Paavo interrupted, seeing the murderous look grow in Angie's eyes. The last thing he wanted was two women arguing about what he was thinking, for God's sake. He lifted one of Angie's suitcases, but as he reached for his duffel bag, Moira beat him to it. She picked it up and held it out to him. His hand joined hers on the handle, not quite touching.

An eternity seemed to pass as Angie watched.

"You're welcome here anytime," Moira said softly.

He nodded. Finally, she let go of the bag.

Angie let go of the breath she'd been holding, then reached for her second suitcase. Danny picked up her third.

"Will you write to me?" Danny asked her as he walked by her side out the door, Paavo following.

"I most certainly will. Just be sure you write back, okay?"

"I will."

She kissed his cheek. He turned twenty shades of red, then smiled, turned, and ran the rest of the way to the car. He put the bag down and hurried back to the house.

Angie noticed Paavo watching him. She glanced back to see Moira, Danny, and Quint standing together at the door. A ready-made family, his for the asking.

Angie's throat felt dry as she studied the pensive look on his face. "Will you ever come back, do you think, Paavo?"

He turned toward her, and slowly a slight, Paavo kind of smile played against his lips. "No. Some ghosts are best dead and buried. And left in the past where they belong."

"Maybe," she said as she gazed at the old house, "*all* ghosts are best treated that way."

He chuckled as he squeezed her luggage into the tight cargo space in the Ferrari.

This vacation had worked out, at least as far as their relationship went, a lot better than she had thought it was going to.

They'd spent a week together, day and night . . . for the most part. They didn't fight much. Or at least, not too much. And they had lots to talk about. She generally listened to what he had to say, and he generally shared his thoughts with her . . . sort of. But most of all, she saw a side of him with Moira, Patsy, and especially with Danny, that she liked and admired. She hadn't given serious thought before to what he'd be like as a father, but now she saw, firsthand, how tender yet strong he could be.

Maybe he wasn't the onion head she'd imagined, but getting to know him seemed like peeling an onion. There were layers upons layers hiding his core. If only she could learn tarot, with all the deep delving Moira had talked about. . . .

No, that wasn't what she wanted from him. This week told her precisely what she wanted. The M word.

"That's a very enigmatic smile," he said.

"Yes," she whispered.

He held the passenger door open for her. "Not going to tell?"

She shook her head. "Not after what I said to Moira about our psychic communication."

As he walked around the car to the driver's side, his empty stomach growled and he suddenly remembered her words in the bedroom. "Got it," he said as he climbed in beside her.

"I knew you would, Paavo." The words all but gushed from her as he started the car and pulled away from the inn.

She smiled at him.

He grinned back at her.

Marriage.

McDonald's.